Sanna Meets Dauntless Swiftsure

by
Roxanna Matthews
Cover Art by Jan York

authorHOUSE®

AuthorHouse™
1663 Liberty Drive, Suite 200
Bloomington, IN 47403
www.authorhouse.com
Phone: 1-800-839-8640

© 2008 Roxanna Matthews. All rights reserved.

No part of this book may be reproduced, stored in a retrieval system, or transmitted by any means without the written permission of the author.

First published by AuthorHouse 10/21/2008

ISBN: 978-1-4389-0670-6 (sc)

Library of Congress Control Number: 2008907171
Cover Illustrations by Jan York

Printed in the United States of America
Bloomington, Indiana

This book is printed on acid-free paper.

Sanna Meets Dauntless SwiftSure

Light flared. I sensed huge movements of energy and seemed to hear a keening that was not sound. Leery was pulling the spirit of the effrit out of my quarterstaff, where I had trapped it. As the effrit no longer had any physical body of its own, it flowed into Leery and began to transform him. He swelled and grew, pulling the staff out of my nerveless grip and absorbing it into himself. His neck stretched, became serpentine, his arms changed to great lizard-like forelegs with long, sharp claws, matching the lizard legs in back. Scales grew over his skin – green and shiny. His face distorted, as long, narrow, toothy jaws extended. And a writhing tail emerged behind him. As he sat on his haunches, his head rose over the battlements – four stories up. He had become a dragon!

"At last!" he exalted. "I am whole again! How could you have known, wretched girl, that after I enslaved this effrit, I left most of my Power with it? And you stole it, trapping it in your staff, hiding it, keeping it away from me! I've been blind and crippled this past year. But now, now I am whole." He cackled with insane laughter, and then suddenly thrust his monstrous head down at me.

"You have thwarted and injured me at every turn. You may have gotten away before, but I have you now!"

He swiped at me with a fore paw. I threw myself backward, but I was weary, stiff, and slow. Instead of impaling me on the sabers of his claws, he managed only to slash me from left collarbone to right hipbone and throw me spinning across the courtyard, where I smashed into a wall.

I landed badly. My pelvis broke, my left shoulder dislocated, and I couldn't feel my legs at all. Blood poured from the slash across my torso. I could see ribs through the wound. My brain slammed a door on the horror and terror of seeing my own body so mutilated. If I was going to survive, I had to be calm enough to heal myself.

Leery stalked slowly toward me, gloating. "I'm going to make your death last a long time." Then he cocked his head and looked at the hot red pool forming around me. "Ah, but you're losing blood too fast. Too bad! At least I can make you suffer a bit more. Let me tell you my plans. After I watch you bleed to death, I'm going to slaughter every living being in this castle -- your brother, your beloved Prince Jerris, your sanctimonious Sorcerer friends, every soldier, servant, horse, dog and cat within these walls. And then I am going to lay waste to every city and village from here to Thon. I was helpless without the effrit, but you brought it back to me, and put it in my hands! You can die knowing that you have brought death to everyone you care about."

Sanna Meets Dauntless Swiftsure

Gasping in horror, I sat up in bed, fighting off the recurring dream. Or nightmare. Or memory. What to call it? Shuddering, I lay back down and cuddled into the warmth and softness of the feather bed and comforted myself with the sound of my brother Jonel's snores from the next room of the inn. Absently my fingers traced the scar from the attack that had nearly killed me. From left collarbone to right hipbone, it was raised and lumpy enough that I could feel it through my cozy linsey-woolsey nightie. I should have spent another six weeks recuperating in Arrex, but I had been absent too long from my classes at the Thon Academy of Higher Magic for Young Ladies of Exceptional Talent, so Jonel had been assigned to take me back to school.

There is a limit to how much healing even magic can do. There needs to be substance in the body to rebuild damaged tissue. It had been over two months since my injury, and I still hadn't replaced all the blood I had lost, even though I had been eating like a teenaged boy. We had been staying in military posting houses on our journey, but last night I was too exhausted to make it to the next one, so we had stopped in the village of Little Dinwiddy, at The Hen and Chicks Inn. I couldn't even walk up the stairs to my room without help and had fallen into bed without eating. And now I was so hungry!

My belt bag was under my pillow, so I reached in, looking for something, anything to eat. My belt bag was the first implement of Power I had acquired, and I always kept it with me. I had made it in embroidery design class, using the cubic illusion stitch. It's bigger on the inside than on the outside and has more than once carried entire picnics. Maybe a chicken wing or a cookie had been left behind? Nothing. Not a crust of bread, not a crumb. My stomach growled fiercely. I shoved the covers aside and stood up – too fast. The room swam around me, and I had to sit down again. Just not enough blood to go around yet. So I sat on the side of the bed and got dressed. I wound up putting on my soft house shoes because Jonel had carried my boots away with him. Then I went padding downstairs. The main room had that frowsy look of an inn that closed late and still hasn't been properly tidied for the morning. Three young dogs curled in a sleepy pile under one bench. Used tankards and plates were stacked at the end of a table. Following the sounds of activity, I opened the nearest door and found the kitchen. A rosy-cheeked woman in her late thirties was ladling hot porridge into a series of bowls.

I spoke without thinking. "That smells wonderful! May I have some?"

The woman looked up in surprise. "Oh, Miss, we'll bring breakfast to your room. I had no idea you would be up so early!"

"Please, may I have some now? I'm so hungry!" My stomach growled again to give added emphasis. Then I turned and saw a gaggle of children lined up and waiting for their porridge. "Unless there's not enough. I certainly don't want to deprive the moppets. I'm so sorry. I shouldn't have intruded."

She smiled at me kindly. "Of course there's enough. Prince Jerris has kept those Golmen raiders well away from us and we have plenty of food here. Sit yourself down."

She dished up a bowlful of steaming grains, drizzled thick dark syrup over it, then added chopped, dried fruits, and handed it to me. The syrup was sweet and strong-tasting, and the fruits added a delightful texture to the meal. As she handed out bowls of porridge to the children, she chattered on, hardly giving me time to answer her.

"I heard that you came from Arrex. Did you see the prince? Is he really transformed into the Golden Dragon? I heard that the Golmen raiders just turn and run when he comes onto the battlefield! My second boy is in the army, and my brother as well. And the man with you, your brother? I could tell he was a trooper the first time he rode in my gate. There's just something about a soldier. My late husband was a soldier, you know. Well, of course, you wouldn't know. But it was his pension that got us the seed money for this inn."

"Did ja see the Golden Dragon?" one young fellow, about nine, asked.

"Don't be rude, Duggers. Let the lady eat."

"But maybe she saw the dragons fight. I bet it was -- horribliffic! With blood an' guts an' stuff!"

"Duggers! That's not nice table talk! This lady will think we're barbarians."

"I have a lot of brothers," I assured her. "All young lads are barbarians. And yes, it was horrible. And it was very, very frightening. The green dragon was higher than the weathercock on your stable. And he was going to kill everyone in the country. He would have been worse than all the Golmen raiders ever born. Then Prince Jerris transformed into the Golden Dragon, and even though he was only half as big, he was twice as smart. He crushed the green dragon's throat in his big lion jaws, and clawed with his lion claws and ripped with his lion back legs. And his Golden Dragon scales helped protect him some from the green dragon's claws -- but not completely. So Prince Jerris was wounded terribly, and it's only because Brother Andra and Master Turik were such mighty healers that they were able to save his life. I have never been so scared in my life!"

"You were *there?*" Duggers asked, with a thousand questions waiting behind his eyes.

I didn't want to deal with all the questions, so I decided to go with an evasion. "I know someone who was. This porridge is delicious! What's this nice syrup?"

"It's sweet-cane syrup," said my hostess. "It has lots of iron in it. You look as if you could use a bit of strengthening. Would you like some more? Nothing like oats and syrup to put the legs back under you."

Chapter 2

I polished off another big bowlful of porridge and asked the woman about the details of running an inn. Her oldest son, Dennies, came in from tending the animals in the stable. He was a strapping lad in his early twenties with shoulders like a blacksmith and big brown eyes with the longest lashes I had ever seen. He too tucked into a bowl of porridge. All the children were rosy-cheeked and healthy, built along the same solid, sturdy lines as their mother. She was wide-hipped, comfortably buxom, and her arms were so beautifully plump that the bone of her wrist didn't show.

Without being asked, the two oldest girls began bringing dirty dishes into the kitchen and filling a basin with hot soapy water.

One of them scolded, "Duggers, quit bothering the lady and start your chores. And sweep the dust *out* of the corners, not into them."

She turned to the dishwashing, and Duggers made a face at her, but carried his bowl over to the wash-up basin and went to fetch a broom.

The day was getting well started. "Jonel never sleeps this late," I remarked. "I'd better get out from under your feet and see what's keeping him."

I slowly climbed the stairs and made my way down the hall to his room. In the light of day I could see that the inn was sturdy, small, cozy and clean even in the corners. I had gotten the sense that Jonel had stopped here before. I began to see why. It was so comfortable.

I tapped on Jonel's door and when I heard a noise, stuck my head around the edge of it. Jonel was still in bed, and the face he turned to me showed red-rimmed, swollen eyes and a nose already glowing from being wiped too often with a rough soldier's kerchief.

"Whad?" he groaned.

I reached into my belt bag and began pulling out medicines.

"So you've come down with a catarrh, have you? Getting yourself exhausted and not eating right. Undo your nightshirt. This ointment will help you breathe easier," I scolded as I opened a jar of pungent goo.

Jonel scowled fiercely. "I'b fide!" he announced nasally. "Just led be go back to sleeb."

"You're *not* fine, and I won't leave till I've anointed your chest and throat. And don't bother going back to sleep, because I'll be right back with some hot tea and a basin of

Sanna Meets Dauntless Swiftsure

herbs so you can steam your lungs clean. And you know better than to argue with a Healer, Commander Jonel!"

He glared at me, but allowed me to smear the vaporous unguent on his chest and throat. This I covered with a square of flannel I had embroidered with the warming stitch, then tucked the covers up closely around him, gave him three soft kerchiefs to deal with the loosening mucus and went off to fetch hot water for tea.

"Mistress Innkeeper?" I said, peeking into the kitchen.

She turned from the chopping block where she was dismembering a chicken.

I exclaimed, "Oh, good! Chicken broth will be the very thing. Mistress..."

"Just call me Cleonie, dear." She smiled warmly at me. "Does your brother like chicken broth?"

"And I'm Sanna." I introduced myself. "No, actually, Jonel far prefers his chicken roasted. But he has a catarrh, and chicken broth will be just the thing for him for a day or two. I think we'll be here at least two more nights. Maybe more if he's very sick. Will that be all right?"

"Oh, the poor man! I thought he looked a bit peaky around the eyes last night. Of course you'll stay here! I'll put lots of garlic in the soup. It's very strengthening. You'll be wanting some wintertea and some --"

"I don't need to deplete your supplies," I interrupted her. "I'm a healer. I brought my own. But a pot of hot water and a cup – "

"I'll bring it right up! Fancy, a young lass like you being a healer!"

Speculation lighted her eye. I thanked her and struggled back up the stairs again. If I were up to strength, I could have spun out the inflammation and healed Jonel in three minutes. As it was, he would have to suffer through a full week of symptoms.

As I neared his room I could hear the disgusting sounds of profound nose-blowing. Good, the ointment was working! I thanked the Good One that I had lots of handkerchiefs!

He was sitting on the side of the bed and had evidently been starting to get dressed when his sinuses opened up. He had his breeches dragged on under his nightshirt, and one boot on. His eyes were watering, his nose running, and he looked thoroughly miserable. I handed over another handkerchief and immediately began scolding him again.

"Now what is the point of wearing waterproof socks that are full of holes? I've been right there at the castle for the last two months with nothing to do while I healed. Didn't I ask if you had any mending or darning you wanted done? Take those socks off and give them to me! I didn't knit you those nice socks so you could wear them into rags. No wonder you're sick -- running around with cold, wet feet."

"You knit waterproof socks?" Duggers had come in the open door behind me.

"Don't you have chores to be doing?" I asked a little too sharply.

"I'm s'posed to empty the chamber pots," he said with injured dignity.

"I'm sorry, Duggers. Here it is." I pulled it out from under the bed, passed the vessel over to him and continued to apologize. "I wasn't thinking. Thank you. I don't think I have the strength to carry this big thing downstairs. Be sure to wash your hands afterward so you don't catch his sickness."

"When I grow up, I'm gonna be a soldier and I'll never wash my hands!" Duggers announced.

"You will if you're in *my* command," said Jonel. "Even with the healers' best efforts, sickness kills more men in the field than injury. If a healer says to wash your hands, you'd better wash them! Got that, trooper?"

Duggers grinned. "Yes sir, Commander! Washing hands, sir!" And off he marched with the chamberpot held as proudly as any company standard.

Jonel snorted – not a good idea with the mucus breaking up and flowing so freely. I passed over another handkerchief. He blew and handed the sodden ball back to me.

"Duggers is a fine lad," Jonel said, smiling fondly. "They're all fine children. She's a widow, you know."

"And she'll be here any minute with a pot of hot water for tea, so off with those ragged socks, off with your breeches, and back into bed. I'm just not strong enough to cure your catarrh. I can make you more comfortable, but the longer you stay on your feet, the longer you'll be sick."

He looked into my face, read the worry there, struggled with his masculine ego and sense of responsibility and was overtaken by a huge, wet sneeze that decided him. He lay back on the bed and began wriggling the breeches down while making sure he stayed modestly covered by the nightshirt. I bent over and rolled off his socks, took the breeches as he handed them to me, and helped him pull the covers decently up to his armpits. And not a minute too soon, as the door swung open behind me and in came Cleonie, laden with a huge tray. She was followed by her daughters, bearing a basket of sand and a long-handled metal pot filled with coals. The basket of sand went into the corner on the far side of the bed and the hot coals were set safely on it to begin heating the room. A small iron pot full of water went on top of the coals to keep the air from getting too dry. Mistress Cleonie obviously had a knack for healing.

"I'm so sorry to hear that you have a touch of catarrh, Commander," she was saying to Jonel," but we'll soon have you back on your feet and fighting-fit."

She pulled a trigger somewhere under the tray, and ingeniously hinged legs folded out so that she could stand it next to the bed. Jonel blinked in some startlement.

"Your sister tells me that she's a healer, but I can see that she doesn't have the strength to deliver kittens right now, so you'll just have to make do with a few home remedies from me." She poured hot tea into a cup, added a spoonful of honey and handed it to him, then smiled at me. "Why should I deplete your supplies while you're on the road, dear? We have a wonderful herb garden here at The Hen and Chicks Inn and more than enough to get us through till next harvest. That's peppermint, Echinacea, chamomile, and ginger-root he's drinking."

"You grow ginger-root here?" I asked.

"Well, no, I had to buy the ginger-root." She looked a bit annoyed at me, then continued, "But I got a wonderful bargain, and I have lots, so don't worry."

Sanna Meets Dauntless Swiftsure

A surge of jealous protectiveness swept me. Who did she think she was, to be taking over care of my brother like this? But she had already turned to fuss over him a bit more, and the wistful tenderness in her voice, the gentle yearning in the way she hovered and touched suddenly got through to me. A soldier's widow, with a fine strapping soldier under her roof again was bound to have -- oh -- responses, if not fully formed intentions. Would I like Cleonie as a sister-in-law? More important, would Jonel like her as a wife? There were, after all, three other inns in the village, but Jonel had passed by the others and come here.

"Cleonie, if you could spare another cup of that lovely tea, I believe I'll leave Jonel in your capable hands and take myself back to bed for a nice brisk nap," I said.

She turned a beautiful smile on me. Jonel, holding his cup of tea in one hand, nervously pulled the covers higher on his chest with the other and looked entreatingly at me. I grinned at them.

Cleonie spoke to her daughters, "MaiRose, will you go fetch the pink cup and the little pink teapot for this lady?"

The older daughter – fifteen or so – cocked her head slightly as if listening to overtones, looked appraisingly at Jonel, smiled slowly, and said, "Oh, yes, Mother! Come along, Aster. You can help me."

Aster began to protest, "You don't need help with that little teapot! I want to stay and talk to Jonel."

MaiRose grabbed Aster by the wrist and dragged her out of the room, saying, under her breath, "Come on, I'll explain in the kitchen!"

Cleonie blushed, but took up a jar of ointment from her tray and said to Jonel, "Now we'll just apply a nice mustard plaster to your feet and you'll feel ever so much better." Deftly, she twitched the bedding away from Jonel's feet. As I left the room, Jonel was clutching the cup and the covers as if his virtue were in danger.

Chapter 3

I was standing beside my bed in the tiny room, having just pulled off my slippers and breeches, and was struggling out of my warm wooly overshirt when little Aster nudged my door open with her hip and backed in, burdened with a teapot, three cups and a small crock of honey, artfully arranged on a tray that was almost too big for her. Pleased with having gotten everything delivered without spills or upsets, she turned around, saw my skinny bare legs showing beneath my linen under-tunic and nearly dropped it all. I caught the edge of the tray as she stared and began babbling apologies. Before Aster could gather her wits, MaiRose entered with another tray, this one laden with freshly sliced bread, a bowl of butter, a pot of preserves and several small knives and spoons. For a minute the three of us juggled trays and exclamations in the crowded space till, laughing, I sat down on the bed and slid my legs between the smooth white sheets.

"Put down the legs on your tray, Aster!" commanded MaiRose. Aster fumbled a moment, then managed to release the catch. The legs dropped down, and with a jiggle and click, they locked into place, creating a small bedside table.

"Do you mind if we join you for just a few minutes?" MaiRose asked me.

"I wish you would," I replied, patting the bedcovers. Aster hopped up and scrambled across my legs to curl like an alert kitten on the foot of the bed. MaiRose handed me the food tray, which I settled on my lap. Then she poured three cups of tea, made sure that I got the thin pink cup painted with delicate flowers, and carefully seated herself on the edge of the bed next to my knees.

"I thought you might be ready for a little snack," she said, ignoring the fact that I had finished two huge bowlfuls of porridge not an hour earlier.

"I can't eat all this alone," I said. "Will you share it with me?"

MaiRose deftly buttered three slices of bread and offered the preserves. "This is peach with raspberry. We make it here from our own peaches and berries. Would you care to try?"

"By all means!" I said greedily.

So MaiRose spread preserves thickly on three slices of bread and handed them out. We all took healthy bites and chewed with pleasure.

I closed my eyes to savor the interesting blend of flavors. I could feel the girls watching me. I swallowed, opened my eyes, smiled, took a sip of tea and proclaimed, "Delicious!"

Their anxious looks dissolved into smiles. They each bit again into their own slices of bread.

Seeing no reason to sneak up on the subject, I remarked, "My brother certainly fancies your mother."

MaiRose, not being a girl to waste time, asked, "Do you think he would be good to her?"

I had wondered if they knew about the potential relationship. Obviously, they were well ahead of me.

"He won't give up his command," I cautioned. "Even when he takes off his uniform, he's still a soldier. He won't be here much."

"When he *is* here," Aster chirped up, "Ma smiles all the time and sings in the kitchen. He spent his two-week leave here last year and helped Dennies re-roof the stable. If they were married, maybe he would be here more often. *I* like him!"

"We *all* like him," MaiRose agreed. "But will he be good to Ma?"

"He's always been a kind brother and an honorable man," I replied. "And he grew up with lots of little kids underfoot. He's oldest, and I'm youngest of seven. And since Father was Head Trainer for the Potentate of Dertzu's racehorses and Mother was Chief Housekeeper for the Potentate's harem, we grew up in the palace with all the Potentate's children and nieces and nephews. Jonel sort of grew up watching over younger kids. I think it makes him a better officer in the army."

MaiRose nodded thoughtfully. But Aster stuck directly to the question. "Does that mean he *will* be good to Ma?"

"I don't know, Aster. I was still a little tyke when he was courting the girls at home. I don't know how he behaves with women. Will your Mother be good to *him*? There's lots of widows who would like to snag an officer's pay packet and have their fun while he's off fighting."

MaiRose and Aster both gaped in outrage at me.

"Ma would never!" MaiRose asserted.

Aster was on her knees, full teacup sloshing quite forgotten in her hands. "She's turned down lots of officers. She could have married dozens!"

"Not dozens, Aster," MaiRose quelled her sister. "Only four if you count that weedy lieutenant. And don't spill your tea on Sanna's feet."

Aster settled back and took a deep slurp of tea, glaring at me over the rim of the cup. "Well, Ma's *not* like that!"

"Sanna doesn't *know* that. And she's right to be worried. For all she knows, Ma could be like that Jillia over at The Badger," MaiRose reasoned with her.

"Jillia is *not* a nice woman," Aster proclaimed. "And she's mean to kitties."

"Jonel likes kitties," I reassured her, then spoke slowly, thinking out loud. "I think he'll be kind to your mother. And you girls are a pretty good advertisement for your mother's honor and good heart. All I need to do is watch her tending Jonel, to see that she'll be kind to him. You know, I think they're probably old enough to work it out for themselves. And I guess they'll do what they want to do without consulting us. But I like the match."

I finished the last swallow of my tea and handed the empty cup to MaiRose.

"The bread and tea were lovely! Thank you so much. Now, if you don't mind, I really would like a nap."

Aster gulped the last of her tea and stuffed the crust of her bread into her mouth. MaiRose nodded at me with a smile that hinted at understanding beyond her years. Then another thought occurred to her. "If Jonel marries Ma, that would make you my auntie, wouldn't it?"

I laughed. "I'm seventeen. Your big brother Dennies is about twenty?"

MaiRose joined my giggles. "He's twenty-one. Your nephew will be older than you!"

Aster scrambled across my legs again, and took the tray off my lap. "You take the big tray this time, MaiRose," she said. Then she leaned over, kissed my cheek, and said, "Sweet dreams, Auntie Sanna!"

MaiRose smiled at me from the door. "Yes, sweet dreams, Auntie Sanna!"

My dreams were sweet indeed.

Chapter 4

I went to check on Jonel when I woke. He turned fretfully as I eased open his door.

"Whad do you wan?" he snapped at me.

"You're not getting better, are you?" I asked, walking up to lay a hand on his forehead. He flung my hand away, but not before I could feel how hot he was.

"Jus lee be alone," he whined peevishly.

"I will not leave you alone. You have a fever. How sick *are* you?" I asked, grasping the hand with which he was trying to fend me off. I sent my Gift into it, through the fibers of his muscles, along the threads of his nerves, into the intricate embroidery of his veins and arteries. If I had been fully up to strength, a single touch would have told all I needed to know, but in my weakened state, it took a full minute before I could properly diagnose his condition.

"You have been out in all weathers for days on end, you have gotten yourself completely exhausted, you frequently forget to eat and you have been worried sick about a thousand things the whole time. Your body is weak and you have finally come down with lung fever. Jonel, I'm not strong enough to *heal* you!"

"I'll be jus fine," he told me, struggling to sit up.

"Oh, shut up!" I growled, shoving his chest with one hand. He was so weak that it knocked him back down. He cracked his head against the wooden headboard, started cursing, then coughing violently. I pulled a big handkerchief out of my belt bag to catch the sparse whitish mucus he was bringing up from his lungs. Cleonie rushed through the door behind me.

"I -- I heard your brother coughing. Is he -- ?"

"He wore himself right down and now he has lung fever." I said with considerable frustration. "I'm afraid we'll be staying with you for a few weeks now. He's going to need lots of good food, lots of warmth and lots of rest. All things he's been missing lately." I tucked his hand back under the covers and adjusted his pillow so he could breathe easier.

"Well, we can certainly provide all of those," Cleonie said, with a look of some satisfaction. Jonel closed his eyes and groaned. Then he opened his eyes and fixed me with a defiant look.

"We cand stay here for weegs. You deed to ged back to the Acadeby. Glasses will be starding soon!" he asserted.

"Classes will just have to start without me. I'm not strong enough to travel by myself, and you're not strong enough to take me, so give it up. I'll get back to the

Academy when I get back there. Now shut up or you'll start another coughing fit."

He drew breath to argue with me, and another violent bout of coughing hit him.

"Onion juice," said Cleonie and headed off to her kitchen.

When the coughing abated, I eased Jonel back down on his pillow, smoothed the hair away from his forehead and said, smiling gently, "It really is lung fever, and the more you fight it, the longer you'll take to get well. Just rest. We *planned* on taking a long, slow trip, remember?"

He nodded, then began to shiver.

"Fever and chills. You're a sick boy, Jonel," I told him.

He just nodded and shivered more. His lips were a bit bluish. I didn't like the looks of him at all.

For the rest of that day, Cleonie and the children and I took turns sitting with Jonel. We did what we could to treat his symptoms, coaxing him to take honey and thyme with onion juice to calm his cough. He absolutely refused food – even the fragrant chicken broth Cleonie had prepared.

The day passed into evening. The family and I feasted on a stew made from the chicken Cleonie had cooked for broth, along with lots of sweet parsnips and carrots. Rosehip and chamomile tea all around as well, to keep us strong, and for dessert, dried apples stewed with cider, cinnamon and a drizzle of honey, then spooned over slices of stale bread. It was a delicious meal, and I was impressed with Cleonie's housewifely thrift.

Sanna Meets Dauntless Swiftsure

Every so often, a neighbor would drop in for a tankard of ale, but the weather kept other travelers off the highway. We were just finishing the last of the dessert when Dennies, the oldest boy, raised his head, listening.

"Someone on the road?" asked Duggers in surprise.

"Sounds like it," Dennies replied. He rose to his feet and swung open the door to peer out. A traveler was coming slowly through the wind and sleet. Dennies stepped out and caught the horse's bridle.

"Here, now, it's not fit out for a breathing soul. Get yourself into the inn, and I'll tend your animal." Then, looking over his shoulder, he called, "Duggers, bring my waxed cape. And wear your own!"

The traveler stiffly swung a leg over the saddle and slid to the ground.

A woman's voice said, "It's thanking you I am," as she stumbled through the door.

Cleonie and MaiRose were on their feet as well, helping the woman shed her sodden cloak and cowl, drawing her over to the fireside to warm up and thrusting a cup of hot tea into her hands.

The traveler was almost as tall as I, with a strong, sharp face and huge, deeply set eyes that might have been all pupil, they were so dark. And though she was a young woman, smooth-skinned, straight and slim, the hair under her cowl was white as frost.

She felt my eyes on her and turned her head to look at me. Embarrassed by my rude staring, I introduced myself. "Sanna of Dertzu, Sorceress Apprentice."

23

I held out my hand. She took it in her thin, cold hand and squeezed firmly. A hot, dry wind seemed to blow fiercely through my nerves for a moment.

"Dauntless SwiftSure I'm called – Messenger for the Headwomen of the Peoples of the Wide Skies."

Chapter 5

"A Messenger?" Cleonie said, as she brought a hot plateful of the last of the stew from the kitchen. "It's an honor, good Messenger!" And she bobbed a little curtsey. MaiRose and Aster curtsied as well.

"A Messenger I am, and cold to the soul!" replied the strange woman. "And couldn't I just be murdering a plate of your fine stew? My blessings you'll be having for giving it to me this night. And would there be any hot cider at all?"

"I'll fetch a jug from the cellar," Aster chirped, and dashed away.

"I'll fetch a pan from the kitchen," offered MaiRose.

"There's a bit of apples stewed with cinnamon if you would fancy it," Cleonie offered shyly, handing over the plateful of stew, then using the corner of her apron to give the spoon a final nervous polish before giving it over as well.

The Messenger smiled broadly at Cleonie and said, "Why, I should be liking it above all things in the wide world. I am dearly loving a bowl of stewed apples at the end of a long, cold day."

Cleonie glowed with pleasure and bobbed another curtsey before hurrying off to the kitchen again.

Dauntless SwiftSure lifted a spoonful of steaming stew to her mouth, paused, then looked around at the remaining two children and me staring at her like shepherds at a raree-show.

"And have you never in your lives seen a woman eat stew before?"

"Never seen a Messenger before," replied the youngest, with eyes big as an owl's.

"I'm sorry to be so rude," I apologized. "I don't even know what or who a Messenger is. And I've never seen anyone like you. But you should eat and warm up first and talk later. The stew really is wonderful."

To give myself something to do, I pulled Jonel's socks out of my belt bag. They had been washed and dried at the kitchen fire (along with any number of handkerchiefs) and it was time to darn them. With the heels worn out, and holes in the toes, they were so ragged that I wondered if it might not make more sense just to cut them off at the ankles and re-knit the feet.

The Messenger snorted. "And that's a fine pair of socks you have there, to be sure."

"My brother's," I replied, shaking my head and starting to pull out stitches around the ankle. "They're supposed to be waterproof, but once he wears holes in them, they're just old socks."

"Waterproof stockings are they? And however might a one obtain a pair of such wonderful things?" she asked, between mouthfuls of stew.

"I've been knitting Jonel's stockings for years," I replied with a shrug. "I have a Gift for it."

Aster and MaiRose came in then, with a small pan, a big jug of cider and a sturdy cup to serve it in. They bustled around the Messenger and were soon joined by Cleonie with a bowlful of stewed apples. I smiled and nodded at Dauntless SwiftSure, then stood and slipped upstairs to check on Jonel. His breathing was labored, and his lips more bluish than ever.

"Sanna? Did I hear someone come into the inn?" he asked, wheezing a little as he spoke.

"It's the most extraordinary woman!" I told him. "She's getting the last of the stew, so if you get hungry, you'll just have to make do with gruel."

"No food," he grimaced, turning his face away.

"Cleonie has some tea keeping nice and warm on your little brazier here," I told him, checking the coals warming the bedroom.

"No tea!" he groaned.

"Do you need the chamberpot? You certainly wouldn't be the first adult male I've dealt with who was too weak to take a leak without help."

"No!" he exclaimed, then started coughing again.

He was trying to sit up, so I helped him. Cleonie appeared in the doorway. Jonel seemed unable to catch his breath at all, and I could hear the phlegm rattle in his chest. His whole face was turning bluish.

"Oh, Good One, help me," I muttered. I was too weak to heal him, but I was going to have to do what I could anyway. I grounded, sending my Talent down into the stone foundations of the sturdy old inn. It wasn't ideal, but it was enough. It gave me a solid footing to start on. Jonel could sense what I was doing and began shaking his head and trying to push me away. Placing my palm flat against his bare chest, I sent my Gift into him, into the meshes and webbing of his lungs, and began pushing out the suffocating fluids.

Cleonie, seeing his protests, rushed over, crying, "Stop! Oh stop, Sanna!"

She clutched at my hand. Strength, health and love just radiated out of her. Without thinking, I began drawing on her strength to work the healing on Jonel, teasing thick, clogging phlegm out of the tiny air sacs of his lungs, twisting it into threads to pull it up the littlest tubes, joining the threads together into strings as the small tubes merged into larger ones, then twining the strings into ropes of mucus and pulling them up his bronchial tubes to clear his lungs. Just in time I shoved a handkerchief into Jonel's hand as he began to hawk and spit, ridding himself of the worst of it.

Cleonie collapsed onto her knees at the side of the bed, looking a bit shaken, but none the worse for the experience, with most of her concern still for Jonel.

"What did you do?" she asked.

Sanna Meets Dauntless Swiftsure

"Since I'm too weak to heal Jonel alone, it seems that I drew on your strength to clear his lungs. I'm sorry. Are you all right?"

We had to raise our voices to hear one another over Jonel's disgusting noises. As his spasm began to abate, I leaned him back against the pillows, took his nasty handkerchief, gave him a fresh one and stroked his cheek. His exertions had started him sweating, but his color was vastly better and he no longer wheezed and bubbled.

Cleonie was looking at him as if he were the only candle in a dark night.

"I would give my right hand and arm to make him well," she murmured, reaching out and caressing his cheek in her turn. He caught her hand to his cheek and smiled weakly at her.

"Yes," I remarked inanely. "Well. Ahhh, Jonel, now that the fever's broken, you should get into a dry nightshirt."

"Don't have one," he told me without taking his eyes from Cleonie's.

"You can wear one of Dennies'," she told him, sighing, and never taking her eyes from his.

Weariness washed through me. My bones ached. My joints felt a hundred years old. Jonel was over the worst and on his way to health, but the work had exhausted me. Even though most of the energy had come from Cleonie, it had required my Gift to draw and spin the congestion out of his lungs, and I had needed to reach into carefully hoarded reserves of strength to do it.

But I couldn't collapse with exhaustion quite yet. Cleonie's gift of health and love had opened doors of understanding between them, and breached walls of propriety. They had things to say to one another, and I needed to leave them alone to do it. Surely I had enough strength left to fetch a dry nightshirt.

"I'll just go ask MaiRose to get it for you, then," I said, and turned to see Dauntless SwiftSure leaning against the doorframe, missing nothing, her frost-white hair stirring in the light draught of the hallway. She stood aside to let me pass and walked down the hall at my side.

"So it's a Shaman that you are, my dear?" she asked me, very quietly.

"A Shaman? I don't think I know what that is," I replied.

"Ah, it's a thing you can be without knowing it at all," she told me, smiling gently, while a predatory bird looked out of her large dark eyes.

Chapter 6

As we came down the stairs, Dennies and Duggers came in from the stables, shaking water off their waxed capes.

"Dennies," I called, "my brother's fever has broken, and his nightshirt is soaked with sweat. May I borrow one of yours? He's used to traveling light and didn't pack a spare."

He grinned. "It would be an honor for me if the Commander would wear my nightshirt. So he's better, then?"

"Your mother healed him." I thought about the tender scene I had just left in Jonel's room, and thought I had better warn Dennies. " Ahh -- you know they – um – they have a deep regard for one another."

He laughed as he hung up his cape. "They've been making sheep's eyes at each other for three years now, but too polite and cautious to do or say a thing about it. I'm hoping he marries her soon. I can't start my own courting properly till I'm sure the old girl's taken care of. I'll just fetch that nightshirt along to his room." And he bounded up the stairs two at a time, whistling.

I turned to the Messenger then. "I hope you'll excuse me. I've been recuperating from an injury, and healing still takes a lot out of me. I need to go lie down before I fall down."

The room was acting all silly around me, with the floor rippling slightly under my feet, and the walls disappearing into roaring blackness. Dauntless SwiftSure slid her arm around my waist, drew my arm over her shoulder, and half carried me up the stairs, murmuring in her lilting, storyteller's way.

"Oh, and it's a weary girl you are now, isn't it so, my dear? It always took Auntie HealWell that way, may her spirit fly with the four sweet winds. And wasn't she always all the stronger in the morning? Sure, my bright girl, let your own brave spirit walk the sweet green grasslands of dreaming this one night. And I'll see that you have two fine fresh eggs with your hearty porridge in the morning, and you will feel the power of life fill you from head to toe tip, see if it isn't so. Truly such a treasure for Tribe Dauntless you might be! Wasn't it the fortunate storm that blew me into this one inn on this one night so that I might meet you? And why shouldn't the Firebird just fly in the ways of her own choosing?"

I had no idea what she was talking about, and was just too tired to care.

She sat me down on my bed, pulled off my slippers, blew out my candle, and walked out of the room, closing the door behind her. I was dizzy with fatigue and with the musical cadence of her speech. Not bothering to pull off my clothes, I slid my legs between the sheets, pulled the blankets up to my chin, crossed my hands on my belly and fell into sleep like a pebble dropping into a well.

I dreamed. The Messenger's words molded my sleeping mind like soft clay. I seemed to walk in grass up to my knees – rich, cool, green grass. When I raised my head, the grassland stretched as far as I could see. There wasn't a hill or a tree or even a bush in sight. I knew I was dreaming because there were no mountains even on the horizon, and I had never been out of sight of mountains in my life. I couldn't even imagine a place without mountains. I began to feel exposed and vulnerable without the proper borders to my world. Then a breeze blew against my cheek. The grass waved like a giant river rippling over rocks. In the distance, I saw something approaching. A rider, on -- what manner of beast could this be? Four legs – yes. Neck far too long and skinny to be a horse. Legs too thick and knob-kneed. Wooly, shaggy, dun-colored hair in long clumps. And the body? It seemed to have two great lumps on the back. The rider sat between them, swathed in dazzling white robes that trailed and fluttered in the wind of her passage.

The beast was ugly, with the most peculiar head I had ever seen on an animal. It had a long, bony skull, no forehead to speak of, and large eyes with impossibly long lashes. And as I stared at the animal, the rider dismounted, then threw off her muffling headdress.

She was an old woman, but her wrinkled skin lay on beautiful bones. Her snow white hair was pulled into a knot at the back of her head and secured with several picks dangling feathers, beads and fetishes. Her eyes were the color of violets. We stared at one another.

"And so you're the one our SwiftSure thinks will be replacing me for Tribe Dauntless, are you? The puny young slip of a thing that you are? How might she be thinking you are to be Shaman for the Tribe when a simple healing of the lung fever leaves you thin and shaking like a leaf of grass? And you had to draw on the loving strength of another woman at that!"

She paced around me in a circle as she spoke. When she completed her circle and stood in front of me again, I was naked.

She drew in her breath, hissing between her teeth as she looked at me.

"Now where would a young lass be getting a great ugly scar like that, and how is it that such a wound was not making an end of you entirely?"

Through my mind flew the story: how the renegade Sorcerer, Leery, had turned my beloved Prince Jerris into a big orange tomcat and announced that only my kiss would break the spell. How, when I arrived, Leery changed himself into a huge green dragon and slashed me with his claws. Jerris, in his cat form, defended me, though he was scarcely the size of the black dragon's eyeball. Using my power gem, which was bathed in my life's blood, and throwing every bit of strength and will into my Talent, I tried to transform Jerris back into a human. "Be your true self," I had commanded. And Jerris, right royal Prince of Arrex, had transformed into the Golden Dragon of Arrex

Sanna Meets Dauntless Swiftsure

– lion head and legs, golden-scaled dragon's body and tail. He vanquished the green dragon!

Jonel, my brother, was the first to arrive at my side. Soldier that he was, he could see my injuries were fatal. I had used every bit of my Healer's art to transform Jerris. I couldn't even halt the flow of my own blood. I asked Jonel to kiss me goodbye, and when he did so, his love was so strong and generous that he gave me enough energy to stop the bleeding. Two of my teachers, likewise giving me the kiss of life, provided me with the will to endure the pain, to keep waking up each morning while I healed. They mended the ruined nerves in my back so that I could walk again, and they fought off the infections that the green dragon's filthy claws had brought, but none of us could spare energy for cosmetic work. I would bear the mark of the dragon the rest of my life.

I knew, in my dream, that the old woman had shared my memories. She seemed taken aback, and my clothing re-appeared. "Indeed, if you are having such a portion of the Power to be transforming a prince into a dragon, if you are having the will to be surviving a dragon's attack, if you are having the knowledge to be working so much healing within yourself, perhaps it's possible that my heedless, selfish niece is right, and it's a fine Shaman you might be making at that. So tell me now, my well-scarred darling, are you knowing the Way of the Winds?"

A storm suddenly blew upon me from all thirty-two points of the compass. My hair whipped my face, and grit filled my eyes and nose. I buried my face in my hands, and the gusts threatened to knock me off my feet as they blew hot and cold and dry and wet, all at the same time. Then, as suddenly as they had started, they stopped.

I was filthy, disheveled, staggering from the assault. The old woman appeared completely untouched.

"Isn't it just as I thought?" she said. "What sort of Shaman is it that isn't knowing the Way of the Winds? And I suppose you aren't knowing how to hold the Heart of the Fire either."

A huge fire rose up before me like some burning city. In the white-hot center of it, the old woman seemed to stand and beckon to me. I could smell my hair singeing, and feel my skin blistering. The heat of the inferno pulled the air from my lungs. I threw my hands up to shield my face and fell to my knees.

The fire was gone, and the old woman stood before me again, cool and completely unruffled. My searching fingers found no trace of the blisters that had been seared on my face an instant before.

The old woman turned and mounted her peculiar animal.

"And how would you be defending your tribe without the Heart of the Fire? Perhaps, when you are getting your strength back, you will be managing the healing as well as ever I did. And in the wise tribe of Dauntless there are many others who know the Way of the Winds. And isn't it true that SwiftSure holds the Heart of the Fire in her two hands every day of her breathing life? But a Shaman, you know, my fine brave lass, a Shaman must lead. Can you be finding your way in the dark?"

Thick, solitary blackness wrapped me round. The air was cold and stale and dead, as still as if I stood alone in a

Sanna Meets Dauntless Swiftsure

closed tomb. I stretched out my hands and felt nothing. I reached out my foot to take a step, and felt nothing! No floor in front of me! Balancing carefully on one foot, I swept the extended foot around. No floor to the side of me either. My heart raced. I began sweating and panting in fear. I might be standing on a shallow step, or on the edge of a hideous precipice. In the muffling, impenetrable dark, I couldn't tell. My head began to spin, and roaring grew in my ears. I held up my hands and cried out to the Good One to help me.

I felt knitting needles being placed into my hands. Automatically, my fingers began to ply them, taking comfort in this act that was as natural to me as walking. Quickly, I knitted up all the slack in the yarn, and in order to continue knitting, would have to take a step in the direction it was stretched. Unthinking, I did so. There was a slight step down. I stumbled ever so slightly, and continued knitting, following the yarn as it stretched away from me. In the darkness, I burst into tears.

Invisible arms hugged me. A gentle voice comforted me. Loving hands patted my damp cheek, and I slipped away from dreaming and into sleep again.

Chapter 7

For the first time in months, I woke filled with energy. I was ready to leap out of bed and seize the day with both hands. And I needed a bath! I spent a teensy pinch of Talent to light my bedside candle, then threw back the blankets, stretched luxuriously and rolled to my feet. As I pulled on fresh clothing, I organized my morning. First I would track down some hot water and bathe.

No, first I would eat. Then I would bathe.

No, first I would check on Jonel. Then I would eat. Then I would bathe. Then I had wads of handkerchiefs to wash. I wished I could hire a laundry fairy to ride around in my belt bag, then giggled at the silliness of the notion. Everyone knows that the only people with a laundry fairy are children and married men.

When I stepped out of my room, I saw that the inn was still dark and all the windows were shuttered. Yet I felt as if I had slept at least ten hours. There was no window in my room, but Jonel's room had a small one. All the more reason to check on him – I could peek outside and see what time it was. I picked up my bedside candle, walked to his room, and gently eased open the door.

The candle next to his bed still burned, shedding enough light for me to see him clearly. His warrior's reflexes had him sitting up and reaching for a sword before he was quite awake. Clearly, he was well on his way to recovery. His color was good, and his eyes had lost that glazed, fevered look.

Then I saw Cleonie's sleep-rosy face peeking out from behind him in the bed. We stared at one another for a moment.

"Now Sanna," began Jonel, "This isn't what it looks like." He was blushing from the neatly buttoned collar of his borrowed nightshirt to his slightly receding hairline.

Cleonie, meanwhile, was scrambling out of the bed. She was fully dressed, if a bit rumpled, and blushing quite a bit herself.

"No?" I asked. "It looks like Cleonie helped Dennies get you into a clean dry nightshirt, then lingered to say goodnight. She didn't realize when I used her energy to heal you that it would make her so tired. You probably both fell asleep whispering sweet nothings to one another. Your instinct has always been to protect her, so in your sleep, you pulled the blankets over her. It looks as if you slept like two weary puppies. Are you sure things aren't what they look like?"

"Well, that's just how it was!" Jonel declared.

"I believe you. But then, I'm your Healer. I know how sick you've been. Even the Great Bull of Bevin would have felt lackluster if he'd had the lung fever as badly as you did. You get no credit for virtue when you're too weak for vice. Cleonie, I think you should make an honest man of my wayward brother before it's too late." I turned to her and held out my arms.

"Oh, I do intend to!" she said, hugging me so hard my spine crackled. There were happy tears in her eyes.

"But look at the time!" she exclaimed, glancing at the little window that showed only slightly grayer than the black shadows around it. "I have to start the kitchen fire and wake the children!"

She turned to Jonel, caught his face in her hands, and kissed him on the mouth. It was one of those kisses that changes as it goes on. First, it was just like an affectionate wife briskly kissing her fond husband. Then Jonel's hands slid over hers, and the kiss began to soften and linger. He slipped one hand behind her head, and the other around her waist, and pulled her down onto his lap. She gasped in surprise, while he grinned at her, pleased with the success of his wrestling.

I stepped to the bed and slapped him on the shoulder. "You behave! Cleonie has things to do, and *you* need to get your strength back. Are you strong enough to stand, or do you need help to use the chamberpot?"

This hideously prosaic question distracted him. Cleonie, who had been working in inns for years and knew the ways of soldiers, squirmed out of his grasp like a plump little bunny. Her eyes sparkled.

Sanna Meets Dauntless Swiftsure

"Why, Commander!" she purred. "I had no idea!" And with that, she sashayed out the door.

He turned a challenging look to me. I smiled blandly.

"Chamberpot?" I asked.

"Get out!" he growled.

"I'll be back in a few minutes to check your lungs," I told him primly. Then I smiled again. "I like her, Jonel."

"I – I love her, Sanna," he replied.

"I can tell. May you have much happiness together!"

I stepped out of the room and closed the door to give him his privacy. The upstairs rooms were all reached by a gallery that ran around three sides of the inn. I leaned against the railing on the inside edge of the gallery and looked down into the inn proper. Below, Cleonie burst into sight, wearing a fresh, crisp apron over her rumpled skirt and bodice, and pinning her hair up as she strode. She threw kindling onto the embers of the previous evening's fire and poked it to a brisk blaze. Then she bustled about, throwing open shutters and making little "tch" noises like a busy sparrow. Dennies came through from the family quarters and reached for his waxed cape, yawning widely.

"Kind of you to let us sleep in, Ma," he said, mischievously.

"Well it's no kindness to the poor cow, so go milk her first thing. I can't think what kept me asleep so long," she answered tartly, not looking at him.

"I can," he replied, and sauntered out the door.

She gasped and threw her head back and her hands onto her hips in a show of outrage, but the door was swinging shut behind him. Did the firelight show a sheepish smile dimpling her cheek?

The Messenger came out of her room on the far side of the gallery and called across to me, "Ah, and so it's the best part of the morning you'll be catching hold of, my fine wise girl! And have you slept like a babe rocked in her pommel basket? You are having the stars in your eyes and the color of a spring sunrise in your smooth cheeks, I see."

How she could see anything of me in the dim light was a wonder. Her white hair, floating loose on her shoulders, was like a drift of moonlight in the pre-dawn dimness, while her dark shirt and trousers blended into the shadows behind her.

"Good morning, Messenger," I replied. "I slept very well, thank you. And you?"

She walked toward me along the gallery, saying, as she came. "Why, I slept as if the soft wind of west by southwest, blowing across 500 miles of rich, ripe vineyards ready to harvest, had picked me up and floated me in the perfume of all those grapes waiting, willing, yearning, to be made into the finest of wines. Such a sweet delicious sleep it was. And were you *dreaming* at all, little doveling?"

I didn't know whether I was more fascinated or frightened by her. I hadn't remembered my peculiar dream till she reminded me.

"I usually do," I answered, trying to be polite. "Did you have pleasant dreams?"

"Oh yes, indeed I did, willow-lass. I dreamed I delivered my message and found my worthy prize and carried the lovely dear thing back to my tribe that is having such deep, deep need of it. And I was set free of the bonds constraining me and allowed again to roam as free as all the small birds of the air. Oh, by the eight little winds, it was a golden pleasant dream! And what of your dream? It is a courtesy and an entertainment for folks to share the stories of their dreaming, you know."

"Sanna!" called Jonel from the room behind me. "Are you coming back or not? Tell Cleonie I'm so hungry I could eat a plow horse!"

"Excuse me," I said to the Messenger, "I need to check on my brother's health," then pushed open Jonel's door.

"I'm sure she already heard you," I scolded. "At least I know your lungs are clear or you couldn't bellow like that."

The Messenger drifted in behind me. Jonel was sitting on the side of the bed, still wearing his borrowed nightshirt. His eyes widened at the sight of her, then he hastily swung his legs up into the bed and covered them with the blankets.

The Messenger hooked her thumbs in her belt and looked with great interest from Jonel to me. "Ah. Well, now this is a thing I've never seen before. How is it, then, that a Sorceress is reading the health of a sick man? Will you be studying the contents of his chamber pot to see what poisons have been taking leave of his body?" she asked.

"No, I won't," I replied, annoyed by her uninvited entrance and by the way she seemed to make the room feel crowded. "And I won't be slaughtering small animals to read the future in their entrails, either. All I need do is set hand to skin and -- well -- I'll *feel* how healthy he is."

"Ah, and isn't that the wonder of all the world? May I be watching this thing that you do, or is it a thing private between patient and Healer? A thing, perhaps, too intimate for a stranger such as myself to be bearing witness to?"

"You make it sound indecent," Jonel snapped. "It's nothing of the sort. Go ahead, Sanna, show her." He grabbed my hand and glared at the pushy Messenger. "There. That's all there is to it. Nothing to see, is there?"

She stepped forward and wrapped her long white hand around our joined hands like an eagle claw clasping a rabbit's skull. I felt as if someone had planted a boot on my backside and shoved me through a door. My healing gift moved faster and stronger than it ever had before. I could read all Jonel's symptoms in a flash. I could see that he was cured of the lung fever but still too run-down and exhausted to be up and on the road. I turned beneath this strange new energy that was pushing me, and began to channel it into him to speed his recovery. SwiftSure snatched her hand away, and the surge of power stopped, leaving me reeling. Jonel was looking dazed by the sudden and peculiar surge of strength I had been able to give him.

"So that's the way of it for a Sorceress, then," she said, massaging her palm as if she had been stung. "Truly, and it isn't at all what I'd heard about the Healers of your peoples. Here I was, the foolish lass, thinking that you dealt all with potions brewed and spells cast, and hadn't a hand at all for the Winds of the Spirit."

My dream came back – the old woman asking, "Do you know the Way of the Winds?" Was this what she had been talking about?

Sanna Meets Dauntless Swiftsure

"Every Sorceress is different," I told her, speaking as one Adept to another. "And not very many are Healers. We all have our own Gifts, and we all use them in our own way. Some healers use potions. Some use spells. I've studied with one who uses a sharp knife and an acute sense of anatomy."

"Sure, and aren't the Winds each blowing in their own way?" she said, smiling wryly and giving her hand a sharp shake as if to throw off water droplets. "What a thing I've been learning this morning! And didn't Auntie HealWell always tell me that a day was wasted if one learned nothing new? See how you've enriched my day, and the cock barely stirring in the haymow yet."

Then she turned and pulled the door open. "Ah, and speaking of that herald of the sweet dawn, wasn't it I who promised you two fresh eggs to go with your porridge? I'll just wander on down and see if I can't persuade the lovely fat hens to be telling me where their nests are. Dauntless SwiftSure keeps her word – see if it isn't so."

And with a cocky salute, she turned and sauntered out, shutting the door behind her.

Jonel, still a bit dazed, looked at me. "What just happened there? That didn't feel like your healing Power."

"I think Dauntless SwiftSure has a magical Gift of some kind, and when she – intruded on us, I borrowed some of her strength to help you."

"Dauntless SwiftSure? That was really the Messenger Dauntless SwiftSure?" he asked as if he hadn't just heard her name herself.

"You've heard of her?" I asked, "Oh, did Cleonie tell you about her?"

"Sanna, everyone knows about Dauntless SwiftSure. She's famous all along the north borders of Arrex. She's the cleverest Messenger the Peoples of the Wide Skies have ever had. You keep a civil tongue in your head when talking to her. She's Important!"

"Who *are* the Peoples of the Wide Skies?" I demanded.

"They're a confederation of nomad tribes," he explained, tugging at his blankets and glaring at them as they became even more rumpled. "They come and go as they please, when they please, on paths that no one can follow. Even the Golmen raiders won't follow them into the Eastern deserts. The Peoples of the Wide Skies come to the borders of Arrex to trade for silk and salt and steel. Their Headwomen never come in off the desert. They send their Messengers to do all their negotiating. And SwiftSure of Tribe Dauntless is the most powerful of the Messengers, so whatever you do, be polite to her. She tells us all the movements of the raiders when she comes to dicker. Don't annoy her, or she might stop talking. Worse yet, she might start lying. We desperately need that intelligence!"

I took the blankets out of his hands. He was only tangling them worse. As I shook and smoothed his bedding, I asked, "Wouldn't it be a good idea just to ally with the Peoples of the Wide Skies against the Golmen tribes, then?"

"Good for us and good for them," he replied, settling back on his freshly fluffed pillows with a sigh. "But the Peoples of the Wide Skies refuse to be bound by any alliances – even mutually beneficial treaties." He frowned, puzzled. "The trading season is over now. I wonder what Dauntless SwiftSure is doing so far south?"

"I'll ask her over breakfast," I said. "I'm going to have eggs – 'see if it isn't so.'"

Chapter 8

I emptied Jonel's chamberpot into the privy, saving Duggers the trip, then looked into the stable to check on our horses. The buckskin gelding I was riding was content to be well fed and lazy, but Jonel's young roan stallion was getting restive after an entire day in one place. I looked in at the Messenger's horse as well – a big bay mare with a knowing eye.

"You look as if you could tell a few stories," I said, scratching her under the jaw.

"And since it is that she is coming from the finest livery stable in Arrex, I'm sure she has seen more things to be telling the stories of than many a horse before her," the Messenger said from above my head.

I followed the sound of her voice and saw her peering down at me from the lip of the hayloft. Spurning the ladder altogether, she caught hold of the edge of the support beam

Sanna Meets Dauntless Swiftsure

under her, then tumbled down to hang by her upstretched arms, a few feet above the floor. She let go of the beam and dropped to her feet as lightly as a raven landing on a branch.

"Do but see what it is that I am finding up in the warm and dusty hayloft among all the bold barn cats and the cowering mousies." She slipped a hand into the front of her vest and pulled out two speckled brown eggs. "Isn't it the fruit of the labors of two canny hens? Laid this very morning and so new the shells are scarcely hard. And how will you be liking them cooked, my poor fainting willow-lass? Will you be having them boiled like a witless bold Golmen raider is boiled in the Smoke Pots of Argrisha? Or would you be eating your eggs fried like a wicked foolish raider might be fried on the hard joints of the Bones? Or will you be taking them raw as a heedless raider caught by a full nest of taureks?"

"If Cleonie can spare this pair of eggs," I said, taken aback by her bloodthirsty images, "I like them best scrambled with onions. But maybe it would be better to save them for the children."

"The children, blessings on the dears, will be a-gathering of the eggs for a fine rich custard for your brother when I tell them where the hens are hiding. And Mistress Cleonie will be sending them out her own self, see if it isn't so."

And so it was. Cleonie was delighted to scramble the eggs for my breakfast in addition to the porridge and syrup. And as soon as breakfast was done, the two littlest children were sent scrambling out to the barn with a basket to fetch in the eggs.

"I'd never have thought of looking for those hens in the hayloft. You'd think the cats would keep them out," Cleonie said.

"Ah, but the wise plump biddies flutter up under the eaves and are nesting on the rafters out of reach of the longest clawed cats, the clever feathered darlings," SwiftSure remarked.

"Oh, well, they're just chickens, after all," replied Cleonie, a bit flustered. "If you'll pardon me, I'll go see if the Commander has finished his breakfast." And she bustled away.

The Messenger and I were sitting in the great room, sharing a small pot of tea. I felt sympathy with Jonel's young stallion, cooped up too long, and was looking for some excuse to get out and get some exercise. And I wanted to think about the Messenger. She hinted and guessed and kept me off balance and dizzy with her rush of words. I wanted to ask her a dozen questions but was sure it would be rude to voice any of them. I fact, I couldn't think of anything to say that was guaranteed not to annoy her. Jonel's warnings had made me extremely ill-at-ease around this strange woman. I put my cup down on the table and gathered my feet under me, but before I could stand, SwiftSure spoke.

"So will you be telling me about your dream now, my fine bright girl? The road outside is a swamp that I'll not be traversing at all this day. And you'll not be traveling without your brother, he too weak to stand and saddle his own horse another three-day at the least. So there is naught before us but a long cloudy day and a great empty inn and only our own two selves for entertainment. If you

Sanna Meets Dauntless Swiftsure

will be telling me the tale of your dream, then likewise I will be telling you any one thing that you might be asking of me."

"What are you doing this far south?" I asked without tact, without subtlety, without forethought.

"Ha! And aren't I hearing the very voice of the Commander in that question?" she laughed. "Well, my bright mirror of wisdom, tell me first the tale of your dream, and then I will be telling you what duty it is that is bringing me along here so far south, and farther still if all the truth should be known."

"Agreed," I said, relieved that she hadn't taken offense at my nosy question. Then I paused, pondered. My dream had been so vivid, but so strange.

"I dreamed about a peculiar animal," I finally began. "It had two big lumps on its back, and an old woman rode between them. I've never seen such an ugly beast, all shaggy and mangy looking, and the color of cow dung."

"The woman was mangy?" asked SwiftSure, with smiles twitching the sides of her mouth.

"No, the animal was. And it had an expression on its face as if it sneered at any creature on two feet."

"Why surely that sounds just like Auntie HealWell's camel, indeed it does. The most arrogant being to ever set foot on sand and evil tempered in the bargain."

"Your Auntie HealWell is evil tempered?" I asked.

SwiftSure burst out laughing. "Indeed she was for a fact, though not a touch on that wicked camel of hers. And did she say anything to you at all while you were dreaming?"

"No," I answered, grinning. "The camel never spoke at all."

"Tcha, be off with you, you slippery bit of nonsense," she chided me, laughing. "Now get along with telling your dream, and I'll rein in my hasty galloping tongue with both hands."

So I told her about my dream. How the Way of the Winds had left me blown almost inside out. How the Heart of the Fire had blistered my face and crisped my hair to ash. How I never *did* find my own way in the dark but had to follow the leading of the Good One by the Gifts she had given me.

"So if a dream does mean anything, I guess it means that I don't know enough to try facing strange new challenges right now," I concluded. "I'll probably be better off with my studies, safely back at the Thon Academy of Higher Magic for Young Ladies of Exceptional Talent."

I sighed. Returning to classes somehow seemed confining now. It had been months since I had had to pay attention to proper deportment, to appropriate behavior, to boring but necessary studies, to acting like a "proper young Sorceress." I had saved Prince Jerris of Arrex at risk to my own life. He was the only man I would ever love, but he was still a prince and obliged to marry another member of royalty to beget legitimate royal heirs. A prince does not marry to please himself.

And I was still a Sorceress, and if I chose to follow my Talent and Gifts, I could not spare the time for a husband, a home, a family. Sorcery is not just a vocation. It's a life.

Sanna Meets Dauntless Swiftsure

So for the noblest of reasons, I had said goodbye to my heart and set out with Jonel to return to Thon. I wasn't quite 18, and I felt life had treated me rather badly.

Swiftsure's voice called me back to our conversation. "Well, there's more than one way of reading that dream of yours, my darling girl. You were after asking me what it is that brings SwiftSure, Messenger of Tribe Dauntless, this far to the south. And the truth of it all is, Auntie HealWell died and left us without a Shaman these next few months until my cousin CureAll grows into her first moon time and becomes a woman. So it is that our Headwoman has sent me to seek out a woman Healer to travel with Tribe Dauntless. And wouldn't you just be knowing that it was to the Academy at Thon she has sent me at the very first."

"Well, I wish you good luck," I told her, "But the Journeywoman Sorceresses get their assignments at Midsummer, and Healers have their pick of positions. I don't know who they might find to help you."

"Ah, but there it is, my green willow-lass. The winds have blown me here, and so have they also blown you here, to my very doorstep as it were, and though you may not be fully fit to be a Shaman, not being born to the tribe, you are Gifted enough to heal us of our ills, such as they are, the healthy and hearty people that Tribe Dauntless is. So think on it, Sanna, you wild young bird, wouldn't you love to leave all your schools and rules and travel free with the Peoples of the Wide Skies?"

Chapter 9

I sat and stared at her. A shouting match started in my head.

"Yes!" bellowed Self-Indulgence, "It sounds like fun. Why should I always have to give up everything that I want to do?"

"No!" yelled Prosaic Common Sense. "I still have three more years of school to finish before I even get my Journeywoman assignment. I'm not fully prepared to be a Sorceress."

"I don't need any more schooling," declared Pride. "It's just a waste of my time."

"Everyone will be so disappointed in me if I drop out now," spoke Responsibility.

"I can't live my life for everyone else. I have to do what's right for myself," recited a Devil of Selfishness, taking truth and bending it to bad purpose.

Sanna Meets Dauntless Swiftsure

"How could I tell the Matron?" asked a Weakening Spirit, sorely tempted.

"Write a letter explaining how desperately I'm needed," whispered a Weevil of Cowardice. "Jonel can deliver it when he's strong enough to travel."

"No! No!" roared my better selves. "It would ruin my life! I mustn't stray from the straight and narrow path. I'll regret it if I do!"

"And has sticking to the straight and narrow made me so very happy?" hissed Resentful Romance. "I did the right thing about Prince Jerris, and I've never been so miserable."

"Oh, pull your socks up. You'll live." I could hear my older brothers mocking my childish troubles. I could hear my hardworking father dismissing my trivial concerns. I could hear my mother being too busy to be bothered with me. My head seemed terribly crowded all of a sudden.

SwiftSure was watching me as keenly as a hawk ready to pounce on a mouse.

"Ah, here's the great fool that I am, asking you to cast off your safe and comfortable life where you know what will be happening in every minute of every day of every week of the year to come, and no surprises to ever break the even tenor of your life, and to go gallivanting off to unknown parts with a total stranger. And you not knowing a thing about Tribe Dauntless or the Peoples of the Wide Skies or even what a camel might be. Of course you'll want to be finding out a bit about us all and thinking over your decision like the wise, cautious girl that you are."

She rose and crossed the room to gaze out the door as she spoke. Then she turned to me again. "It's looking as if the wet winds have ceased their weeping for this small while. Would you be liking to escape from under this dark heavy roof and walk about a bit in the open air? And while we are so beguiling ourselves, stretching our legs and loosening our backs, I can be telling you anything at all you might be wishing to know about me and my people and how we are living bold and unfettered on the Northern desert and on the gentle grasslands."

It seemed as if there wasn't enough air in the room. I jumped up so fast that I knocked over my stool and ran through the door.

The town of Little Dinwiddy, had grown up around the joining of three major roads. From here one could go north to Arrex, south to Thon or east to Dianos. Cleonie's inn-yard was a cobbled triangle with the inn along one side, the stable along the second, and the road to Arrex along the third. The buildings were whitewashed, with the door and window frames painted a friendly dull red. A pair of benches stood on either side of the door. Barrels full of dirt had held bright flowers in summer. It was a cheery, tidy-looking little place. Over the door hung a charming sign, showing a mother hen surrounded by chicks. A wreath of hops had been painted around them to show that ale was served inside.

Looking up and down the road I could see other inn signs. There was The Badger (where Jillia, who was "*not* a nice woman" resided), The Raider's Head (with a ghastly rendering of a swarthy turbaned man, eyes rolled up white, mouth agape, and blood trickling from the ragged stump of his neck) and beyond the market square on the road to Dianos was The Rose. In spite of the soggy roads, several riders and even a few wagons splashed by. Women carrying market baskets picked their way among the puddles. Children scampered around, their shouts and laughter ringing in the cold wet air. The sky was a low gray blanket of clouds, thick enough to block all trace of sunshine. I didn't even cast a shadow.

Dauntless SwiftSure was also looking over the scene. "Tcha! And a nasty, sniveling sky that is, I'm thinking," she declared. "Too lazy to throw up a proper storm, but only moping and drooping and weeping like some city maid crossed in love. Well, it looks to me as if the road to Arrex is less of a muck than the others. Shall we be taking our stroll in that direction, my fine willow-lass?"

She gestured, I nodded and we turned north, toward Arrex and my adored Jerris and all the sweet, impossible fantasies of love I had abandoned.

"How does a girl of Tribe Dauntless behave when she is crossed in love?" I asked.

"Well, and doesn't that all depend on the crossing?" the Messenger said, leaping across a real boot-sucker of a mudhole. "She holds her own life in her own two hands, and if it's just a matter of other people forbidding, while she and the lad are willing, then she takes him regardless. And she throws back her shoulders and takes whatever comes after, as well. The women of the Wide Skies make no promise lasting more than a year and a day, and a girl can bear anything for that long."

"Your marriages last only a year and a day?" I asked, aghast. "But what about the children?"

"It is to me a great puzzlement how other people will be considering their children," she said. "Among my people, the birth of a child is nothing less than a gift to the tribe. It is an honor and a pleasure to be sharing in the care and the loving of a babe. We are all her aunties and kindly cousins. And if her mother and father decide that the passion they felt is maybe not so strong as they thought it would be at the end of a year and a day, if he farts too pungently and she snores too loudly and they can no longer bear to live together, then they separate. Does the Heart of the Fire thereby grow any colder? Do the fine trade routes become longer, or the strong arms of love grow weaker? Does the pommel basket cease to rock the darling child?"

"Well, uh, I guess not – but who does the child go with?" I asked, a bit bewildered by the transitory sort of life SwiftSure was describing.

"Why, the child is born to the tribe, as I was after telling you, foolish girl," the Messenger said. "The father comes from another tribe of course, to be keeping the bloodlines clean, and if he wants to be staying with his child, then he is staying with the tribe, though mayhap not with the mother of his babe. He might tent with the bachelors, or another woman may choose him for a year and a day. It is entirely up to him where he goes. But the babe stays with the tribe."

Then she put one hand on my shoulder and pointed at the sky. "Look you now at that fine strong eagle!"

We had made our way out of Little Dinwiddy as we talked, and a view opened out before us. The road to Arrex wound north between two ridges, and a tiny black speck floated in the wind between them, almost invisible against the gray bellies of the clouds.

"How can you tell that's an eagle?" I asked. "From this distance I couldn't tell a crow from a buzzard."

"Ah, well, and doesn't the Firebird know all the beings of the air?" she said. She seemed almost pulled onto tiptoe by longing.

"What?" I quacked. Then, remembering my manners, I amended my question to, "I beg your pardon. I don't know what the Firebird is."

"It is looking to me as if rain bids fair to return on the shifting of the wind," she said, which was no answer at all. "Best we stretch our strong, long legs and make our way back to the inn with all haste, lest we be drinking the sky's tears from our own cheeks before we find shelter." And with a wide, sweeping gesture, she linked her elbow through mine, looked again toward the eagle, bobbed her head in a sort of exaggerated nod, then turned me around and rushed me back into town too quickly for speech.

SwiftSure had read the weather accurately, and we made it into the courtyard just as the drizzle began again.

"That little trot has me sweating like a pony," I said, disengaging myself from SwiftSure's hold. "If you'll pardon me, I'll go have a wash before midday meal."

She smiled brightly. "Isn't that the lovely thought, my clean willow-girl? Why, I believe I'll just be joining you and we can wash one another's backs like the one hand washing the other. This fair wee village of Dinwiddy has a grand fine bath house, see if it isn't so. Do you be asking Mistress Cleonie for towels and I'll see to fetching a change of clothes for us both. Where might you be keeping your things, my darling girl?"

"Oh . . uh, thank you but . . . well, I'd rather not, thanks. I . . . I have some scars. They're pretty ugly. People will stare. I'll just take a pitcher and basin up to my room. You have a nice wash though. I'll tell Cleonie that you need a towel." And I bolted into the sanctuary of the kitchen.

Chapter 10

"Why, Sanna, what is it?" asked Cleonie, turning from her cooking as I hurtled through the door.

I could feel my face flaming with embarrassment at my rude behavior. But I couldn't help myself.

"The Messenger – Dauntless SwiftSure – she wants to use the bathhouse. May she have a towel?" I babbled.

"Of course. But dear, what's the matter? You're frightened."

"She – she makes me feel like a mouse in the shadow of a hawk. I feel like I'm going to be caught!"

SwiftSure's voice came from the doorway behind me, "Ah, now, my green willow-lass, how should I be catching you? I admit that I would like it fine if you would come to serve as Shaman to Tribe Dauntless, but I scarce can snatch you up and carry you there against your will, the clever, strong Sorceress that you are. It well may be that

I have pressed my friendship too forcefully upon you, us being the only two idle persons in town this day, and none but each other to beguile our waiting, but blame that on your own thoughtful questions and forgive my excess pleasure in the answering, won't you just?"

I was adrift in the wash of her words. I just nodded mutely.

SwiftSure smiled at me, then turned to Cleonie. "Then, inn's mistress, if you would be so kind as to be making me the loan of a towel, I'll just be off and enjoy the glories of Little Dinwiddy's bathhouse before our midday meal. And the modest young Sorceress will be washing in her room, I'm thinking. Isn't that so, bright Sanna?"

Again, I nodded. Cleonie fetched a ewer of warm water and a basin for me and towels for both of us. SwiftSure stood at the foot of the stairs, watching me till I closed the door to my room. And the little mouse heart in my chest just pitterpatted in panic.

The rain continued with a steady dull patience. After the midday meal was finished, I went up to my room and took a nap, sleeping most of the afternoon. When I woke, the sun was slipping long fingers under the edges of the cloud cover and prying it up for a brief, brilliant sunset. I was standing in the door of the inn, watching the changing colors in the clouds overhead when Dauntless SwiftSure came up behind me again.

"Well, and doesn't it look like a dry night and a fair day tomorrow? With this kindly warm wind blowing, we might set out on our road before midday, I am thinking."

Sanna Meets Dauntless Swiftsure

"You move silently as a hunting owl!" I snapped, startled by her unexpected appearance. "Jonel won't be ready to travel for at least a week, so he and I will be here long enough for another storm to roll in. All this rain keeps things nice and green, but it sure is gloomy."

She threw her head back in a laugh, and her dark eyes glittered in the last rays of the sun. "Your brother will feel no gloom, basking as he will be in the lovelight of our inn's mistress. While as for you and me, sweet willow-lass, we shall be riding well away from this rain, in safety and all comfort. I've spoken with your careful brother, don't you know, darling girl, and offered to take you on into Thon along with myself. You couldn't be safer in your own mother's arms than you will be in traveling with Dauntless SwiftSure."

Chapter 11

I stared at her in astonishment. Then I babbled, "Oh, I couldn't put you to so much trouble. Jonel should never have asked you ---"

"Now don't be putting the blame on the poor lad," she interrupted me. "He was just a-lying there quiet and sleepy as any fat ground squirrel with a larder full of grass, and in comes I upon him and says to him, 'Commander, I've a long ride to Thon that I must be making as soon as ever may be, and there's your little sister who is also bound for Thon, and don't you know, I've taken a liking to the girl (as who wouldn't, the fair bright lass that she is) and I'm here to be asking you to give me the pleasure of her company as I ride along. I'll be caring for her as if she were my own darling sister, seeing to her ease and comfort before my own, and I will guard her with my very life, on the word of SwiftSure, Messenger of Tribe Dauntless.'

"And then I said a hundred other things all of the same kind until I covered him with my words and wishes and wore him down, and so, weary of my ways, he has turned the care and feeding of you over to me. And now you may be returning to your lessons and your well-led life all before the turn of the spring equinox, see if it isn't so. We bid fair to set out tomorrow, so smile, green willow-lass, and come along to the fine dinner inn-mistress Cleonie has prepared, the wonderful cook that she is."

"I'll just have a word with Jonel first," I said, turning toward the stairs with fury in my mind.

SwiftSure darted in front of me, blocking my way. "Now there isn't a thing you might be saying to him that wouldn't be the better for a smallest bit of a wait and a sound meal in your belly, isn't it so? And wouldn't it just be rude to let our good dinner go cold while you have your argle-bargle with your weak, bedeviled brother? You know everyone sitting to table can hear every word that the two of you speak with your fine, strong voices, and won't you be speaking the fine strong words, the pair of you? Do you but sit this small while and think over this plan and mayhap it might not be so unwelcome to you after all. And Mistress Cleonie has made dumplings for our stew that are so light and delicious that they will truly lift up the tongue in your mouth, see if it isn't the truth that I'm telling you this day. Come along now and just sit you down and take a mouthful of this elegant, beautiful stew."

Well, she was right. I could certainly argue with Jonel later, and I was so hungry that my stomach was trying to crawl up my throat and go foraging for itself. I allowed her to herd me over to the table where our meal was set out, wreathed in fragrant steam. The dumplings were superb, floating on a stew of vegetables and rabbit.

I thought as I ate. As long as I had to go back to school, sooner was probably better than later. I sighed, drooping my head a bit. Jonel was probably right to agree to send me on with SwiftSure. Then I looked up and saw her watching me as intently as a falcon. Her eyelids flicked shut and open so fast I barely saw it, and the predator look was gone. She gave me a wide easy smile and went on with the story she was weaving for the children.

After dinner I trudged upstairs to Jonel's room. He was drowsing, but roused when I opened the door. His look of pleasurable expectation crumbled when he saw it was me, and not Cleonie. I shut the door carefully behind me and sat down on the foot of his bed. We stared at one another in silence for a minute, searching for words.

"I *am* an adult now, you know," I said, jumping right into the middle of it.

"Sanna, if I could travel, we'd have been on the road today. I'm responsible for getting you back to school. SwiftSure can get you there safely and in good time. And it's a terrific honor for you to travel with her. You mind your manners around her! If I can't deliver you myself, then --"

"I'm not a parcel, Jonel. You don't have to deliver me. I'm perfectly capable of making my own arrangements. I *am* seventeen now. I have to start taking care of myself sometime!"

"Well, don't you want to go with SwiftSure?" he asked.

"She makes me uncomfortable," I replied. "And you know what, Jonel? I'm a grown-up now, and I can deal with that. I would rather travel with you, but if I can't, it makes sense for me to travel with SwiftSure. But," and here I stood and just roared at him, "how *dare* you make plans for my life without consulting me?"

Anger washed red into his face. He struggled to sit upright. "Don't you talk to me like that!" he yelled.

"I'm *going* to do what you wanted," I shouted back. "What do *you* have to be mad about?"

Cleonie burst in. "We can hear you two all over the inn!" she said in alarm. "Lower your voices. What are you fighting over?"

My eyes were filling with tears of rage. I was shaking with it. "He's treating me like an infant! He's made plans to ship me off with SwiftSure tomorrow without asking what I wanted. It's my life, and I'm old enough to have a say in it now. People can't just tell me what to do anymore. I'm an adult."

"You're not acting like one," Jonel said, trying to untangle his feet from the sheets and stand up.

"Neither are you," Cleonie said tartly, "Now calm down, the pair of you. Jonel, even if Sanna were eleven years old, she still should have been consulted, and you know it. You owe her an apology."

"I just wanted to do the best for her," he grumbled.

"Good for you," Cleonie said. "But Sanna is not one of your troopers, and she gets a say in decisions concerning her. Right?"

"But she's so young," he whined.

"Jonel, she's an adult. Your baby sister is an adult, and you can't tell her what to do any more. She deserves an apology." Cleonie patted his shoulder and looked kindly into his eyes.

"I'll remind you of this when your girls turn seventeen," Jonel said to her, then looked at me. "Sorry, Sanna. I'm used to giving orders. And I'm not used to being yelled at. You need to learn to control that temper of yours."

"You need to learn to quit telling me what to do," I snapped. "I'll see you before I leave tomorrow." And I stomped out of the room.

I'm sure he could hear the creaks and groans of the old bedframe in my room next door as I threw myself under the covers and began thrashing around, trying to find a comfy spot. An angry bed always seems full of lumps and wrinkles. I didn't sleep well at all.

Chapter 12

The next morning, I woke feeling sorry and unrested. I could hear Cleonie bustling around downstairs so I knew night was over. I rolled out, dressed, and took my chastened self over to Jonel's room. I knocked tentatively at the door.

"Come in," his pleasant baritone voice called.

I opened the door slowly. "How's my patient this morning?" I asked, trying to be cheerful.

He sat up in bed. He was stronger than the day before, but I could see he hadn't slept well either.

"Why don't you want to go with SwiftSure?" he asked. "It really is a great honor for you, and you might even learn something useful from her."

"Jonel," I said tiredly, "I'm mad because you didn't ask me before you made your decision. And I'm going, so let's not fight anymore, all right?"

"You said she made you uncomfortable," he persisted. "If you really don't want to go with her, I suppose we can work something else out. But how to keep it from looking like an insult..." Concern put a crease between his brows and pinched the corners of his eyes.

I leaned over and hugged him. "Jonel, it's all right. I just feel smothered by all her words sometimes. And she talks around and around a thing until I'm so dizzy I don't know where I stand. But what difference does that make? We'll just be traveling companions for a few days. It's not as if we were going to be spending years together. I can let her talk."

"Well, if you're sure," he said. "But you don't have to go if you don't want to."

"That's what I was trying to tell you last night," I said. "And I'm sorry I yelled at you."

"Aw -- you always were a scrappy kid," he said, ruffling my hair. I grinned and swatted his hand away, then laid my ear against his chest to listen to his lungs. Nice and clear. Holding his hand, I wove my Gift along the fibers of his body, assessing his strength and health. There were scars from wounds I would have healed more neatly for him, broken bones I might have knit together more strongly, the stains and knots of long-gone parasites and illnesses. But he was as sound as I could make him now, although he had no reserves of strength and needed quite a lot of building up.

"I think, if Dennies will give you a hand, you can start walking out to the privy today," I told Jonel. "The exercise will do you good, but don't get chilled. I'll tell Cleonie."

"I'm going to marry her," he said, smiling with pride.

Sanna Meets Dauntless Swiftsure

"Have you asked her how she feels about it?" I teased.

He blushed.

"You haven't actually asked her yet? Jonel, you do it! She's a treasure! If you don't grab her fast, someone else may discover her."

"I just need to find the right time," he mumbled, plucking uncertainly at his blankets.

"Well, if you can meddle in my life for my own good, surely I can return the favor," I said, and marched out of the room calling, "Cleonie? Would you come up here a moment?"

"Sanna, no!" Jonel cried behind me as Cleonie came hurrying up the stairs.

"Is something wrong?" she asked a bit breathlessly.

"Jonel has something he wants to ask you," I said, ushering her into his room.

"Sanna, how dare you?" he snarled at me.

"What is it, Jonel? Is there anything I can do for you?" Cleonie, in her haste, had carried along the broom and dustpan she had been wielding. A clean apron swathed her plump curves, and concern for my stupid brother wrinkled her wide, smooth brow.

I took the equipment out of her hands. "Hold his hand, Cleonie. He's terribly frightened," I told her.

"Oh, my dear!" she exclaimed, falling to her knees beside the bed and taking Jonel's hands. "What is it?"

"Shall I tell her?" I asked brightly.

"Just get out!" he snapped.

I stepped out and kicked the door shut behind me, then, leaving the broom and dustpan on a bench as I went through the main room, made my morning trip to the privy. Scraps of clouds blew across a clean blue sky, and the bite in the wind told me that winter hadn't finished with us yet. Before returning to the inn, I went to check on the horses, singing snatches of "The Old Man's Wedding" as I patted and inspected them.

"Ah, and isn't that the sprightly tune of all the world," said SwiftSure from behind me.

I spun around in startlement and snapped, "Just once in a while, I would like to see you coming,"

She laughed. "Ah, there you have a great deal in common with many a dead Golmen raider. But have no fear, Sanna-me-lass. It is only the best of all things that I wish for you. And what is the cause of your merry chirruping this fine morning?"

"Oh, you might say a family issue has been resolved," I said, with a smile. "Shall we go in to breakfast?"

When Cleonie came out of the kitchen with our bowls of porridge, she put her arm around my shoulders and kissed my cheek. "Thank you, dear. He did rather need a push," she said.

"Have you set a date?" I asked. "Don't let him keep you dangling."

"Two weeks next Restday," she answered. "By then he should be strong enough to stand up and say 'I will' in a loud, clear voice."

"Oh, I wish I could stay!" I exclaimed. "I'm so happy for you both!" We hugged, and smiled into one another's eyes. Then she patted my cheek.

Sanna Meets Dauntless Swiftsure

"Thank you, dear. But since you do have to leave today, I'll go pack a little food for you." And she bustled out to the kitchen again.

When she left, SwiftSure raised her eyebrow at me questioningly. "And has the Commander finally brought his shy and timid self to plight his troth with our worthy inn-mistress?

I stuck a spoonful of porridge and syrup into my mouth and nodded smugly.

Chapter 13

Cleonie gave me enough food to feed three fifteen-year-old boys for five days. If I hadn't had my magic belt bag to carry it all, we would have needed a pack horse. SwiftSure was ready in no time at all and waited while I hugged Cleonie, Aster, and MaiRose. Dennies had helped Jonel downstairs, and again I presented my cheeks to my brother so he could kiss me goodbye. I read the worry in his eyes and assured him, "I'll be fine, Jonel. What could happen to me with Dauntless SwiftSure at my side?"

"Indeed, Commander, I shall be cherishing your dear sister and guarding her as if she were the most valuable of treasures," SwiftSure called from atop her mare. "Now let us be setting off, Sanna. We are having a good long day ahead of us."

Sanna Meets Dauntless Swiftsure

The road had dried overnight. It was still a bit boggy in the low spots, but the rest of the time it was easy going. I pulled my hat low on my forehead, wrapped a scarf around my face and ears, and fastened my cloak tightly against the wind. SwiftSure rode with her head and throat bare to the cold, her soft white hair blowing around her like war-banners. Dark firs and pines shaded the road, stands of aspens shimmered their yellowish spring green. The rich smell of the earth rode streamers of mist in the cold, damp air.

About midday, we came to a small trail branching off to the side of the road. SwiftSure drew rein.

"Shall we just be going the smallest way down this little trail?" she asked. "There is the loveliest sheltered little glade that I'm knowing of where we might be sitting a brief while in the sun, sharing a beautiful lunch and taking the smallest rest, for I'm thinking that yourself is looking the slightest bit weary. I could draw water from the dear little stream that trickles through, and then I could be making a tiny fire and heating the water and giving us both the strong cups of sweet tea to bring back warmth to our cold bones."

I could see the glade in my mind's eye, and my cold bones yearned for it. We had made good time that morning and could spare an hour or so for a break. "Good idea," I said, and followed her down the trail.

The place was everything that SwiftSure had promised and more. There was a shelf of bare black stone along the side of the stream, making a dry, clean place to sit and bask in the sun. The shoulder of the hill broke the force of the wind, and we arrived to find a man and woman already picnicking there with a fire burning briskly and a kettle simmering over it. They were wearing long, brightly striped robes of a style I seemed to have seen before but couldn't quite recall where, and they sat on an intricately patterned rug spread across the black stone.

SwiftSure called out, "Why, RugMaker! It's yourself, is it? And doesn't the sight of you just bring joy to my heart? And did you bring the stalwart SeeFar with you, as well? Oh, the glory of it! Why, do but see here, I have the little Healer named Sanna with me, isn't it the wonder of all the world?"

The two waved and beckoned us over.

"You know these people?" I asked, swinging a leg over my horse's back and dismounting.

"Why, I know them as well as I might be knowing my own brother and sister," she said. "SeeFar is the finest Warleader that Tribe Dauntless has brought to birth, and that is no little thing, I'm telling you. And fair clever RugMaker is maker of aerial rugs. And as you may be wondering why they are here so handily waiting for us, I'll just be telling you. But sit your weary bones down on this beautiful rug and take a sip of this lovely tea while you're hearing my tale."

As usual, when dealing with SwiftSure, I felt dazed and uncertain. But the thick rug looked soft, the sunshine falling on it looked warm and the tea smelled delicious. My stomach growled, putting in the deciding vote. I sat down, took a sip of the tea (mountain camellia leaves, rose petals, lots of honey, a splash of milk and a pinch of something I couldn't quite identify--cardamom perhaps?) and began pulling food out of my belt bag.

"Now hasn't the good inn-mistress done well by us this fair day?" said SwiftSure. "SeeFar, do but taste the hearty bread she has made, and take a slice of her savory cheese there. Look you, isn't this a feast fit for the finest of folks? Drink your tea, Sanna-me-lass. It will take the chill from out your poor cold belly."

And when I had drunk off the delicious, warming beverage, she filled my cup again.

"Now I will be answering all the questions that are crowding behind your sweet open face," SwiftSure said to me. "And you needn't even be asking the most of them."

"SwiftSure will talk your ear off," said SeeFar, in a light tenor voice. "We are by way of needing a Healer for these two weeks past. SwiftSure was sent to find one for us, and here are you. Will you be coming with us till our cousin CureAll is old enough to be Shaman?"

"I can't," I said, feeling oddly calm, and taking another sip of the delicious tea. "I'm not even a Journeywoman Sorceress yet. I have years more schooling ahead of me."

"Do but listen to the modest little willow-lass," said SwiftSure. "And isn't she the very one who turned the mighty Prince Jerris into the Golden Dragon of Arrex? And didn't she then give him the power gem to change himself from dragon to man and back again? I my very self have seen her work magical healing, and though she may be weak in body at this moment, she has the spirit of a mighty healer in her scarred and skinny chest."

"We are knowing who she is, SwiftSure," said RugMaker, and her voice was like velvet and smoke. "The ghost of HealWell has been speaking in my dreams and has told me all. And are you sure young Sanna will not be coming willingly?"

"Noooo," I drawled happily. "I won't come willingly. Are you going to snatch me up and carry me kicking and screaming all the way to the high desert?" and I fell back, squealing with laughter.

SeeFar stood up. "I'll just be fetching a quilt, then," he said, and walked over to the horses.

"It's the sweet high air for me," declared SwiftSure. "Oh, and glad I am of it!"

She stood up and stretched her arms over her head, sighing, "Yesssss!" And her arms grew longer, brighter, wider. Heat began to radiate from her. Her arms were transforming into wings, her feet into claws, and her soft white hair was turning into a covering of soft white feathers.

"Yessss," she cried again, and brought her wings down in a mighty stroke as she leapt into the air. She burst into white hot flame and flew, burning and exalting into the sky. SwiftSure had turned into a Firebird!

"Oh, and haven't I told her a thousand times not to be taking off from one of my rugs!" grumbled RugMaker. "She will be scorching the nap, the heedless wight."

"She never is scorching it, though, is she?" said SeeFar. "And will our fair worthy prisoner be needing another cup of tea before you are carrying her away?"

"The longer she lies quiet, the easier it all will be," said RugMaker. "But take no liberties with the helpless lass."

SeeFar sat down behind me and pulled me up so I lay partly across his lap, leaning back against his shoulder. My arms lay limp, and my boots dragged like there were

Sanna Meets Dauntless Swiftsure

no muscles left in my legs. SeeFar reached for the cup RugMaker handed him, and my head flopped back and bobbled loosely so I was staring up his nose. A nice, strong beak of a nose it was. He was beardless and blonde with the same dark, dark eyes that SwiftSure had.

He lifted my head gently back upright, set the cup to my lips and poured a sip of tea into my mouth. I drank like a good child.

"What's an aerial rug?" I asked, before he could put the cup against my lips again.

"You'll be seeing that in no time at all," RugMaker said.

Again I was given a draught of the tea, and again I drank it down. I rolled my eyes so I could look toward the strong handsome face, so close to my own that his breath caressed my cheek.

"I want to go back to school in Thon," I said, clearly. Then my eyes rolled closed. SeeFar slid me down to lie comfortably on my back, and I felt him kiss me lightly on the mouth.

"When CureAll is taking her place as healer, dear girl, I'll be seeing to it that you are going anywhere you like, if you'll be wanting to leave us by then," he murmured into my ear. Then he covered me with something soft and warm, and I heard his footsteps moving away.

"I'll be catching up with you when I've taken the horses back to the stable," SeeFar called.

"I'll be watching for you," RugMaker replied.

The ground underneath me began to tremble, then suddenly fell away. Surprise opened my eyes against the strength of the drug. The treetops were dropping down

79

toward us! I mewled and tried to force my arms around my head. All I could do was flinch and jerk. And then the treetops somehow slid past. I felt as if I were lying on a hammock. Wind blew past my face.

RugMaker spoke with a laugh in her voice, "An aerial rug, my dear, is by way of being a carpet that flies."

Chapter 14

I slept. It was almost evening when I woke. I felt a merry, rosy glow.

"I'm going to wet all over your nice rug if you don't let me off soon." I said happily.

"So yourself is awake at last, are you?" said RugMaker. "Well then, let you off I shall."

The rug tilted under me. I started to sit up to see what was happening.

"Lie still!" RugMaker ordered. "Look you, it is especially important to be balancing the rug during take-offs and landings."

Suddenly, a snow-covered crag reared up before my eyes. I gasped. Then there was a thump, a skidding sensation, and at last the carpet came to rest. I threw off the soft warm quilt SeeFar had placed over me and rolled to my feet. We had landed on a mountain snowfield. On one side, cliffs dropped precipitously away. On the other side, the peak that had so startled me raised itself in icy glory.

I stepped off the rug and pulled down my breeches but was more light-headed than I had realized. I lost my balance, tangled my feet in my pant-legs, fell and began rolling toward the drop-off. RugMaker managed to snag a handful of shirt sleeve before I had skidded too far and dragged me ruthlessly back to the rug. I was giggling helplessly.

"This is quite a remarkable drug you've given me," I chortled. "I should feel scared to death and furious, but all I feel is giddy. Wheeee! Boompsadaisy!

"Oh, but you should have the drug out of you entirely by now," RugMaker said, white-faced with anxiety and frowning at me. "Just be doing your business so I can be getting you safely back in the air."

"Oh goody! Back in the air. Back in the air. Back in the air," I sang as I answered nature's call.

As soon as I had re-adjusted my clothes, RugMaker grabbed me by the belt and dragged me into the middle of the rug. "Now sit you still!" she ordered.

I wrapped the quilt around my shoulders and sat, beaming with idiot glee.

RugMaker sat carefully in the center of the leading edge, picked up the long corner tassels in either hand, and gave them a lifting little jerk. The carpet began to rise and slide forward, toward the cliff. The world dropped away below us, and we were sailing as fast and as freely as any hawk. The wind whipped my face and was cold enough to freeze my nose hairs. RugMaker, though, sat as if in the stillest sunny courtyard. Her headdress neither ruffled nor lifted. Her robes moved not a whit.

"How come there's no wind where you are?" I shouted above the gale.

"When I was knotting the rug, I was also tying in a good many of my own hairs," she replied. "So I am by way of being part of the magic, and the magic is shielding me. And you, slight willow-lass, will be much the warmer if you will be lying down."

I flopped down onto my belly with my chin propped on my hands. The rug radiated a pleasant slight warmth. Clouds and mountain peaks and startled birds slid past us.

"Now *this* is the way to travel!" I crowed. "No saddle sores, no trail mud, no branches in the face, no sweat, no flies, no dirt, no achy muscles, no horse poop, no ---"

"Yes, mouseling, this is in all ways the best means of travel. Now do be keeping quiet, will you not?"

I lay there obediently silent for over an hour, contentedly watching the scenery passing. I noticed one bird that did not swerve away from our carpet. In fact, it seemed to be pursuing us. I watched it for a while as it followed us, gaining very slowly.

"Hello eagle," I caroled, waving cheerily.

RugMaker seemed to come back to herself from a deep meditation. "An eagle? Oh, and where are you seeing the creature?" she said.

"Wayyy back there," I replied, pointing.

She looked, muttered, "Oh, may all the wicked black effrits be flying away with me!" and gave one of the tassels an extra twitch.

The rug swooped around on its side and went rushing back the way we had come. We passed the eagle, turned again (with me laughing in glee at our aerobatics) and came up behind and under the great bird, slowing till it was directly over the rear of the rug. It just stretched out its legs and landed. Then its wings lengthened and consolidated into arms and hands, its legs grew, claws transformed into feet, feathers turned back into long blonde hair, and suddenly SeeFar was dropping down beside me.

"And weren't you just going like a bat with its tail on fire!" SeeFar complained. "Is this how you go about watching for me? I could scarcely be keeping up."

"Yes, well, our new young healer is still feeling the drug, though you know full well that by now, she shouldn't," RugMaker said.

I reclined, leaning on one elbow, and smiled, twiddling my fingers at him in a coy little wave.

"That couldn't be so," said SeeFar. "CureAll said it would be keeping her compliant for no more than the brief hour. Hasn't she slept at all?"

"Oh, sleep she has indeed, and the whole time she was snoring like a camel!" said RugMaker.

"Isn't it possible that she's just shamming her weakness until we are letting down our guard," SeeFar suggested.

"Oooo," I cooed, "that's a wonderful idea! Do you think it would work? I wish I'd thought of it. But RugMaker? -- RugMaker? -- RugMaker? Oh, RugMaker?"

"What is it you're wanting now?" she asked me.

"I'm going to be sick." And I was -- repeatedly -- casting a quantity of greenish fluid onto the carpet. SeeFar pulled away in distaste, gagging and covering his nose with the quilt.

"Get your useless self over there and be helping her!" RugMaker yelled at him.

"Helping her? And what should I be doing to help her? Am I a healer to be tending the noisome sick?" SeeFar yelled back.

"You might be holding her head up so she isn't choking on her bile, you great stupid lout!"

"Don't you be calling me stupid! Who was it that was outwitting the Golmen raiders the last time they were attacking Tribe Dauntless?" he shouted at her.

"A sheep could outwit Golmen raiders, you great dummy! I am thinking that the eagle you were was merely shitting in fear, and only by luck was it striking the Golmen leader full in the face to be blinding him. There was no whit of wit or aim about it at all, but only the kindness of the Good One to us."

"Oh, the foul liar you are, sister mine! You will be taking that back!" he bellowed, throwing off the quilt and jumping to his feet. The carpet pitched and bucked. I had been on my hands and knees and was thrown onto my side where I curled in a moaning, shivering ball of misery, still retching occasionally.

RugMaker glanced back at me. "Look you, SeeFar, she is ailing sorely! And won't SwiftSure be skinning us alive if anything is happening to her foreign Shaman? You must be taking to the air again so that I might be flying the faster and taking the lass to CureAll with all speed."

The quilt was flipped over me and the mess I had made, then the rug beneath me bounced once, and the rush of wind around the corners of the coverlet became a howling gale. I was too weak and racked with stomach cramps to try to see what was going on. All I could do was lie there, using what I could of my Power to trace this illness and deal with the symptoms. But I was airborne. I couldn't ground myself and pull power from the earth. I could sense the tiny gray tendrils of poison worming their way through the tissues of my body, but I had no strength to stop them. I was going to die a long way from home, and no one would ever know what had happened to me.

Chapter 15

It was dark when we landed. A babble of voices surrounded us. The quilt was pulled off me.

"Agh! And isn't that just the stench of all the world?!" someone said. "Where's CureAll?"

"Here I am. Just be letting me through!" a stern young voice said.

"She isn't shaking off the drug, little Cousin CureAll." RugMaker was saying. "And hasn't she just been puking and puking --"

"I am seeing that," the young voice said. "But this shouldn't be happening. She should be back to normal by now. You weren't by way of adding anything to the tea I gave you, did you?"

"No, I was doing just as you were telling me. And I left SeeFar to be flying back all the weary long way on his own two wings so I might be bringing the poor mouseling back to you as quick as ever I could," RugMaker said.

I felt a soft, small hand on my forehead.

"Earth," I whispered. "Put me on earth."

"Let us be getting her off this rug," the young voice said. Many hands lifted me, laid me on the ground – on the sand. Shifting, sterile, useless desert sand! No strength for me there.

I sobbed in despair. Then a hand landed like a claw on my shoulder, and a flame of strength seared into me.

"She can be learning the Way of the Winds," I heard SwiftSure say, "but the poor slip of a lass is too weak to rise to the path alone as yet. Do you but give her one feather from your wing of power, Cousin CureAll, and you will be seeing how well she soars back to strength."

The small soft hand was on my forehead again. She didn't give me a feather. She gave me strength. She poured it into me through her touch, as did SwiftSure. I seemed to feel winds blowing through me. Strong winds. Clean winds. It was not the steadfast strength of the earth such as I was accustomed to finding when I grounded, but it was a strength I could use. At first, my awareness tumbled through my poisoned body like a tuft of wool blowing around the spinner's feet when a door is opened. Then I caught one of those gray cobwebs of poison and held on.

I felt SwiftSure's hand clench bruisingly on my shoulder as she began prying her way into my consciousness, dragging CureAll's smaller, softer awareness along with her.

Sanna Meets Dauntless Swiftsure

"And what might this thing be that our green willow-lass has snagged herself upon, CureAll my dear?" I heard SwiftSure ask.

CureAll's awareness touched the poison, then jerked back in fear and horror. I heard the young voice gasp, "It's .. it's Amanita. Poison mushroom. I was using the dried Agaricus mushrooms in the compliance tea you were giving her, and -- Agaricus and Amanita are looking so much alike when they're dried -- all it would be taking is one..."

SwiftSure's presence in me went icy cold. I felt her dismay, her anger. She seemed to snarl inside my head, "You'll not be dying on me now, Sanna-me-lass. I've far too much need of you for that!"

Then my ears heard her speaking in a strong calm voice, surrounding CureAll's presence in me with warm encouragement, "And what might the remedy be for one who has a sip and some of the Amanita tea, CureAll my dear? Surely you have helped Auntie HealWell with the occasional poisoning, have you not?"

"Yes, but – no – I don't -- I can't be curing *Amanita* poisoning. There is no healer who can." I didn't need to hear the panic in her voice. It was running through me from her touch on my forehead. SwiftSure gripped my shoulder till the bones ground together, and her desperate need and determination poured through me so cold it burned. Her Firebird claws clenched on the core of my being and refused to release me, no matter how much I suffered. It wasn't fair!

Well, then, she would have to pay for my pain.

If I could have grounded, I could have found a stable point, and from there I could have spun the poison out of my system, wound it into a ball of venom in my stomach and vomited it out entirely. But there was no solid earth to draw strength from. I would have to use the Power I had available.

"SwiftSure," I whispered, "hang on." And drawing avidly on the fire of her being, flying on the winds of healing that CureAll blew through me, I began to burn the poison out of myself.

It was as if I was drawing a red-hot needle rapidly along every nerve and vein in my body. If I lingered at all, the heat would char flesh. I had to speed, speed along, just fast enough to burn the poison, but not so slow that I damaged myself. It was like creating a tightly focused, killingly high fever - now in my right shoulder, then in my left lung, then darting on to the next concentration of toxins. I felt my skin blistering as the poisons boiled and disappeared. I began sweating from every pore, and the sweat stank of sickness. My liver had been struggling to filter out the nasty stuff, and was nearly clogged full. I made darting passes through it, flashing in and out before any one section became hot enough to roast. My kidneys were overwhelmed. I seared the cobwebby gray fibers to dead ash. Oh, I was breathing out smoke before I was done, screaming and writhing and clinging to those two strengthening hands, drawing on them greedily for the Power I needed. They were as aware as I of my pain, my misery, the fearful desperation that threatened to upset the essential delicacy of my touch and timing. And to their credit, they stuck with me through it all, giving without stint, though CureAll was trembling with fright and exhaustion at the end.

When I let go of their hands, SwiftSure sat back on her heels, cursing gently and shaking her hand as if stung. CureAll folded over her knees and rested her forehead on her crossed wrists, drawing shuddering gasps of breath.

"Water." I croaked. Someone raised my head. Someone else held a waterbag and deftly squirted it into my mouth. It was tepid and stale and tasted of leather. It was wonderful. I drank till my stomach swelled.

I was dripping with oily stinking sweat. The burned poisons were passing out through my skin. Self-pity flooded me. And a niggling sense of guilt that I might have brought all this on myself by showing interest in SwiftSure's offer to take me away from obligations and responsibilities. I tried to be furious about my kidnapping, but I simply couldn't find the strength.

"Curse you, SwiftSure," I groaned. "Why have you done this to me?"

Her face looked like three days of warfare, and her voice betrayed a hint of shakiness, but she put cheery confidence into every word.

"Ah well, does the one speck of rat dung spoil the whole kettle of porridge? This was by no means what I had planned for you, willow-lass, but we've brought you through it alive and proved your worth into the bargain. If you're one as can cure Amanita poisoning, which no other Shaman has ever done at all, why then, you are just the Shaman for Tribe Dauntless!"

Then she stood and commanded, "Take her to FearNaught's tent. CureAll may then handily tend to them both."

In the darkness, through the leaping shadows from a dozen fires, under the cold sharp stars, I was carried by muffled forms, then laid down on cushions. Some kind soul began pulling off my noisome clothing – soaked with sweat and vomit and other excrescences. She paused with a gasp when she revealed my scar, then hurried to strip away the rest of my garments, bathe my sticky skin with warm water, and wrap me gently in soft linen sheets. I begged again for water, was given it, and slid into a frightful, fitful semiconsciousness.

Chapter 16

Again I saw the old woman in the white robes. At first, all I saw was her elegant, leathery face framed in a white turban, and behind her head, a fiercely blue sky. Then my focus drew back, as it will in dreams, till I could see that she was sitting on a rock at the edge of an infinity of broken black boulders. I seemed to be lying on the ground at her feet. She spoke.

"Oh, and it's a wicked wrong thing that SwiftSure has done to you, my girl, make no doubt about it. And my poor little CureAll, with no intention whatsoever to harm, has done you any amount of damage. Truly it was entirely by accident that the Amanita was mixed into your tea. You do believe that, don't you?"

"Yes," I said.

"And the strength, the Power of you to heal yourself of the poison -- " she continued, but I interrupted her.

"That wasn't my strength. I used SwiftSure's Power, and CureAll's. I'm not a mighty Healer. I'm sick, I'm frightened and I want to go back to Thon."

"Ah well, as to that ... no ... no, I'm thinking that as long as you are here, and Tribe Dauntless is so much in need of a healer till CureAll reaches her moon time . . . It was wrong to steal you away like that, but you're stolen now and stolen you must remain."

"*No!*" I cried, struggling to sit up, waking myself from the dream. A small oil lamp on a low table beside me showed my surroundings dimly. A nest of soft cushions beneath me, a length of soft wool thrown over me, mounds and walls of shadows around me. Then RugMaker materialized out of the darkness.

"Ah, poor doveling," she murmured, "and have you a pain, or is it a fearful wicked dream? Tell RugMaker, and she will make it better."

I burst into tears. "HealWell won't let me go home," I wailed.

RugMaker stiffened slightly, then patted my shoulder and murmured as I wept, "So you've been talking with HealWell, have you? Then truly, it's a Shaman you are, for all your foreign birth and training. And Tribe Dauntless is in sore need of a Shaman and a Healer just now. You rest, little one. Gather your strength. In the morning, you may speak to FearNaught, our Headwoman."

"Why should she be waiting, RugMaker?" a weak voice said in the darkness. "I'm wakeful now, and so is she. SwiftSure, give us some light."

SwiftSure's hand burst into flame. She touched and lit several oil lamps. As my eyes adjusted to the sudden brilliance, I saw I was in a large tent, rich with brilliantly colored rugs and fabrics. On a bed near the center lay a woman, thin as bone, taut as a lute string and as white-haired as SwiftSure, who was standing beside her. But the woman on the bed was ill. Her hair was rough. Her skin was pale and loose, as if the flesh behind it had been gnawed away. Her eyes blazed with fierce will but carried a shadow that told me she knew her fight was ending soon.

"Are you sure you are having strength enough for this, Mother?" SwiftSure asked.

The woman on the bed spoke with iron control, though her voice was breathless and gasping, "My dear girl, I need to be making use of the little time I have left. You've kidnapped this poor woman here against my wishes, and now I must be dealing with her while I can."

RugMaker helped me over to a pile of cushions near the bed and let me collapse. I was critically dehydrated, so dizzy that my ears were ringing and my vision narrowed into a small tunnel directly in front of me. I couldn't even sit upright but had to lie down on my side. Then blood rushed up to my brain, and slowly sight and sound returned to normal. I raised my eyes to the face of the woman on the bed above me.

"SwiftSure, what were you thinking?" the woman asked. "She's useless, and now we have a helpless mouth to feed."

"Ah, but Mother, hasn't she just cured herself of Amanita poison this very evening, as no other Healer has ever been known to do, and hasn't she fought a dragon and doesn't she bear the scars on her body even now? Hasn't she transformed the Prince of Arrex into the Golden Dragon and taught him the way to be controlling his form? Her body may be weak as thrice-thinned broth just the now, but she is in spirit a most powerful Healer!"

"Yes, and wasn't she just telling me that HealWell won't let her leave?" added RugMaker. "And Mother, if she is talking with your sister, dead these two weeks, then doesn't she just have the power to be our Shaman? Besides, when have you ever known it that Auntie HealWell has not gotten her way?"

"I don't know this 'Way of the Winds' that seems so important" I protested. "I can't hold the Heart of the Fire, whatever that is. I can't find my own way in the dark. I haven't even finished school yet. I want to go back to Thon."

"I remember what you told me of your first meeting with HealWell," said SwiftSure. "And haven't I just been watching you this whole time? You know much of the Way of the Winds, though you call it by other names, and RugMaker can teach you much more. As for the Heart of the Fire, why, who else needs hold it while SwiftSure her bold self is about?"

"But if she can't find her way in the dark . . ." said FearNaught.

"Ah, but she needn't find her own way if she has the wisdom to trust and be led, isn't it true?" SwiftSure said. "Mother, you must be holding on these few days more, and Sanna, our green willow-lass, will have the healing of you accomplished."

FearNaught dropped her hand over the edge of the bed and stretched it out toward me. "Tell her," she commanded.

"If you can read the Winds of the Spirit, then tell my daughter how I may be healed."

I reached out my hand and took hers. It was rough, dry and hot. But I didn't have enough Power left to read her. I shook my head and released the feverish claw. Then SwiftSure stepped over to me and, grasping both FearNaught and me by the wrists, she joined our two hands together again. SwiftSure's Power was frightening. No wonder she could transform at will into the Firebird. I felt as if I had been thrown onto the back of a mighty horse. With luck, I might keep my seat, but not for long could I control her against her will.

When I first saw how withered FearNaught appeared, I had begun to suspect her illness, so I guided SwiftSure's awareness and cascade of strength to the inner organs. The tumor squatted crablike in FearNaught's womb, with legs and claws embedded all through her body. How she had stayed alive so long was a wonder to me. Even at my strongest, I could never have cured a cancer so great.

"Look, SwiftSure!" I commanded her. "Look though my eyes and see what I see!"

If I had been riding a horse, I would have dropped one rein to haul back on the other with both hands and all my strength, to turn the horse, will-she, nill-she. I did something of the same with SwiftSure, making her aware of the damage done, the pain endured, the flickering fires of life in her mother.

SwiftSure tore away from me, dropped our wrists and fled from the tent. Through the slit of the doorway, we saw the flash of brilliance as she burst into flame and flew, wailing her denial into the night.

"Ah, so great is the suffering of my big sister SwiftSure," said RugMaker. "But surely, time it is that she realized that we all die, even the mighty FearNaught."

"Time it is," FearNaught agreed.

"When she comes back, if she will loan me a touch more of her Power," I offered weakly, "I can stop the pain for you."

RugMaker said, "If you can truly do that, willow-lass, then SwiftSure was right indeed to be bringing you here."

"I won't be having my mind dimmed!" declared FearNaught.

"I'll just weave protective sheathes around the nerves that carry your pain," I told her. "The damage will go on, but you won't have to feel it."

"Truly, can you be doing such a thing?" asked FearNaught.

"Working with fibers is my Gift," I explained. "And your body is a network of scars. I'll just tease out threads of scar tissue and weave it around your nerves like bandages around a burned hand. You may lose muscle control, but your mind will stay clear and the pain will stop."

"I've lost use of my legs these two years past," FearNaught said, "and it's been a shameful three months now that I've been diapered like a baby. I've little left to lose. The mighty Dauntless FearNaught is dying by inches and must soon be turning over her Headwoman's position. My willful daughter SwiftSure is rightwise my heir, but without a Shaman, I cannot be properly passing the care of my tribe on to her. And she has fought me. She would not be bound by responsibilities as she has seen me bound.

She would fly the hot winds at will, as I have not flown them since she was conceived in me."

FearNaught seemed to be talking to herself, her gaze unfocused, her thin hands wandering like spiders across the brilliant embroideries on her coverlet.

"Ah, but Cunning StrongHand was worth the loss of flight. Almost unheard, too, a Headwoman to marry the same man seventeen times over, each time the year and a day was over, but StrongHand was ever the right man for me. Ever and ever. And three fine children we made, didn't we? SwiftSure and SeeFar and RugMaker, the splendid get of our joy. And I'd be married to StrongHand still had that Golmen arrow not bereft me of his strength. I think it was then I began dying. It was then I began following him on..."

She drifted into murmurs, then silence. RugMaker rose, settled me more comfortably in my cozy nest of pillows next to FearNaught's bed, tucked a quilt 'round me and began blowing out the lamps surrounding the bed. Darkness fell through the tent like ashes.

Chapter 17

There was a pre-dawn freshness in the air when SwiftSure slipped back into the tent. FearNaught roused at SwiftSure's arrival and stretched out her hand to her troubled daughter. SwiftSure fell on her knees at her mother's side and pressed the withered hand to her cheek.

"I'm sorry, Mother. 'Tis time and past time, and it's a wretched, selfish, stubborn vermin I've been to deny it."

FearNaught stroked her other hand across SwiftSure's feathery white hair and said, "Ah, my darling girl, and doesn't the Firebird ever fly in the way of her own choosing? And haven't you brought a Shaman to Tribe Dauntless to work the Passing for us? All will come well, my dear. All will come well. And our willow-lass here says she can muffle my pain, if you will but lift her Power to the task."

Sanna Meets Dauntless SwiftSure

SwiftSure turned her face to me. "Is it even so? Can you truly ease the pain? I would give you this arm of mine entire if you need it to work such good."

She held out her right hand to me. I raised my own hand to grasp hers. "I won't need your whole arm," I told her, "just a pinch of your strength. Carry me again as you did last night."

Instantly, I seemed to be on that powerful horse again – but a horse tamed and trained and biddable. I called on her Power to do my work as I reached my other hand out to touch her mother. FearNaught must have been a fierce warrior once. Her body was white with knotted scars, her muscles bound and shortened by her injuries. There was more than enough fiber to draw out and weave into sheaths around her tortured nerves. I could feel the ease moving through her as I did my work.

At last, "That's all I can do," I said, releasing both women's hands.

FearNaught drew in a deep breath and blew it out in a huge sigh of pleasure. "Oh, it's almost merry you have made me feel, willow-lass. I had a fire inside me, and you have quenched it with clean, cool water. There's not a one could know what a gift it is to be pain-free, save those who have suffered without surcease. Truly, it's a Shaman and a Healer of worth you are!"

"Fine for you," complained SwiftSure, "and isn't it myself that's left feeling I've suckled a camel every time I give the girl my hand? I'm withered and empty as the last waterbag carried across The Bones. She's taking more than I'm wanting to give."

She had just said she was willing to give her whole arm. It seemed that Swiftsure was one of those people who talk a good fight, but cry like puppies when the first blow is struck.

"Then it's a fine rich stew you'll be wanting to build you up again," RugMaker said from the door of the tent. "And don't I always know what you'll be wanting after one of your wild flights? There's mutton stew and some fine red wine for all three of you weakened women."

The smell of the stew hit me and I began gagging.

"No stew!" I begged. "Oh, get me away from it! I'll pay for your trick with that tea for months, SwiftSure. Get that stew away from me!"

SwiftSure pounced, grabbed me by the wrists and pulled me out of my cocoon of sheets and blankets, then dragged my backside across the carpets and onto the cold sand outside the tent. I lay there, nauseated, gasping the cold, clean air, till SwiftSure grabbed a handful of my hair and lifted my head so she could hiss into my face, "How dare you? How *dare* you insult RugMaker that way? It's all commands and demands and complainings from you, as have no place nor power here, but are ever sucking the life out of me to be doing your works. You may have been soothing my mother's pain, but if you'll not work the curing of her, then I'd as well not have brought you here, the needy, crossgrained whelp that you are!"

She was shaking me by that fistful of hair, and I wondered, in a far little corner of my brain, if the scalp would tear, or if the hair would just pull out, leaving me a bald patch. The Good One knows I couldn't have spoken right then to save my life.

Sanna Meets Dauntless Swiftsure

"Stop it, SwiftSure!" CureAll's young voice commanded from behind us, and SwiftSure released me.

"You don't know what this ungrateful spider has done!" she snarled, smacking me across the mouth with the back of her fingers. "She spurned RugMaker's fine and glorious mutton stew and made as if to vomit in the very presence of FearNaught!"

CureAll said, "That cursed tea I made and you gave her has ruined Healer Sanna's liver. The very smell of fat will set her retching. And doesn't RugMaker make her stew with the fat floating in rich shiny drops upon the surface? No wonder Shaman Sanna spurned it. And you, you heedless wight, the cause and foundation of all her sickness that you are, you are now the one to abuse her? Oh, it's a fine compassionate leader Tribe Dauntless will be having, I'm thinking!"

CureAll dropped down to her knees beside me, confronting SwiftSure across my body. I felt like a soft white grub lying between an eagle and a young falcon. Their faces were fierce with outrage. Then CureAll softened.

"You've been flying the night through, haven't you?" she said. "Do you go and eat, and send Cousin RugMaker out to me. I know the Firebird still beats her wings in your soul. I spoke without thinking. It's a fine, splendid Headwoman you will be when the time comes to it."

"Yes, well, the time is coming far too fast for my liking," SwiftSure snarled. "I've knelt to take the saddle, but I'm not liking it in the least."

Chapter 18

SwiftSure strode into the tent without another word. I looked at my rescuer. The sky behind her head was white with dawn. Her dark hair was pulled into a bun and secured with several picks from which dangled feathers and fetishes. Her face was smooth and rounded, but the bones were those of the old woman in my dreams. A few things fell into place for me.

"HealWell was your mother?" I asked.

"Yes," CureAll replied. "She told me you have been speaking with her. It's so sorry I am to have been a part of this terrible thing we have done to you ---."

I interrupted her. "Your mother is dead, but she's speaking to you and to me in our dreams?"

CureAll nodded, her eyes dark with pain. "She may not fly with the winds till Tribe Dauntless has a Shaman in her place. And I can't be Shaman till my first moon time."

I looked more closely at her, squeezed my eyes shut, then looked again. "How old are you now?" I asked.

Her chin came up a bit defiantly. "I have seen eleven green times," she told me.

"And you expect your periods -- your moon times -- to begin when?" I asked. "Next year? The year after? So your tribe will take two or three years out of my life, then send me home when you're done with me? Why should I do anything to help you people?"

"Because you are a Healer and a Shaman, and this is what you have been called to do," CureAll said, with sorrow beyond her years. "We are needing you, Healer Sanna, and you are so made that you cannot be denying us."

RugMaker came out then, laden with blankets and apologies. "You poor dear mouseling. Had I realized it was your liver that was bad I would never have brought such a burden of fat near you. I've never known a one to be cured of Amanita poisoning and had no idea it left you yellowish. But then, you must be eating something. CureAll, what shall we be feeding her?"

As she spoke, she was deftly swaddling me in soft warm blankets and tucking a cushion under my head.

"I don't know," CureAll replied. "Momma never told me about liverish problems."

"Well, I'll tell you, then," I said. "I can eat boiled grains and greens and perhaps even beans. I can drink any strengthening tea you can make. But I can bear no fat whatsoever, and wine would kill me just now. As weak as I am, you had better boil my drinking water, too."

"And, CureAll," said RugMaker, "while you are doing all these things for our new Shaman, you must also be strengthening her and teaching her the Rite of the Passage."

CureAll's little face crumpled with grief. "Oh, poor Auntie FearNaught! No wonder SwiftSure was so knaggy."

"Yes," said RugMaker, caressing CureAll's cheek. "But it's time and past time, and as well as I do you recognize this passing for the blessing it is. Now I'll be sitting with the willow-lass, and you go give your greetings to FearNaught. I think you'll be seeing a good thing in her this day."

CureAll slipped into the tent, and RugMaker sat behind me, pillowing my head on her lap, and gently stroking my face with her fingertips. Ease and rest followed her touch.

"You're a Healer," I said after a few moments. "Why can't *you* be Shaman for the tribe?"

"I'm not so great a Healer as all that," she said. "I can be encouraging you to strength and health, but I am not finding nor curing the sicknesses themselves. And it takes a Healer of Power to be Shaman. Now look you, at the glory of this day's sunrise."

Clouds above the horizon were glowing red, orange, coral, incandescent gold. Then the sun crested the rim of the world, and light spilled like a stormwave across the earth to splash, hot and yellow, up against us.

CureAll stepped out of the tent, stood blinking in the brightness a moment, then dropped to her knees beside me and bumped her forehead against my feet.

"She is free from pain. Even HealWell herself could not be easing the pain, but you have released FearNaught from its bondage. Please be teaching, me, Healer Sanna. Please be teaching me."

"Stop that!" I snapped. I'm sick, and I'm tired and I need to eat. I used SwiftSure's strength for everything I've done in this camp, and I'm just an Apprentice Sorceress and you're asking too much of me. I'll let you down. I'm not the person you need! This isn't fair."

"Hush now, mouseling," murmured RugMaker, gently stroking both hands over my ears. "Hush and rest. CureAll will be bringing you a lovely bowl of boiled grains and a jug of fine healing tea, won't you, CureAll? And then we'll be finding you a nice shady bed and leaving you to your rest. So very weary you are now and such a great lot of work you have done."

CureAll hurried off while RugMaker sat with me, gentling my distress and easing away my aches. And the rising sun began heating the oven of desert we camped in.

Chapter 19

I ate, I drank, I held it down. SeeFar, the eagle-man, arrived and swept me up in his arms.

"What a bony bundle you are, to be sure," he said, "but a light little load to carry thereby. CureAll says you're to be resting in her tent, and I'm to be sitting right outside the tent door to be guarding your sleep and serving your every wish." He smiled charmingly down at me.

"Well, don't do anything stinky," I told him, "like curing leather or farting the alphabet, or I'll be puking all over again."

His face twisted with distaste. "And aren't the Sorceresses supposed to be such refined and elegant creatures?" he asked.

"I'm *not* a Sorceress, just a raw Apprentice," I snapped. "Where's this bed I'm supposed to be resting on?"

Sanna Meets Dauntless Swiftsure

With injured dignity he carried me through the camp. I saw now that FearNaught's tent was the largest and most decorated, with standards and banners set in front of it, and intricate designs painted on the walls. The other tents were smaller, but no less brightly colored. This one was painted with flowers, that one was covered with geometric patterns, the one over there in simple bold vertical stripes. The people of Tribe Dauntless dressed themselves as brightly as their tents, with long brightly striped robes under short embroidered waistcoats, and long, patterned vests; with plaid scarves and checkered sashes, fringed headdresses and vibrantly colored bangles and jewelry. As we passed, each woman who saw us paused and touched the notch of her collarbones with her left hand.

CureAll's tent was white as dust. Glaring, starkly white. SeeFar deftly elbowed open the tent flap and carried me through. Then he stood a moment, till his eyes adjusted to the sudden dimness. The bed was next to the door, so he knelt down and laid me on it.

"Sleep well, willow-lass. Dream of me," he whispered, and leaned over to kiss me.

I blew a strong puff of fetid breath into his face. It startled him enough so that he drew back.

"Stop that," I told him. "I'm *sick*! Do you think you're so wonderful that your very presence cures my nausea? Go away."

He gaped, flushed, then jumped to his feet and left. It was all I asked of life right then. I slept.

I dreamed. HealWell wouldn't leave me alone. She was in the dim white tent with me. I couldn't see her, but her voice spun through my mind.

"That was well done with SeeFar," she chuckled. "The lad grows too full of himself, though he is of a surety as handsome as ever his father was. But you are right to seek your rest. Now you must soon be working the Rite of the Passage for FearNaught and SwiftSure, and I'll be telling you the way of it.

"All the fires in the camp must be extinguished and the ashes buried as deep as your arm is long. New fires must be laid for every tent in the tribe, with wood that has never been charred. CureAll knows the herbs that must go for each fire, according to those living in the tent. FearNaught and her bed must be carried out of sight of the camp: You. CureAll and SwiftSure must go with her. Send you then all other attendants back to the camp and when they arrive, let them begin the mourning chant. There will be only you, CureAll, SwiftSure and FearNaught. When you hear the mourning chant, do you begin to pour the oils over FearNaught. Then give them time to warm, for if the oils are too cold, they will not properly ignite."

"So you cremate your dead?" I asked.

"Why, no - you must perform the rite before she dies," HealWell said. "Wasn't FearNaught the Firebird before SwiftSure ever became the Firebird? How did you think the Headwoman of Tribe Dauntless passes her leadership to her heir?"

"How should I know?" I barked. "You think everyone should know everything about your peculiar ways and want to follow them. Up until I saw SwiftSure transform,

I thought the Firebird was a myth. I've been kidnapped by a fairytale, and by her sister who flies an aerial rug, and by their brother who turns into an eagle; and they poisoned me. No one who loves me knows where I am. I'm sick, and I'm alone, I'm only half-trained, and I'm frightened. And you're dead, by the way. Dead people can't go around harassing live people like you do. I need my rest. Just go away and leave me alone."

And for a wonder, she did. But when I woke, I somehow knew how the Rite should be carried out to its finish, and it wasn't a pleasant thing to know.

Chapter 20

CureAll brought more food and healing tea. The tea tasted vile, but I could feel my strength returning with every sip. I drifted in and out of consciousness in the stifling hot tent. Occasionally, I could hear people speaking outside, but I couldn't hear what they were saying. Now and then, a shadow would slide across the canvas beside me. In the distance, I heard the peal of children's laughter.

And then RugMaker woke me, and through the tent door I could see the colors of sunset staining the sky.

"Here, my little mouseling," she said as she helped me sit up, "do but see the fine lovely meal that I have brought to you to make you strong and brave and gallant. But first, our wise little CureAll tells me, I must give you a cup of this excellent tea which will be whetting your appetite like a knife against a smooth stone. When your hunger is so cunningly sharpened, then you will eat more and hold it down, and so will you grow well."

The tea, this time, tasted surprisingly pleasant, with anise and raspberry leaf and a bit of honey. I drank it greedily, then began devouring the bowlful of grains and greens. It was completely unseasoned, and I was astounded at how delicious plain boiled grains tasted.

RugMaker chuckled, "Ah, and hasn't CureAll's tea done the fine work, now? She has here two other teas for you to be drinking as well. First should you be drinking all of the elixir in this blue bowl as you are eating your meal. Then for your dessert, do you sip the contents of this little white cup. It will strengthen you for tonight's ceremony."

Ice stabbed through my stomach. "Ceremony? What ceremony?" I demanded.

"Why, the ceremony of introduction, when you will be made known to all the members of Tribe Dauntless as their Shaman. What ceremony did you think it would be, that you should be so fearful of it?"

"The Rite of the Passage."

"Ahhhh. And yet, that ceremony must come soon as well. FearNaught is burning her life like a pitch brand now that she is free of pain. She will have all things in order before she goes. Now do you be taking a sip of this tea and leave all worrying to RugMaker this little while. You are to be doing naught but eating and resting and regaining your strength."

Darkness fell as I ate. All too soon, SeeFar came for me, and carried me through the camp again. FearNaught was propped up on her bed in front of her tent. SwiftSure stood at her right, and CureAll at her left. SeeFar settled me on a pile of cushions on the ground at SwiftSure's feet, and sat behind me, letting me lean against his broad, muscular chest. The rest of the tribe gathered in front of us. Three tall oil lamps stood on the sand beside me.

FearNaught spoke, in a voice belying her physical weakness. She spoke like a queen, like a warrior, like a woman used to being obeyed. "My heir and daughter, SwiftSure, has traveled far and found for Tribe Dauntless a most puissant and powerful Sorceress to act as our Shaman until CureAll may assume her rightful place. Last night, saw you all how this Sorceress did heal herself of a foul poison, which no Shaman has ever been able to do before in the history of all the Peoples of the Wide Skies. Know you also that HealWell herself has claimed this willow-lass as our Shaman. Tonight, it is time that your new Shaman should come to be knowing you. Who will first greet her?"

There was a shifting and a bit of muttering among the people where they stood with the lights from the oil lamps flickering on their faces. Shadows leapt and twisted among them. Then a lean woman with a long scar across her cheek stepped forward, dropped to one knee, touched her left hand to the notch of her collarbones, then extended her right hand to me.

"Who else should be first to greet you but FirstForth? 'Tis myself that is welcoming you to Tribe Dauntless." She smiled crookedly around her scar. I grinned back at her and took her hand. A spark seemed to leap between us and I felt a flush of courage surge into me from her touch.

Sanna Meets Dauntless Swiftsure

"Thus do you know FirstForth, bravest warrior of Tribe Dauntless," said FearNaught, as First Forth stood and stepped back, to be followed by a youth in his teens.

He took my hand, and wholesome good nature trickled into me. "It's WillingStrength that I am, and happy to be giving aid where I may," he said. I couldn't help but smile at him as well.

"Thus do you know WillingStrength, son of FirstForth and worthy man of Tribe Dauntless," FearNaught told me.

And so it went into the night, as all-fifty two members of the tribe came to take my hand and tell me her (or his) name. The women all first saluted me with the touch of the left hand to the base of the throat. And with every handclasp, a taste of their spirit flowed into me. Some were bitter, many were worried, one or two were bent in their souls. All been appropriately named. Even the toddlers, such as little HappyGirl, looked into my eyes, touched my hand, and thereby shared a bit of themselves with me. I felt crowded when SeeFar finally carried me back to CureAll's tent. CureAll brought me yet another cup of tea, this one rich with chamomile, and tucked me warmly into her bed.

"I'll be staying by Auntie FearNaught tonight," she told me, "but SeeFar will be sleeping just outside, so if you need anything, you have but to call."

"Or do but sigh deeply," SeeFar's light tenor voice spoke from outside the tent, "and I'll be at your side before you can draw breath again."

"Don't do that, SeeFar," I groaned. "When I want you, I'll call you by name."

"Oh, and sweet it sounds on your kissable lips," he said. "Do you but call my name whenever I might be the smallest bit of good to you."

I rolled my eyes in disgust, and CureAll giggled. Then she took the cup, and as our hands touched, a spark passed between us. Grief, anger, sympathy, resignation surged within us in a maelstrom, and we clung together till they subsided. I was seventeen, she was eleven. We were both bereft, frightened and ill-prepared for the job we needed to do. And, as I held her little hands, I realized that I was going to do it. I was going to be the Shaman for Tribe Dauntless till CureAll was old enough. They needed a Shaman, and I was so made that I could not deny them. They were good people, and by the ceremony that night, they had become *my* people. I would do my best for them and pick up the pieces of my life afterward. I heaved a huge sigh.

"Did you call me, fair willow-lass?" SeeFar called through the tent.

"My name is Sanna, and I *said*, when I want you, I'll call you by name!"

CureAll hugged me, rose silently and left.

Chapter 21

I slept dreamlessly. The next morning, I woke feeling light of heart and ravenously hungry. And I felt stronger. Carefully, I rolled out of bed and climbed to my feet. I was a bit shaky, but I could stand and even walk a few steps. I tottered to the tent door, raised the flap and looked out. People were stirring in the pre-dawn chill, and I realized with a start that I knew each one. The middle-aged woman tending the fire over there was SmartFingers, a notable seamstress. Her grown daughters were ThreadBender and HarnessMaker. The man going out to milk the goats was LongRider LoveSinger. He had been born to Tribe LongRider, then married Dauntless SweetSavor for a year and a day. They allowed their marriage to lapse, but he remained with the tribe to help raise his son, the sturdy fifteen-year-old

Dauntless RunningFast. Everywhere I turned my eyes, I knew each person and their place in the tribe.

Looking down, I saw SeeFar rolled into his blankets at my feet. He was resting on his back, breathing unevenly. Under his closed lids, I could see his eyes moving rapidly.

"What does an eagle dream of?" I whispered.

His long blonde lashes flew up, and as I stared into those startled, startling eyes, I was suddenly awash in a sense of falling, tumbling, plummeting toward the hard rocks below . . .

I lost my balance and fell forward across him, catching myself on my outstretched hands. He rose beneath me and pulled me all the way down on top of him in a close embrace.

"CureAll said you would have more energy today," he said, smiling smugly.

I shoved away from him. "Oh, don't get ideas! I just lifted the tent flap and lost my balance."

"And that is the tale I will assuredly tell everyone," he said, lounging in his bedroll and laughing at me as I fought with the tent flap and my swaddling blankets.

"SeeFar," I said, "I need a set of ceremonial robes."

"And robes you shall have just as soon as morning is fully upon us and we have broken the night's long fast," he said, snuggling back into his blankets with a prodigious yawn.

"Now!" I barked, and the spirit of FearNaught and SwiftSure and even HealWell spoke their authority through me. SeeFar scrambled to his feet in shock.

"Now?" he asked, hesitantly.

"SmartFingers is awake. Ask her if she will spare me a few moments of her time," I told him.

He turned his head, looked around, and saw SmartFingers coming out of her tent with a kettle in one hand and a spoon in the other. He looked back at me with eyes wide and uncertain, then walked over to speak to her.

SeeFar had slept in nothing but a pair of lightweight loose trousers, gathered on a drawstring around his lean hips. I saw that his shoulder blades were tattooed with a pattern of feathers like widespread wings. His long blonde hair floated in the morning air.

When he spoke to SmartFingers, she nodded, handed him the spoon, pointed to her kettle on the fire, and came striding across to where I sat in the doorway of CureAll's tent.

"So it's the robes of a Shaman you'll be wanting, is it?" she asked me as she ushered me into the privacy of the tent.

"One set for ceremonies, if you would be so kind," I answered, "but the rest of the time I can wear my own things. I'll only be Shaman till CureAll is old enough, so there's no sense wasting all that fabric on me."

The tension I had sensed in her eased. "CureAll's a darling of a girl," she said. "I'd not like to see her supplanted as senior Shaman in Tribe Dauntless after she's old enough to do the work. And that by someone outland born as you yourself are, meaning no offense, but there's no gainsaying that you're not of the Tribe and like to be leading us in foreign ways without the knowing of it. But as it's only the few years you're intending to stay, why one fine set of robes shall I be making for you, and that with a right good will. Let us be measuring you."

She pulled forth a piece of string and began looping it around my wrist, my neck, stretching it along my arm and across my back, around my chest, my waist, my hips, and down the length of my leg, muttering notes to herself as she did so.

At last she tucked me neatly into my blanket again and said, "There, then, you long-legged skeleton-lass. I'll be making robes to be covering your thin bones, and I'll put in pleats to let out as RugMaker fattens you up. But however did a city lass like you get such a monstrous scar, and however did you survive such a wound?"

"I was attacked by a dragon, and healed by Master Sorcerers," I said.

"Ahhhh," she breathed, "now there's a tale for a quiet night. I'm eager to be hearing it soon. But now, I'd best go rescue my porridge before SeeFar burns it black as the Bones."

SeeFar returned looking disgruntled, shrugged into a long shirt and short waistcoat and said, "I'll just be telling CureAll that yourself is up and about, then." And off he strode, chest out, head up, with the rising sun lifting flashes of light in his fair hair.

Chapter 22

And back he strode, scowling in annoyance.

"It's your great self I've been commanded to carry back to FearNaught's tent," he grumbled, stooping and hefting me in his strong arms again. "There's some nonsense about a bag that can't be moved and only our Shaman-lass can solve the riddle."

"It's my belt bag," I explained, as I clung to his neck. "It's magic, and it's theft-proof. I'm the only one who can carry it, open it or find anything in it. And it's bigger on the inside than on the outside."

He thought. The scowls cleared from his face like clouds blown away by a greedy wind. He turned a charming smile on me.

"Sanna, my darling, my lovely light willow-lass, kindest and fairest of all Shamans ---"

"No," I said.

"Ah, but if you would just be considering what I have to say ---"

"There's no way you can get a bag like that. It's the only one of its kind. I made it, but I can't make one for you," I told him sharply. "I'm only half trained. I don't have the skills to make magic belt bags for other people. I probably don't have the skills to be a Shaman, either, but I'm all you have for the time being. Get used to disappointment. And put me down. I can walk from here."

We had arrived at FearNaught's tent. RugMaker, hearing our arrival, was lifting the tent flap.

"Ah, sweet willow-lass. It's stronger you are looking this fine morning. Put her down, SeeFar, and off with you to the bachelor's tent for your breakfast. We'll call you if needed." She held one hand out to me and made little shooing motions at SeeFar with the other.

At the word, "breakfast," SeeFar's stomach rumbled, casting a deciding vote. He bent and lowered my feet to the ground, but continued to clasp me against his chest with the other arm, so that he held me in a close embrace when he stood upright. I was taller than he by maybe four finger-widths.

"We'll talk more later, sweet star of the dawn," he murmured. Then he tried to kiss me again, but I turned my head and pushed away from him.

"Stop that! What's wrong with you? I'm *sick*, for pity's sake," I snarled.

"If I wait till you're well, you'll not have time for poor little SeeFar. I must woo you while I can," he replied, roguishly, and with a jaunty salute, strode off.

"Ah, it's hard for SeeFar," said RugMaker, helping me into the tent. "He can't dally with any girl of Tribe Dauntless, being cousin to all. And yet he can't bear to be leaving us to be taking a wife. Now aren't you just the answer to his problems? He's hoping to marry you and get children so that you will stay on after CureAll becomes rightwise our Shaman. And with the single women of every tribe on the catch for his handsome self every time we meet with them, he knows himself to be utterly irresistible."

"If I marry anyone, it will be Prince Jerris of Arrex," I said, dropping down next to my belt bag and pulling out breeches and tunic. "And no doubt I'll be marrying Prince Jerris shortly after goats grow fins and swim in the seas."

With RugMaker's help, I dressed and tied my belt bag around my waist, then tottered outside to sit in the sunrise and enjoy another meal of boiled grains and teas. CureAll came to join me, setting a finger to the pulse in my wrist for a moment, then nodding to herself.

"You're stronger today," she said, smiling. "Are the teas agreeing with you?"

"You're a wonder with your brews," I told her. "I'll have to study under you while I'm here. Do you gather all your own ingredients?"

"Only such things as can be found in the desert. The rest we must trade for, like that cursed contaminated Agaricus mushroom powder that poisoned you. Never again will I use that wretched risky stuff. It is too easy to be confusing the Amanita with the Agaricus and tainting the whole. I have vowed to forsake the brewing of compliance tea altogether, and Agaricus is good for nothing else. It's sore sorry I am ---"

"Don't," I interrupted her. "You didn't mean to hurt me. Mistakes happen. And without that compliance tea, SwiftSure would simply have carried me kicking and screaming the whole way. Will you please stop apologizing?"

Her sweet young face twisted. Tears filled the large violet eyes. "I don't know *what* to do," she wailed.

I took her little hand and squeezed it gently. "When I feel like that," I told her, "I find it helps to take a deep breath, blow it all out and become aware of the strength inside me. Then I ask myself what's right. Not how to get what I want, but what's right. Mostly, I just make it up as I go along. *Nobody* knows what to do *all* the time. "

"SwiftSure does," CureAll replied.

"Ha!" I snorted. "Just because she's sure of herself doesn't mean she's right."

SwiftSure's voice rang out from inside the tent. "CureAll, don't you have sick people to see to?"

CureAll turned a worried face toward me, then raised the tent flap and went in. I could hear parts of the ensuing conversation.

" --- asked them to come here so Healer Sanna might see to their ills without wearying herself going from one to another," CureAll murmured.

"--- see to FearNaught," SwiftSure replied.

FearNaught spoke clearly and firmly, "And what would you have the frail stick of a lass do for me now? She's freed me from pain, and she'll help my Passing tonight. Today she should see to her Tribe as the Shaman she is."

"Tonight?" SwiftSure cried, "Oh, Mother, not tonight!"

"CureAll, will you leave us now? There is much that SwiftSure and I must say to one another," said FearNaught.

Chapter 23

CureAll slipped back outside, tied the flap shut and settled down beside me, saying, "Look you, here is coming SweetSavor. This has been a difficult pregnancy for her."

I have heard that you should never trust a skinny cook. SweetSavor would have been eminently trustworthy. She was in her early forties, and the weight of the baby growing in her, combined with all the extra pounds she usually carried, was exhausting her heart. Her current husband, Eldritch Smith, helped to lower her onto the rug in front of us, then silently hunkered down beside her to watch and listen.

SweetSavor was breathless and red-faced. "Ah, it's the headaches and the backaches that are plaguing me this day," she sighed. "And I can't do the walking as you told me to do, CureAll, because of the pain it is bringing to my feet."

She rolled onto her side and extended a foot to show us. It was purple and horribly swollen. Her ankle was nearly the size of my knee, and the bones showed as dimples in the inflated flesh. When I pinched the place over her big heel tendon, I left white indentations as deep as my first finger joint which took several worrisome seconds to disappear. She was retaining fluids to a dangerous degree, and her kidneys could be failing.

"I've been treating her with strengthening teas and herbs and trying to get her to eat less fat and salt," said CureAll.

"Some of those herbs were so foul they scoured my mouth," complained SweetSavor. "And what sort of cook would I be, I'm asking you, to be foregoing fat and salt in my cooking?"

"You might be a cook who lives to see her grandchildren," I told her. "Smith, I don't have the strength right now to heal SweetSavor. Will you lend me some of yours?"

"No," he said, and shut his lips as if words were gold and he had spent too much already. Then our stunned silence and our shocked stares pried his mouth open again.

"You're not proper Tribe bred," he muttered to me, "and I won't have your foreign fingers stirrin' through my soul."

"Oh, and it's the fine loving husband you are, then!" shrilled SweetSavor. "Tribe Eldritch was never known to be generous, but I am sore sorry to think you a coward as well. Woe is me, birthing the get of such a gutless, selfish hulk, and like to die of it. But will he trust our rightwise

Shaman to help in the healing of me? Not the mighty Smith! No, let SweetSavor die and good riddance to her. There's many a tribe as would be wanting the worthy Smith of Tribe Eldritch. He can marry where he will. I am too swollen with his babe to be cooking the meals he loved me for, and now he wants free of me. Oh woe! Oh woe!"

Lying on her side on the carpets, SweetSavor pulled a fold of her headdress across her face and wept noisily. Smith, meanwhile, went crimson in the face, but let her rant on without moving a muscle in response.

"Oh, by the Good One, I wish I had my strength back," I groaned. "Slap her, CureAll."

She hesitated, eyes wide with dismay.

"She's hysterical," I said, gritting my teeth with impatience, "and in her condition, she'll hurt herself and the baby with too much emotion."

Eldritch Smith pulled SweetSavor to a sitting position and CureAll smacked her on the cheek. The sting of it broke the desperate rhythm of her sobs. She gasped and sat sniffling, nose and eyes streaming.

RugMaker, drawn by the noise, came bustling out of the tent.

"FearNaught is trying to rest and here you are, SweetSavor, screaming like a goat with its hind leg caught in a thornbush. We can be hearing you all over the camp. You know how uncanny all of Tribe Eldritch is when it comes to the Ways of the Winds. Smith scarce would let our doughty HealWell treat him, so of course he won't be giving trust or strength to our willow-lass here. But *I* will."

She turned to me and continued, "I've strength enough for any healing you'll be wanting to do, Shaman Sanna of Tribe Dauntless. How can I be lending it to you?"

"Put your hand under mine, here, and CureAll, you put your hand on top of my other hand. I'll draw on RugMaker's strength, and show you how to read an illness."

Smith was on one knee with SweetSavor leaning against his shoulder while he tenderly wiped her wet cheeks and runny nose with the corner of his vest. I picked up her pudgy hand and held it with my right hand on top and my left hand underneath.

They did as I asked, RugMaker sinking gracefully to sit at my left side, CureAll scrambling on her knees around to my right. I took a deep breath, and slid my consciousness into SweetSavor's suffering flesh, following the threads of blood vessels and the fibers of nerves. I wanted to spin out the deposits that constricted her veins, and to darn the weak spots in her heart, but it was her overtaxed and failing kidneys that needed immediate help. I mended and re-wove the torn and brittle meshes that filtered her blood. I spun out poisons into her urine and quenched an infection that was starting. There was so much more to do, but I could sense RugMaker beginning to weaken. I barely had strength enough to sit up, so I drew out our combined Talents and released SweetSavor.

"The backache's gone!" she exclaimed. "And the thundering in my brain is fading as well! Oh, it's truly the Healer you are, foreign-born Sorceress though you be!

"And it's truly the shrew that I am to you, my darling Smith," she continued, freeing her hand to stroke his bristly, scarred cheek. "Can you ever be forgiving me and my cruel angry tongue?"

He kissed her on the mouth and helped her to her feet.

"I'm coming with you," declared CureAll. "And I'll be making you a broth to be cleaning your blood, and you'll be drinking every drop, see if it isn't so! And moreover, I'll be taking away all your salt and lard and anything that is bad for you to be eating. If you had seen your insides as I have just, you couldn't swallow another bite of fat in your life!"

Smith and SweetSavor lumbered away like two orchard-fatted bears, with little CureAll scolding after them like a squirrel.

Chapter 24

RugMaker sighed beside me. "Ah, it's a good child, CureAll is," she said, "and so brave, withal, being so recently orphaned."

"How did that happen?" I asked.

"Why, didn't it happen when the Golmen raiders last attacked us? May their feet rot off them within sight of water, the skulking jackals! But the way of it is this: HealWell trusted in the safety that all accord to Shamans in the desert. None will harm those who wear the white robes. SeeFar and FirstForth and our other doughty warriors had vanquished the vile raiders and driven them off. But one lay behind, his leg crushed and pinned beneath his dying pony. HealWell bent over him to ease his pain, and then the wretch reached out and stabbed her to the heart. He turned the dagger on himself straightway, the sneaking serpent that he was, and cut his own throat so deeply that his neckbones showed, escaping thereby, the blood price I would have taken from his miserable hide. A curse on his despicable spirit, may it blow forever though the seven ovens of hell!"

I had begun to think of RugMaker as a tender and gentle being. The grief and fury that blazed in her eyes frightened me. Nothing is as fierce as a loving woman defending or avenging those in her care.

"Calm down, RugMaker," I cautioned her. "I drew deeply on your strength to help SweetSavor. You're too exhausted to be this angry."

"I'll be as angry as may be when it is coming to wrongs done to my family, young willow-lass, and don't you think to be speaking me calm," RugMaker flared at me. "And won't the sweet winds of this morning just be blowing the Power back into me in no time at all? I've strength and to spare for the raging of my grief."

Her face was scarlet and her pulse was racing. I tried to think how to distract her. "Are you telling me that you get strength from the wind?" I asked.

"Of course I do! How can you be riding the winds of the spirits and not be drawing the strength from them?" she snapped.

"I take my strength from the stones of the earth," I answered. "But there's no stability or strength in all this sand. Will you show me how to draw Power from the wind?"

I held out my hand to her, allowing it to tremble with weakness a little more than it might have.

Her face softened. The mad light in her eyes went out, and she took my hand gently.

"Ah, and it's the lost little mouseling you are now, aren't you, young Sanna-lass? And suffering for the sorrow and damage you had no hand in creating. Yes, I'll be showing you the Way of the Winds, just as I've shown every Gifted child of Tribe Dauntless these past ten years and more. Look you, do but turn your face into this sweet breeze." She took my hand in hers and closed her eyes.

The threads of her spirit intertwined with mine, supporting and guiding it, like a lattice supporting a climbing vine. I closed my eyes as well and concentrated on the soft movement of the warm desert air across my face.

Her voice was velvety as she spoke, "You are feeling the stroking of the air against your skin as it moves across the outside of you. And your weary spirit is closed inside your skin like a city wife closed inside her house. But if you are coming outside of your skin just the littlest bit . . ." she lifted me outside myself as if spirit had become a nimbus of some sort extending two finger-widths from my physical self " . . . you will be feeling the mighty winds blowing *into* you, carrying away the troubles and cares, filling you with their clean power and strength."

I *was* feeling it. As if I were a mildewed old blanket being spread to fluff and dry in the sun, I felt myself growing cleaner, fuller, stronger. From a distance I heard RugMaker ask, "And how are you liking this feeling?"

I didn't answer her. My voice seemed somewhere miles away, and I wasn't much interested in using it. The wind was intoxicating. It was like drinking hot spiced wine when you have been cold and thirsty for hours. It filled all my senses, met all my needs. I wanted to run and dance and yell and ... and ... I wanted to blow away in the wind and feel like this all the time!

"Oh, you are taking to this like the Shaman you are." RugMaker said. My ears registered her words, but my spirit was tugging and struggling, greedy for more of this wild energy. RugMaker restrained me, kept me tied to my thick cold body. "Ah, no. If I were to be letting you frolic free, you would surely perish. You must remain with your body, for spirit and body are both part of the whole. Neither will survive without the other. Now, you must be drawing back into yourself."

She was easing me back inside my skin as she spoke, and I saw how she did it – how to extend out and how to withdraw to safety. And as she pulled me back, I became saner, realizing that without RugMaker's protection, I would have let go of my body and ceased to exist.

RugMaker patted my hand and laid it gently on my lap as she whispered to me, "Do you be using this new strength to heal and to grow in Power so that you will have strength for tonight's Rite of the Passage."

Comfort and peace seeped into me. I dozed.

"Shaman Sanna?" CureAll was hesitantly patting my hand. I looked around for RugMaker, but she had risen and left me sleeping. The nap had done me good, and I felt stronger.

"Oh, CureAll, I fell asleep. And I'm so thirsty!" I exclaimed. "Have you gotten SweetSavor dosed and settled?"

"Yes, and scolded into eating properly for the next few days at least. Little RunningFast was such an easy baby for her, but Tribe LongRider are lean people, and their babes often small. Tribe Eldritch has big, heavy bones and such big babies --- and SweetSavor is years older now. She didn't expect such difficulty this time."

"Well, I've been delivering babies since before I was your age, so she's in good hands when her time comes," I assured the worried CureAll. "Is SweetSavor our only patient today?"

"Oh, a few children drank direct from the springs and had the flux, but I've been dosing them with tea and they're cured, though pulled down a bit. The poultice I used on RunningFast's bruised foot has taken away all the swelling. Those who were wounded in the last battle with the raiders are healing cleanly . . ." she trailed off, swallowed, then seemed to take herself in hand.

"So it's time that I fed you again, and then we must begin to prepare for tonight's ceremony of passage. Mother says you know what to do."

I closed my eyes in resignation, and the soft desert breeze kissed my cheeks. I drew in a deep, dry lungful of air and blew it out in a huge sigh. Without opening my eyes I said, "I am Shaman of Tribe Dauntless, and I know how the Rite of the Passage must be executed." And like an ember that someone blows upon to waken it to flame, my Power glowed brighter.

Chapter 25

Each family of the tribe snuffed their fire and dug a deep hole in the sand to bury the ashes and last coals. New fires were laid for each tent, and CureAll strewed herbs across each in preparation for the flame that would be brought. As the sun was setting, the Tribe gathered in front of FearNaught's tent. The tent flaps were thrown back, and FearNaught was carried out on her bed, born aloft on the shoulders of her children and the stalwart warriors of the Tribe.

    RugMaker began a chant, describing the heroic deeds of FearNaught. The other bier-bearers responded, "Hail, Dauntless FearNaught," to every verse. Chanting, they carried FearNaught completely around the perimeter of the camp, while the weeping people bid her farewell. Then FearNaught and her entourage set out across the sere and bitter land toward the sullen glow of the sunset, leaving her Tribe behind her in the lowering darkness.

I stumbled often in the dusk. CureAll led me and let me lean on her, but still it was hard going. The sand gave foothold to brittle clumps of bleached grass, stunted, scrubby trees and dry skeleton bushes bearing a rich harvest of stickers. SmartFingers had basted together a white robe for me in the few hours available to her, but it was soon soiled from my frequent tripping over unseen obstacles. I turned often to see if we weren't out of sight of camp at last, but every time, the tents showed pale through the sparse trees.

RugMaker continued her chanting. Her voice plucked at the strings of my soul. SwiftSure keened her responses, "Hail, Dauntless FearNaught," like a stormwind howling through the mountains. Streaks of tears glinted on SeeFar's face. A thin cold wind sprang up around us. I paused a moment and breathed it in.

"Here," I said. "Now. This is the time and place."

"We haven't gone far enough!" SwiftSure declared. "I can still . . ."

She turned her head and saw that we had crested a small ridge. The camp was hidden behind it in the darkness. It seemed we had been walking for hours, but we were still so close that I could hear little HappyGirl's piping voice asking a question, then being shushed.

I seemed to feel HealWell hovering behind me, guiding me as I began the ceremony.

"Warriors of Tribe Dauntless," I proclaimed, "you are honored to have brought your leader to her passing. Bid her farewell."

They set the bed down, then one at a time offered their right hands to FearNaught who grasped them between her own bone-thin hands. A spark seemed to pass and each warrior stood straighter as he or she stepped away from the bed.

I turned to RugMaker and SeeFar and spoke at the ghostly promptings of HealWell, "Surely you are the most fortunate of children, for you have the opportunity to take leave of your mother in peace and dignity."

SeeFar was weeping. He fell on his knees next to the bed and buried his face in the covers. "Mama," he sobbed. "Oh, Mama." FearNaught rested her hand on his head, stroking his long fair hair. The wind strengthened. SeeFar heaved a deep sigh, was still for a moment, then raised his wet face to look his mother in the eyes. "I'll be giving you a lot of grandchildren," he promised her. FearNaught smiled at him.

RugMaker took his place. FearNaught placed her hand on RugMaker's head also. The love in their eyes glowed so brightly that I could almost see the blessing pass between them.

Then they all turned and began walking back toward the camp, leaving SwiftSure, CureAll, and me alone with FearNaught. I opened my belt bag and pulled out the first jar of oil. SwiftSure eased her way into the bed with her mother and settled herself with FearNaught held in her arms.

We waited in the cold night while the moon rose, washing the world in silver light and black shadows. Then, in the distance, we heard the combined voices of the entire tribe beginning the mourning chant. I opened the jar and poured the oil over the old leader and the new, soaking their clothing and hair with the scent of olives.

CureAll strewed herbs and incense as I poured the second jar of oil over the bed, saturating the linen bedding and flock mattress. All wool and silk had been removed, leaving only things that would burn quickly and completely.

"Shaman Sanna," said FearNaught, as I prepared to complete the ceremony, "take my hand."

I took her long hand, slick with oil, hot with fever and little more than skin over brittle bones. And a jolt of Power surged into me. This was Power like SwiftSure carried, but steadier -- not as potent, but more reliable. I gasped with the shock of it.

"My thanks to you," she whispered as she released me. "Care for my people."

SwiftSure, her face as hard as the stony cliffs of Thon that I yearned for, began to glow, then flames ran across her skin. The oil-soaked fabric of the bedding and clothing caught and blazed brightly. FearNaught, clasped in SwiftSure's arms, cried out and writhed as the fire enveloped her. SwiftSure held her tightly. There was an explosion of flame, and carried to the peak of it I saw a Firebird – no, *two* Firebirds! One blazed with the red fires I had always seen with SwiftSure. The other burned white-hot, silvery hot. She burned like liberation from bondage, and joy too great for the body to hold. They danced together in the blazing inferno of the pyre as I spoke the final words of the Rite of the Passage, "From death to life, reborn in the fire, mother and daughter and leader of Tribe Dauntless, the Firebird flies ever in the ways of her own choosing."

The bed had become a furnace, but CureAll and I stood close, squinting into the light and heat. Somehow, a cold, clean wind seemed to blow from the fire into our faces, and I drew it deep into my lungs with each breath.

Quickly, the oil-soaked pyre burned to coals. As the flames died down, the silver Firebird soared into the skies with the last of the smoke. The red Firebird settled down as if nesting on the glowing embers. She raised her head to the white sickle moon and from her throat rose SwiftSure's voice in a rending, wailing cry.

Chapter 26

CureAll and I turned back toward the camp. The orange light of the collapsing pyre threw our shadows leaping up the ridge before us. The cold, white moon laid distorted gray shadows beside us. Stumbling between my two shadows, I felt brittle as an empty gourd. I wondered why the wind blowing past my ears didn't whistle over the hollow spaces inside. I had just helped a woman burn her mother to death -- and it was the right thing to do. I had accepted a position of authority in a culture that was completely strange to me. I was sick and weary, and no one who loved me even knew where I was. And beside me, CureAll began to sniffle.

The poor child had lost her mother, and now, two weeks later, her aunt, the tribal leader. And she was only eleven. I didn't know how to comfort myself, but I needed to comfort CureAll. I reached out my hand to her shoulder.

She turned to throw her arms around me and bury her face against me, and we clung together on the crest of the ridge for a moment, shivering and trying to work up enough courage to go forward. Behind us, with a final fountain of sparks, the last of the pyre fell and died, and our long shadows stretched up, then vanished. Lighted by the rising moon, attended only by our puny side-shadows, we walked back to camp.

When we arrived, RugMaker brought the mourning chant to an end. People rose from their knees, wiped their eyes, blew their noses. We stood silent, with only an occasional sniff or a baby's querulous whimper piercing the dark. Then SwiftSure the Firebird rose above the ridge in flaming red glory and flew like a comet to the camp. She landed in front of her tent, atop the carefully laid pile of wood for the Headwoman's fire. The wood burst into flame beneath her. She stepped regally out of the fire and transformed to human. SeeFar gave his hand to SwiftSure.

"SwiftSure, Headwoman of Tribe Dauntless, I give you the honor and fealty of the bachelors' tent," he said.

"This honor and fealty I gladly accept," she told him. "Take you my fire for your living."

SeeFar turned, took a burning branch from the fire, carried it over to the bachelors' tent and lit their hearth.

The same actions and words were repeated for each separate family, with the exception that every other person pledging honor and fealty was a woman. (The husband was part of her family, not the other way round.)

CureAll nudged me several times and when I finally caught on to what she wanted, I hissed, "It's *your* tent! You take the fire." Looking uncertain, she did so. SwiftSure accepted her pledge but gave me a hard look over the child's head.

And then, when all the tribe's fires had been lit, it was time for the funeral feast. "It's glad I am to be Headwoman of such a valorous and honorable people," proclaimed SwiftSure. "Do you be enjoying this feast to the fullest, but linger not over long. For it's true that we have dallied here these past weeks when by rights we should have been out upon the trade route. It is time and past time that we should be on the move, and the taureks are nesting beneath the sands even as we sleep. Tomorrow, we must set out with all the speed we may make before they hatch and swarm and we are cut off from the summer pastures. Tomorrow, we move."

Her words were greeted with cheers.

And HealWell (blast her ghostly strength) opened my mouth and used me to say, "We must wait two more days."

SwiftSure turned a glare on me that should have incinerated me on the spot. But I stood cold beneath it. Having spoken, I knew I was right. We had to wait two more days before we moved. I didn't know why, but I knew it was true.

"So!" flared SwiftSure, "You pledge me none of your fealty and give me no honor of your own, but hide behind the skirts of poor young CureAll. And now are you thinking yourself free to steal my authority? That you'll never do, foreign witch that you are, for the peoples of Tribe Dauntless will never be heeding your words over mine. You will be doing as I say and coming or going at my will, and there are strong arms and rope enough to carry you kicking and screaming if you will so have it. Tomorrow, we move!"

I thrust out my hand to her. "Here's my hand. Until you have another Shaman for Tribe Dauntless, I will give you my fealty and honor."

SwiftSure grabbed my hand and I felt her trying to draw the Power out of me. But I have been a knitter all my life. I have unexpected strength in my hands and forearms. I squeezed her hand and ground the knuckles together. The pain threw her off. She didn't flinch or grimace, but I saw the flash of surprise in her eyes, quickly masked by iron control. We released each other.

"But if you will take my advice as from the Shaman of your people, you will not move the Tribe for two more days," I said.

"Take the advice of a foreign Sorceress?" she spat at me. "Best you be saving your breath, willow-lass, for you are too green to be giving advice to any but the babies. Do you tend to the healing and the ceremonies, and leave the leading of Tribe Dauntless to those as are born to the Tribe and know our ways."

With that she turned on her heel and strode into her tent.

Chapter 27

The next morning, in the cold of dawn, CureAll woke me with a steaming cup of tea in hand.

"I let you sleep as long as ever I might," she said apologetically, "but look you now, it is time to be folding up the tent. Do you drink this good tea and dress yourself, and then come forth and see how Tribe Dauntless sets out."

I knew we shouldn't leave, but I didn't know why. And since I had agreed to care for the tribe, I was going to have to go with them. I considered pulling on a pair of fast-foot socks to speed my steps but then realized that the tribe would move no faster than its herd of goats. Between CureAll's teas and gruels, and the extra power I was getting by dribs and drabs from the people of Tribe Dauntless, from FearNaught's parting gift of power, and even from the wind, I felt strong enough to walk at least part of the day. And if I grew too weary, perhaps I could ride on RugMaker's aerial rug. Sturdy boots, gray linen trousers and a white linen shirt were what I decided to wear.

I lifted the tent flap and stood amazed at the scene of bustling activity before me. Tents were collapsing like pricked waterskins. Bundles were being tied up. Sleepy children huddled around fires, slowly eating their morning porridge while their mothers bustled about, cleaning and packing the cooking pots. A hideous bawling roar drew my attention to the edge of camp where LongRider LoveSinger was riding in on one of those peculiar ugly beasts called "camels" and leading another sixty or so behind him. Their complaints were loud and continuous. People ran up and began leading their own beasts to their campsites. CureAll brought three of the creatures to our tent. Two to ride and one to carry the tent and furnishings. We soon had these stashed, and after I had been helped onto the back of my beast, and my camel's reins tied to CureAll's saddle (till I learned the way of riding and guiding the awkward animal) we were ready to set out. Before the sun was three fingers above the horizon, Tribe Dauntless was on the move. No one walked. Even the shepherds rode camels. Toddlers rode with parents or aunties or older cousins, and children not much older than seven were put atop heavily laden old beasts and given the reins. To avoid the dust kicked up by our progress, we rode side by side in one long line, all headed north. We spread across the bitter land, and I concentrated on staring at the horizon and keeping my breakfast down. Riding a camel involves dipping, swaying, rocking, pitching and lurching. The real trick is keeping your stomach from being shaken loose. I could have walked faster, but as the sun rose and began bearing down on us, I was grateful to be able to save my strength.

I reached into my handy belt bag and drew out the white headdress that SmartFingers had made for me. It was a large square of fine, soft wool, folded into a triangle and draped over the head, then held in place with a padded circlet of cording. I looked to right and left of me and saw that everyone had drawn one side of her headdress across her face, leaving just her eyes showing, and had tucked the loose end into the circlet of cords. I tried this. It took me quite a bit of adjusting and fiddling, but it did shade my eyes better, and it kept the hot wind from drying out the lining of my nose.

No sooner had I gotten things arranged to my satisfaction than I was assaulted by thirst and had to tear all my careful pleats apart to get the waterskin to my mouth. Fidgeting with my headdress kept my mind off my nausea, though, so I didn't mind it too much.

We didn't stop to eat, but munched leftovers from the previous night's feast as we rode along. Then, in the middle of the afternoon, Eldritch Smith came racing up to CureAll and me.

"SweetSavor!" he gasped. "She's started. It's too early!"

Without a word, CureAll dragged her camel's head around and slashed its flanks with the long springy stick she carried. Since my camel's bridle was tied to CureAll's saddle, we were dragged along with her.

SweetSavor's camel was kneeling next to a small tree, and SweetSavor was lying in the scant shade it offered. She was leaning on one elbow, throwing up. I had no idea how to make my camel kneel, so I jumped off while it was still standing, and ran to SweetSavor's side. Her face was gray and her skin was clammy. She wailed as a contraction took her.

"Boil some water and salt it heavily," I commanded Smith. "Then put up some kind of shelter. We'll be here a while."

"But we're miles from our next camp," he protested.

I was checking SweetSavor's pulse. It was rapid and weak. "If she travels any farther, she and the baby will die," I said. "CureAll, we'll need anti-hemorhagics, a good heart strengthener, and what do you have that's calmative?"

SweetSavor was weeping in great gasps. "It wasn't like this the last time," she wailed. "This hurts so much!"

"Well, you're older now, dear heart," I said as helped her roll onto her back. I was sending a feeling of comfort and peace into her with my touch, my voice, my healing Gift. "But you're not the oldest mother I've helped. We'll do fine. Let's just see how things are going here." And I lifted her skirts to check the progress of the birth.

Before I had finished, CureAll was holding up SweetSavor's head, giving her sips from a small vial and murmuring quietly.

"The birth will go easier if you can sit up," I said. "You have a strong little girl in a good position, but a long labor will be hard on both of you."

Then, as if things weren't difficult enough, an eagle dropped out of the sky and transformed into SeeFar.

"What are you doing?" he demanded. "You're falling too far behind the tribe. Camp is miles away yet!"

"SweetSavor is having a baby, and her husband and healers are with her," I told him before anyone else could speak. "You can help us, or go on without us, or fly in ever decreasing circles till you disappear up your own backside for all I care. Now lend a hand or get out of the way."

SeeFar got. Eldritch Smith, using his magical Talents with fire and iron, had a small cauldron of water boiling by that time and was efficiently staking out a square of canvas to shield and shelter us.

"Good job, Smith," I exclaimed. "As soon as you've finished that, bring a saddle over here. We can use your strong arms and back."

He looked puzzled but did as I asked without saying a word. As soon as the saddle was placed to my satisfaction, I had him help SweetSavor to her feet, then sat him down on the saddle sideways, not astride. He spread his legs for balance, and I sat SweetSavor down on his lap, with her back to his chest and her knees outside of his.

"Now wrap those strong arms around her, whisper sweet things into her ear, and when you feel her belly get hard, push down on the top of it." Anxiety looked out of his eyes, but he followed my instructions. As his rumbling bass voice murmured comfortingly to her, and his brawny arms held her secure, SweetSavor began to recover her panic and get into the work of birthing.

CureAll and I used compresses soaked in the hot salty water to help the birth opening relax and stretch without tearing. I was fishing another compress out of the boiling pot when a ball of flame hurtled down from the cloudless expanse overhead. SwiftSure had to stick her beak in.

But she surprised me. Rather than demand that we get right back on our camels and follow the tribe, she first went to SweetSavor, dropped to one knee beside her and spoke gently.

"Ah, sweet cousin, and is this the glorious day of your babe's arrival? It's sorry I am to have been chivvying you along on such an auspicious occasion. See you now, I am sending SeeFar and RugMaker and FirstForth and WillingStrength to guard you through the night. And LongRider LoveSinger himself will soon be at your side, as well, for the persistent love he bears you, the rogue that he is. And if you are having need of me, I will come my own self as fast as wing can carry me, see if it isn't so!"

SweetSavor smiled, then her face puckered as a contraction took her. Smith pressed on her belly as I had instructed him, and raised his voice slightly over her whining moan. "There, my sweet dumpling," he said. "There, my brave and tasty girl. Oh, what a good strong girl she is." SweetSavor slid her hand around his neck, and as the contraction passed, relaxed against him with a sigh.

SwiftSure stepped over to me and snarled, "You contrary vermin! Why didn't you say that her time was upon her when you gainsaid me last night?"

I hissed, "It wasn't! If you had waited two days, as I suggested, she would have been strong enough to carry the baby to term. I didn't know she would go into labor. I just knew that something bad would happen. I'm not a fortune teller – I'm a Healer!"

"You're a bad bargain to me all round," she growled, and burst into flame so close that she singed my eyelashes as she flew away.

Chapter 28

Soon SeeFar returned as an eagle, followed by RugMaker on her carpet.

"Why do we have to have this mob of people?" I asked. "You won't be any help with the birthing."

RugMaker looked taken aback. "Why, to be guarding you all from the Golmen raiders and the wild dogs of the desert and the night-flying effrits. And it's few enough we are for that, but more warriors here would leave the tribe vulnerable."

Suddenly I saw the solution to our problems. "Well, let's put SweetSavor on your carpet and fly her to the camp!"

"Ah, and wouldn't that be the very thing if only my carpet could lift so much weight. But were it not for the fact that you are the leanest bit of bone I've seen to stand and walk, I could not have carried both you and SeeFar at one and the same time. SweetSavor weighs more than the three of us together. No, if things go badly here, then I'm to carry you and CureAll off to safety, and no argumentation about it – the tribe must have its Healers!"

SweetSavor cried out, and I went to her. There would be no argument from me if things went badly. I would die before leaving someone in my care.

CureAll and I continued working with the hot compresses, and the birth progressed steadily, but slowly. Between contractions, we massaged SweetSavor's feet, hands and belly, wiped her sweaty brow and neck with cool moist cloths, gave sips of teas to her and to Smith. CureAll had several small kettles going, and her potions were working wonders, but I worried. SweetSavor's heart wasn't strong, and her kidneys weren't drawing the poisons from her blood the way they should. The longer the labor went on, the weaker she grew.

The warrior FirstForth, her son WillingStrength, and SweetSavor's first husband, LongRider LoveSinger, arrived about an hour before sunset. They immediately set about fortifying our little site, cutting and dragging the spikey thornbushes into a wall encircling us, maybe twenty paces from one side to the other; making the riding camels and the baggage camels kneel down around the front of the shelter to conceal the fire's glow with their shaggy bodies. The camels belched and grumbled and chewed their cuds. And LoveSinger's voice pealed out in a sweet baritone, singing blessings as he worked. RugMaker joined with him in song, and I sensed a shield of protection building and settling above us.

SeeFar flew overhead, keen eagle eyes searching the horizon for dangers. The sun sank in the endless white sky and set with a suffusion of gold. But long after the cold blue evening shadows had rolled across us, SeeFar hovered high above, glinting in the final high rays of light.

SweetSavor labored on. I poured more of my own strength into her as the night lengthened. When I began to weaken, I would step outside of the shelter and open my spirit to the cold wind, feeling it blow the weariness and worry out of me, and fill me with energy and certainty. But, toward midnight, the wind carried something … not right.

SeeFar should have been guarding, but instead, was chuckling and telling stories with WillingStrength. I dashed over to them and grabbed each by the shoulder.

"Face the wind!" I ordered, and when they did, I demanded, "What is that?"

SeeFar stared into the darkness as if he could see the very shape of the air. "Raiders!" he whispered. "The vermin are skulking between us and our main camp. WillingStrength, be waking the others. Sanna, do you be sending CureAll out here, and yourself set about keeping SweetSavor quiet if it can be done. If the Good One is generous to us tonight, they may be passing us by altogether.

But when I slipped into the shelter and muttered to CureAll, "SeeFar wants you," SweetSavor began to fret.

"What is it that's happening now?" she demanded. "Why is SeeFar wanting to be speaking to CureAll?

There's a thing that is sore amiss, I am feeling it in the wind."

"Nothing for you to worry about, little mother," I crooned, stroking the side of her face and sending as much serenity into her as I could. "Just you focus on helping that lovely daughter of yours into the world. What will you call her?"

"I'm not to be naming her," SweetSavor snapped, then gasped and groaned as another contraction took her.

"All babes in the tribe are given their names by the Shaman," said CureAll, slipping a long knife under her belt as she stepped back into the shelter. "It's you that will be naming this wee one. And it's sure you are that we have a girl here?"

"Oh, yes, a big strong girl with all her fingers and toes and everything where it should be," I answered, hoping to keep SweetSavor distracted. "You know how I can go into a body and read its illness. I can also read a body inside a body. And this body is ready to be born. Are you starting to feel the need to bear down during your contractions?"

SweetSavor nodded, panting with the work she was doing. I reached into my handy belt bag and pulled out a birthing rope – a length of rope with the ends worked into padded handgrips. I threaded the rope under the saddle that Smith was sitting on, and gave the handgrips to SweetSavor.

"When you want to bear down," I coached her, "take a deep breath, then pull on the rope while you push out the baby. We'll count for you. At ten, stop and breathe ten times. Then take a deep breath and push again. Understand?"

She nodded, squeezing the handgrips. "But it wasn't this hard when RunningFast was born," she whimpered. "And my head is pounding fit to burst already."

"There, now, my tender cutlet, my sweet morsel of joy," soothed Smith, caressing her swollen belly with his great, burn-scarred hand. "You'll soon be done with this, and everything will be well. Hush you now, my succulent one." For a man who seldom spoke, he certainly knew the right thing to say when he had to.

SweetSavor strained and groaned and was unable to keep from occasionally crying out with pain.

SeeFar stuck his head around the edge of the shelter once. "Can't you keep her quiet?" he hissed.

I held out my hand to him as I rested the other on SweetSavor's rippling belly. "Come over here and carry her pain for a few minutes, then tell me how to keep her quiet." SeeFar jerked back and disappeared like a tortoise into its shell. I snorted at him, but Smith glared at me.

"What?" I asked.

"Why haven't you given her pain to me?" he asked.

"I can't. Each person must bear her own pain. No other can bear it for her. No Healer can give it to another. I just said that to chase him away. But if you will share your strength with SweetSavor --- "

She cried out, and pulled on the ropes, her face growing almost purple as she bore down.

"..eight, nine, ten! Now breathe!" I ordered, panting along with her.

The sense of things not right grew behind my shoulders. I put my hand on Smith's wrist and begged him, "Please, Smith, I may be foreign to you, but I'm the only Shaman you've got. SweetSavor needs your help. You've got to trust me."

"Give her my strength then!" cried Smith, clutching my hand in a bone-crushing grip.

"Ten! Push!" I said, drawing strength from him, black and red, alternately pliant and rigid – strength like hot iron and cold steel, and feeding it to his weary wife. "Bear down again! Pull on that rope! One, two, three . . ."

"I see the head!" cried CureAll.

A hideous shrieking split the night, and sounds of combat swept around us.

". . . nine, ten! And breathe. One, two. .."

The camels lurched to their feet and stood bawling defiance into the darkness, then kicking, spitting, lunging through the leaping shadows of our small fire, they fought to defend us. I saw one fasten her long yellow teeth into the shoulder of a small, dark form and lift it as it shrieked with pain, then drop it and trample it beneath her great splayed feet.

". . . ten. And push!" I ordered again, flooding SweetSavor with Smith's determination and strength.

"Here she comes!" called CureAll. "One more good push like that will do it!"

"And breathe! One, two . . ." I could hear war cries, roaring camels, shrieking raiders, a thundering of horses' hooves and the hair-raising *'sssik'* of arrows flying past.

"And push!" I demanded. SweetSavor gulped air, clenched her jaw and pushed fit to burst her heart.

"Yes!" cried CureAll, lunging on her knees to hold the slippery infant, "It's a girl!"

The thin wail of a newborn rang out. The sounds of battle stilled a moment as the tiny cry was repeated, stronger, louder, longer. Our defenders cheered. Then I heard a raider shout a rough, guttural command, followed by a receding drumming of hooves.

Chapter 29

I didn't have time to celebrate, though. As CureAll held the little girl, I tied off the umbilical cord and cut it, then placed the baby in SweetSavor's arms.

"Dauntless SweetSavor, Eldritch Smith, here's your daughter, PeaceBringer."

The parents gazed awestricken at their tiny child as the baby found SweetSavor's breast and began to nurse. And CureAll and I worked like furies. SweetSavor was bleeding too much, and we had to get it staunched.

"Smith, she needs to lie down on her back. Slip something under her hips and hold her feet up," I ordered. Startled, he jerked into action.

We tried. We did everything we knew and everything we could think of, but at last, SweetSavor's exhausted body just gave up. She grew paler and paler while the smell of blood filled the air.

"I'm sorry, my darling," she whispered at last, stretching out a hand to Smith. "I won't be baking you a honeycake tomorrow after all."

"SweetSavor!" he cried, clutching her hand. "Shaman, do something!"

I had already sent my Talent into her, knotting off all the veins to her womb. She was no longer leaking blood, but still the life was ebbing out of her. Her overtaxed heart fluttered like a moth.

"She's out of my reach, Smith. The Good One didn't give me Power over death."

"Give her my life! Take it! I don't want to live without her."

SweetSavor breathed out and did not breathe in again.

"Do something, Shaman! Do something!!" Smith grabbed the front of my robe and began shaking me. He was massively strong. My head snapped back and forth like a rag doll's. I used both of my hands to bend his little finger back till the pain got through to him and he released me. CureAll, holding the sleeping baby, huddled wide-eyed in the back of the shelter.

Smith fell to his knees beside the body of his wife, wailing, "SweetSavor! Oh SweetSavor!"

From out in the desert, his cries were echoed by a feral howl.

"Dogs!" shouted SeeFar. "Now it is we must be standing together, to be guarding one another's backs. LoveSinger, do you be calling in the camels. RugMaker, it is now that you must be taking our healers to safety."

Sanna Meets Dauntless Swiftsure

A fierce wind was blowing from the east, filling me with a wild vitality. When RugMaker flew up on her carpet, I bundled CureAll and the baby onto it, saying, "I can handle a few dogs. Fly fast and bring help. Don't waste time arguing with me. Save your Shaman and the newest member of Tribe Dauntless. Go!"

RugMaker knew enough not to waste breath or effort. The carpet soared high and arrowed off through the night. I saw its silhouette dwindle against the setting moon.

I pulled my quarterstaff from my belt bag, exulting in the excitement pouring through me. I was sick and tired of being sick and tired. It was time to strike back!

FirstForth blinked in startlement as I joined her in the skirmish line. We could hear the dogs growling and snuffling outside the thornbush wall.

"Will the wall keep them out?" I asked her.

"Only for the smallest part of an hour. They'll dig under it, the canny beasts, or leap the low spots or simply break through where it's thinnest." Then eying my staff skeptically she tapped it gently with her bow and asked, "And have you any great skill at all with that?"

"Good enough. It's an implement of Power. It helps me read and direct energies," I answered.

"Might it be that you can throw a few small lightning bolts with it?" she asked, hopefully.

"I'm not that potent," I said. "If someone throws a bolt at me, I can re-direct it, but I can't create one for myself."

Then I looked around, counting heads. "Was anyone hurt by the raiders?"

"WillingStrength had the poor luck to be too slow to duck the Raiders' wicked arrow altogether, but the good luck to have a great, thick skull. I don't think the wound is so very bad, but if you could be taking the quickest little look at him . . ." I could hear the brusque warrior and the worried mother struggling for dominance in her voice.

"Where is he?" I asked, and she nodded toward where her son stood in the shadows, while LoveSinger bound a bandage around the wound.

"Healer's here," I announced and joined them. The wound was just a graze - clean and shallow, though like any head wound, it had bled terrifically. I staunched the last of the bleeding, approved LoveSinger's bandaging and turned to see where else I might be needed. The twang of a bow and a canine shriek of pain brought me around. FirstForth's keen eyes had detected a wild dog wriggling through a shallow hole under the thornbushes. Now, the dog blocked that hole with its body. Her skill with the bow explained why she had let LoveSinger tend her injured son.

SeeFar yelled and pointed to where other dogs were leaping over a low spot in the wall. FirstForth took one with an arrow, SeeFar felled another with a well-cast spear.

"If the thornbushes won't keep them out," I said, "let's see if fire will." SeeFar looked at me in puzzlement, but FirstForth saw my intentions instantly. She grabbed a burning brand from the fire and hurled it into the wall of thornbushes, which began to blaze. WillingStrength and LoveSinger followed her lead, and then SeeFar caught on as well. Soon we were surrounded by a ring of fire, and the wild dogs milled around outside, screaming their fear and anger. We formed a defensive ring around the shelter where SweetSavor's body lay. The camels stood with us, trembling with fear.

SeeFar spoke to Smith, got him to his feet and shoulder to shoulder with us. But when he tried to place a spear in the man's hands, Smith shoved him away with a snarl, then stood, glaring at the fires around us, clenching his fists and growling deep in his throat.

As the flames burned lower, we began to see the wild dogs circling outside the wall. They were dark, shaggy-coated beasts, and I could see only glimpses of slinking, long bodies, with occasional flashes of firelight reflected from white fangs or mad green eyes. One of the largest and boldest leapt the fires, caught an arrow in the chest, and crumpled a spear's length from our feet.

"How many arrows do you have left?" I asked FirstForth.

She ran her hand across the top of the quiver slung over her shoulder. "A dozen – maybe fifteen. But look you, I have also this fine long dagger, and a warrior of Tribe Dauntless is ever to be reckoned with, even bare-handed."

"Hmm – we have fifteen arrows, four or five spears, a quarterstaff, an unarmed madman and nine camels against thirty or forty wild dogs. Do we have a plan?"

"Why yes, it's the simplest plan in the world, fair bold Shaman," said FirstForth. "We just keep killing the foul brutes till they give up with their wanting to be killing us." Her confident grin twisted the scar on her face. In the leaping firelight, she looked terrifying. With her on our side, the plan just might work.

Dogs began leaping the embers all around us. FirstForth's bow sang like a harp beside me, but she couldn't kill them all. I lashed out with my staff, breaking necks, skulls, legs of the hulking brutes; guarding her side as she nocked, drew, and loosed feathered death upon them. At my other side, a lean, quick dog leapt for Smith's throat. Smith wrapped his hands around the creature's neck and squeezed. The dog thrashed, then went limp. And with a roar, Eldritch Smith changed into a huge yellow dog and turned ravening jaws upon the other dogs attacking us.

Chapter 30

Two of the camels had gone down, screaming, under the dog's assault. The spears were gone, and FirstForth had nocked her last arrow. Smith was the center of a baying, screaming, thrashing ball of teeth and destruction as he tore into the wild dogs. But we were done for. Then I began to hear the sound of arrows again. The dog lunging at me suddenly sprouted an arrow in its back, and fell away. The hideous shrieking began once more. It was the Golmen raiders, returned to hit us again! I threw my life into the hands of the Good One and stood my ground. The dogs drew back, died under the rain of arrows, finally turned and fled. Smith stood amid the carnage he had created, one of his hind leg dangling broken, his muzzle dark with blood. The raiders on their stocky ponies circled us.

SeeFar stepped forward with his long knife clenched ready in a bloody hand and demanded of them, "And how will you be dealing with these warriors of Tribe Dauntless now?" he demanded.

The Raiders mumbled among themselves, then one called out, "This is a birthing?"

"Yes," I spoke up. "But the mother has died and the babe has been carried to safety."

"You wear Shaman white. Why you let her birth here?" he accused.

"I didn't know she would," I said.

"You not good Shaman," he replied. "Tribe Dauntless – Shaman is good Shaman. All know HealWell. Who you?"

"I'm Sanna, Sorceress Apprentice from Dertzu, and if one of you raiders hadn't killed HealWell, none of us would be here."

"Liar!" he cried, and raised his little, recurved bow and aimed an arrow straight at my heart.

"I am LongRider LoveSinger," spoke the sweet-voiced shepherd, "and I swear by the truth of my right hand that a raider killed Dauntless HealWell."

"LongRiders not lie," asserted another of the Raiders.

"Raiders honor a birthing," another said.

"Birth done," said the first. Then, scowling fiercely at me said, "Shaman. Come." And he crooked his long-nailed finger at me.

I felt the push of HealWell again, and submitted to her ghostly lead. Absently, I slipped my staff back into my belt bag, rousing gasps of astonishment as the six-foot length of bone white wood disappeared into the two-foot long bag dangling from my belt. Breathing deeply of the pre-dawn wind, I strode up to the leader's stirrup, put my fists on my hips and cocked my head at him. "Well?" I demanded.

He thumped two fingers against his chest. "Heal," he commanded.

"Give me your hand, then." I said, and he stretched out his grimy, callused fist.

I touched his skin and slid my awareness into the fabric of his flesh. He was early fifties, and tough as an old boot, but an infestation of tapeworms was quickly sapping his strength. Surely CureAll would have a potion for this common ailment, but she was gone, and he wasn't likely to take anything that might be poison. How could I deal with tapeworms by myself?

I thrust my right hand up into the wind and willed inspiration to come to me. And wonder of wonders, it did! I slid my awareness into the tapeworms, one at a time, to bind off their tiny appetites. They detached from the walls of his intestines, and began to die. Quickly, I fled their bodies before I could be trapped by their deaths.

At last I looked the raider in the eyes. "You're healed," I told him. "But you won't know it till you start crapping worms tomorrow. Oh, and I fixed your infected toenail as well. If you would just clip them straight across, they wouldn't get ingrown like that."

He continued to grip my left hand as the tip of his boot rose and fell a few times while he wiggled the injured toe. Then he nodded, released me, shouted another guttural command and wheeled his pony to race away with his fellows.

Chapter 31

I wanted to collapse into a trembling heap on the dirt, but Smith needed my help, as did SeeFar and FirstForth, who were also injured.

When I approached Smith, he hobbled away, growling and bristling. Well, if I couldn't go to him, perhaps he would come to me. I sat on the ground and held out my left hand, palm up. "Eldritch Smith," I said, as calmly and matter-of-factly as I could manage, sitting there amid dead dogs on the ground turned muddy with blood, "Eldritch Smith, you must be healed."

I held up my right hand and began siphoning Power from the steady wind. Smith approached as if against his will. When I finally touched him, he transformed to a human and crumpled on the ground beside me.

Tearing open the side of his pants, I set hand to skin, sent my Talent into the mangled flesh and pinched the nerves to his leg, temporarily knotting off his pain like a strand of embroidery silk. "Now don't move!" I ordered him. "If you start thrashing around, I won't be able to hold you." Quickly, I grabbed the ankle of the broken leg, braced myself for the effort and pulled the leg straight, ignoring the sound it made as the broken bones grated against one another. He grunted with surprise, but held himself dead still.

It was a nasty, splintered break. I eased the shards of bone into alignment and took materials from the rest of his sturdy frame to knit the fractures together, re-embroider the delicate traceries of blood vessels, darn the torn muscles. Then I told him, "Lie still a bit longer. You're healed, but you'll be dizzy for an hour, and sore and weak for several days. I'm going to give you control of your leg again, and it's going to hurt."

I released the pinch from the nerves and watched him carefully. His face paled, he gasped, and clenched his hands, then blew out his breath and closed his eyes. His body was strong and would recover well. I hoped his spirit would survive the mauling it had taken that day.

My healing Power was returning to its old strength and skill. Like a muscle wasted with disuse, the only way to strengthen it was to use it again. I turned to FirstForth to tend her injuries. The worst was a nasty tear on the inside of her thigh. It had missed the big vein, but was ragged and dirty and needed careful attention or would leave a binding scar.

Before I had finished with FirstForth, a blazing light flew through the sky. SwiftSure to the rescue, but much too late.

She transformed to human and began speaking to us. "Torn I have been this past hour, and make no mistake about it. A whole troop of those foul Golmen raiders was sneaking past our camp, as silently as the vile spiders they are, when I saw your fire blaze up and knew it to be a signal that you were in dire need. And then, who should come flying out of the darkness but my own fair RugMaker with CureAll and the wee new lass for Tribe Dauntless. They told me that it's safe from raiders you were, but savaged by dogs in the darkness. But look you, I couldn't leave the camp until I was sure Tribe Dauntless was safe. When I saw the raiders well away and our guards well prepared should they return, I took flight to aid you."

Her long speech had given me plenty of time to finish knitting up FirstForth's torn flesh and spinning out all the dirt and infection from the wound. I quickly mended a few shallow scratches on her arms and left her rubbing the newly healed skin and squinting at it in the firelight.

SeeFar had thrown all his spears and had ended up fighting the dogs with his long knife. The brutes had inflicted cruel scratches with their powerful blunt claws. The injuries weren't life-threatening, but they were bloody and ugly. SeeFar looked a mess. He stood, dirty and battered, facing SwiftSure with his fair head at a defiant angle.

"So it's torn you were?" he said to her, then flung out his mauled left arm so quickly that the blood flicked off it and spattered against her shirt. "And it's torn we were also, though I see no blood of yours. You were cautiously guarding our camp against the vicious raiders, while those self-same raiders were rescuing us from wild dogs. Raiders honor a birthing, Headwoman, as do all the peoples who cross the deserts. But did you place the birthing signs to ward us? I saw none, though I looked with diligence as I flew above to watch over those in my care. Raiders honor the safety of the waterholes, and were merely passing you by, yet you set fearful guard against them, and left us to the teeth of wild dogs while you crouched in your fear."

"And all peoples who cross the deserts honor those who wear Shaman's white," snapped SwiftSure, "and yet wasn't it our own Auntie HealWell who was slaughtered before our very eyes by the dastardly villainy of a raider? How am I to be trusting them to honor anything now?"

LoveSinger stepped between them, making patting-down motions with his hands.

"Yes, yes, I'm sure you both have the wonderful weight of bitterness to be sharing with one another. But at the end of it all, our darling SweetSavor is dead, and the sun is rising, and Tribe Dauntless has need of their Headwoman and their Warleader. This thing between you will not be sorted any time soon, so I'm thinking that you might just be putting it away for a time and tending to your rightful duties now, isn't it so?"

SwiftSure snapped her head around to measure the rising sun, then strode toward the shelter where SweetSavor's body lay. As she passed Smith, she knelt down, touched him and spoke to him, but he lay unmoving, staring at the fading stars overhead, opening and clenching his fists while tears rolled un-heeded down his face. SwiftSure went on to the shelter and stepped behind its screen. Then a strong white light began to glare forth.

I looked at the rigid Smith, then laid my hand on SeeFar's arm to draw his attention from his anger.

"SeeFar, RugMaker needs to return with little PeaceBringer as soon as possible. Her daddy needs her."

SeeFar looked over at Smith, took half a step toward him, stopped, then transformed to eagle and flew off.

WillingStrength was next closest to me, so I turned to address his injuries, cleaning and darning the bites and tears on his legs and arms.

"What do you turn into?" I asked him as I worked.

"Turn into?" he said.

"SwiftSure turns into a Firebird, and SeeFar turns into an eagle, and Smith turns into a mastiff, and LoveSinger probably turns into a camel. So what do you turn into?"

"Nothing," he said, a bit nervously. "I am ever and always only Dauntless WillingStrength. There's no Power or Gift of shifting in me, and glad I am of it. Those born with the double nature have much the harder life than the rest of us, look you, for they are ever of two minds, with the beast tainting the human part of them, and the human contradicting their animal self. It's a wonder to me indeed that they can get through a day, let alone work the good that they do.

"But LoveSinger doesn't shift. The Gift of Tribe LongRider is the power of their speech. A LongRider will hold her right hand up to the eight sweet winds and the eight bitter winds, and the word of truth will fill her entirely. If a LongRider swears by the truth of her right hand, then you may believe her as if the Good One and all Her angels confirmed it."

"And Tribe Eldritch?" I asked.

"Ah, well, Tribe Eldritch is that fey, don't you know?" he answered, glancing at the great bulk of Smith nearby. "They travel in the Wildings and are dealing with effrits and Sorcerers and who knows what other strange creatures. They are uncanny souls, though powerfully attractive. There's a girl of Tribe Eldritch with a smile like music and the sway of her walking is like the play of the little winds over the long grasses of spring - ah, but I don't know that I'm willing to spend a year and a day in the dark of the Wildings, be the girl never so lovely."

We set to packing up our camp. I picked up CureAll's small kettles and boxes of potions and tucked them into my belt bag, then had to explain its magic properties to WillingStrength and the others.

The sun was two fingerwidths above the horizon when SwiftSure stepped out of the shelter and began taking it down. I strode over, thinking I might be needed to lay out SweetSavor's body. But the body was gone! Where SweetSavor had lain was just a mound of gritty, ashy white sand.

SwiftSure handed me a rope as I stood there, staring in amazement. "You might be coiling this up if you would be useful, Shaman."

"What happened to SweetSavor?" I asked.

"It is the way of the Firebird to transform the bodies of her people when they die," SwiftSure said. "I have burned her to clean ash so that she might fly freely with the loving winds. And were you thinking we would be leaving her body here to be torn by the wild dogs and fought over by the carrion birds? Do we seem such savages to you, haughty Sanna of Dertzu, great Sorceress that you are?"

Her face was drawn, and behind the anger in her eyes I saw – guilt. SwiftSure was the tribe's Headwoman, and because of her error in judgment, SweetSavor had died. Suddenly I was profoundly grateful not to have SwiftSure's burdens.

"I'm so sorry about SweetSavor," I said. "We did all we could to save her life. Her body just gave up."

"So said CureAll, the poor dear child," said SwiftSure. "And you may be assured that I hold you blameless for this death. You spoke well when you called for the two-day delay, and I heeded you not. And hadn't Auntie HealWell been fretting over SweetSavor through every month of this ill-fated pregnancy, worried she would come to such an end regardless of Healer's skill?"

We were folding up the tarp now, but wound up twisting it between us as we each bent to the right to bring the fold up to the free corners. I dropped my corner and bent to the left to pick it up straight.

"We need to work together. You lead," I said.

SwiftSure looked affronted. "I was not waiting on your permission to be doing so," she said, dropping the tarp and striding away from me.

By the time RugMaker and SeeFar had returned, the tiny camp had been struck, the surviving camels had been loaded and we were mounting, ready to join with the rest of the tribe. SeeFar and I got Smith onto his feet, then I took PeaceBringer from RugMaker and tucked the sleeping infant into Smith's huge arms.

"Smith," I spoke to him, cupping the side of his face with one hand and reaching through his grief and pain as best I could, "You're all she has now. You need to take care of your daughter. She's so small and helpless."

PeaceBringer stirred, opened her little rosebud mouth in a wide yawn, blinked at Smith, then smiled that smile that midwives say is only gas, but every parent knows to be a sign of unconditional trust and contentment. With a shudder, Smith seemed to break through the paralysis of sorrow that had frozen him. The look of tender wonderment in his eyes was like the beginning of a spring thaw.

"Oh, and isn't my SweetSavor's daughter just the little beauty of all the world?" he breathed, stroking his great work-blackened fingertip so gently along her tiny cheek.

PeaceBringer was undersized, purplish red, and wrinkled like a walnut. Her head was still a bit misshapen from the birthing, though I knew it would soon round out nicely. As we gazed at her, she squeezed her little face into a pucker of concentration and soiled herself.

"Yes," I agreed. "She's a beauty. Let's take her home."

We mounted our camels. Smith refused to put PeaceBringer in her pommel basket but carried her instead, in the crook of his arm, next to his heart.

Chapter 32

We arrived at the oasis by midday. When I first joined the tribe, they had been camped at a desert well. This oasis was quite a different place. There was greenery! Trees and bushes with great fernlike arching leaves. I hadn't realized how my eyes had yearned for the color green. I feasted on it. Green and shade and even a small pool of standing water. The tribe's colorful tents looked like flowers blooming here and there. Laundry was drying in the hot breezes. Men and women stood chatting, and children scampered around, squealing with glee. Our arrival brought everyone running, and we dismounted into a sea of helping hands.

CureAll greeted me with a strengthening tea and a bowl of fresh crispy shoots and tender buds. "These will be doing your liver a world of good, Sanna," she told me. "And there's a pallet in the shade by the water when you'll be wanting to lie down. I've set RunningFast himself to watch over your resting then. He was demanding it, when I told him how it was with the passing of his mother, and how loving and gentle and strong you were, and how you even drew the strength from Smith to try to be saving SweetSavor's life. I'm afraid RunningFast is feeling a bit guilty, the poor wight, that he was riding with his friends and didn't miss SweetSavor till it was too late to turn back. I've told him he wouldn't have been a bit of help, but be that as it may, he thinks he should have been there. And him not quite fourteen and no hand at all with a weapon. What would he have done but get underfoot?"

As she talked, she was shepherding me toward the deepest foliage and the solemn-faced lad standing there.

"RunningFast," I said, juggling bowl and cup into my left hand and laying my right hand on his shoulder, "SweetSavor said to me, 'Tell my darling boy that he was ever the joy of my heart. It's an ease to my passing to know that he is safe.'"

I ignored CureAll's look of surprise. SweetSavor had said no such thing, but I was no relation to the LongRiders, and I could lie whenever I wanted.

The lad's eyes began to fill with tears. He turned his head away so I wouldn't see them. I squeezed his shoulder and said, "I don't really need a guard, but I think Smith will need help setting up the tent. And he would love to show you your baby sister. For SweetSavor's sake, please be kind to the baby, RunningFast."

He sniffed mightily and replied with a watery, "I will, Shaman," then sprinted away. He was aptly named. His robes billowed behind him and he fairly flew through the undergrowth.

CureAll led me to the pile of rugs she had laid for me, nestled deep under a shady bush, then left me to nap. Oh, I needed it! A birth, a death, Golmen raiders and wild dogs – I felt as limp and wrung out as a cloth used to scrub stone steps. I stretched till my joints crackled, then relaxed and barely had time to appreciate the glory of being able to lie down, before I fell asleep.

Something was tickling my face. I tried to raise my hand to brush it away, but there was something blocking my arm. I pried my eyes open to see SeeFar's face, scant inches above my own. It was his breath on my face that had woken me. He was hovering above my body, braced on his hands and toes. I had fallen asleep with my legs sprawled apart, and my hands loose at my sides. His boots were between mine, his hands outside my arms, and I was caged under him in a most compromising position. I drew in a breath, and my breasts just brushed his chest. We were both fully clothed, but my traitor body responded, and my nipples tingled. Smiling into my eyes with cocky self-confidence, he slowly lowered himself on to me, a fraction at a time. His arms quivered with the exquisite control exerted, until I bore the full, muscular weight of him on top of me. And I *liked* it! Heat surged through me, my face flushed, and I heard myself moan.

Suddenly I knew what it was like to have a dual nature. My brain told me to throw him off. My body insisted on savoring the feel, the scent, the delicious manly weight of him just a little longer . . .

"Arrrgh!" I planted one foot on the ground beside his knee and pushed hard to roll over. But as I shoved, he clasped me to him and I wound up lying on top of him, trapped in his powerful arms, my own arms pinned to my sides. My heart was thundering, and I was breathing hard.

"Ah, slight willow-lass," he was purring. "There's a fire in you after all. And if you'll be throwing me onto my back, why then, I can be giving you a ride such as you've never had before." And he rocked his pelvis under me so that I felt the swelling urgency of him pressing against my lap.

The place between my legs throbbed with warmth. It felt so good! I wanted more. I had grown up in a harem, and heard the wives and concubines talking about the pleasures of love, but I had never experienced them myself. SeeFar, I was sure, knew how to bring those pleasures.

"SeeFar, let me go or I will hurt you," I said, managing to put enough conviction into it to make him stop that distracting gentle rocking against me.

"Ah, dear Sanna, and why should I be stopping when the shortness of your breath and the rising glow in your cheeks tell me you are enjoying this as much as I am?" And slowly he rocked his pelvis under me again, the sensation even more intense because of the pause.

I gasped at the thrill of reaction that twitched inside me. Then I twisted one hand up behind my back to touch his hand where it held me pinned against him. Skin-to-skin is the only way I can use my Gifts. I was going to sting him senseless, but found I didn't want to. Instead, I took all the wild excited urges and sensations pulsing through my body and sent them into him in one intense, sudden jolt.

He arched into a bow of ecstasy. "Ahhh, ahhh, ahhh," he cried softly, then collapsed, his arms falling limply to his sides. I planted my hands on his chest and shoved myself to a sitting position, straddling his belly.

"Oh, sweet Good One!" he gasped. "I wasn't ready for *that*! Oh, Sanna!"

He began to raise a hand to caress me. And finally, my brain took over completely from my roused body. I scrambled to my feet, and ran.

Chapter 33

I said nothing to anyone of the encounter but stayed close by CureAll the rest of the afternoon and never saw flesh nor feather of SeeFar. It was a good thing I didn't have much work to do because I was completely distracted. SeeFar was undeniably attractive, and he *roused* me so that I was half dazed with desire and the memories of his lean, hard body pressed against mine.

A Sorceress never marries, so I had always thought I would have to choose between love and Magic. It appeared that Shamans were welcome to mix the two. Marriage and children? The pleasures of love and the comfort of a man's company? Did I want this? Did I want SeeFar? Did I want to remain with Tribe Dauntless as a Shaman even after CureAll was old enough to take over? I thought about it a lot, dozed where I sat in the stuffy heat, and dreamt of being swept away in a great, warm river of honey.

At sunset, SwiftSure summoned the whole tribe together.

"And so it is," she said to us, "that we have each in our own way, been mourning the passing of SweetSavor. If there is blame to be borne, then I must be taking it, for our Shaman warned me to wait, but I was too fiery impatient to heed her."

"If SweetSavor had heeded HealWell and CureAll, she would never have come to such a pass," said Smith. "It's sore I'll be missing her, but I'll be blaming none, nor hearing word of blame, neither. We need now to be caring for this scrap of sweetness she has left to us." He smiled down at PeaceBringer, still cuddled in his left arm.

"And we need also to be caring for this great lad," said LoveSinger, with his arm around the shoulders of his son, RunningFast. The boy was being brave, but you could see it took everything he had.

SwiftSure asked, "Well then, LongRider LoveSinger, will you commit for a year and a day to care for RunningFast and PeaceBringer as if you were equally father to them both?"

"And haven't I made Tribe Dauntless my home these many years already? If my deeds speak too quietly, then I swear by the truth of my right hand that I will care for RunningFast and PeaceBringer as far as my strength will carry me, and my spirit will watch over them when I die."

The tribe gasped and murmured. Evidently this was quite an oath.

SwiftSure then asked, "Eldritch Smith, will you commit for a year and a day to care for RunningFast

Sanna Meets Dauntless Swiftsure

and PeaceBringer as if you were equally father to them both?"

"For a year and a day and all the rest of my life," said Smith. "I will care for SweetSavor's children in whatever way I can, as father and Smith and Eldritch yellow hound."

"Well and good then," SwiftSure said. "The family of Dauntless PeaceBringer is established for a year and a day and for all time after that. Let us be going to our rest and dreaming sweetly."

I bent over PeaceBringer and laid my finger against her tiny palm. She curled her fist and gazed at me with her wondering, unfocused eyes. Gently I slid my Power into her, reading her health and strength, floating for a moment in the quiet blue mists of potentialities that she held. Then I slipped free and withdrew my finger from her grasp.

A fresh breath of night wind whispered across us. "I need to be making you a blanket," I said to the drowsy babe. "I'm very handy with the self-heating stitch."

"Why yes," said SwiftSure at my shoulder, "You are the fine, fair, knitting mistress, are you not? Though I doubt we'll be having much need of the waterproof stockings out here in the desert."

Smith gave her a cold look, then turned and carried PeaceBringer off to bed.

I sighed at SwiftSure's pettiness, then said, "I don't want to tell you what to do," I said to her, "but we really need to leave tomorrow. I don't know why . . ."

"I'm knowing the reason," said SwiftSure. "The taureks may be nesting already, and the longer we wait, the more dangerous they become. But you seem to be finding your own ways in the dark, so I'll be leaving the reading of the winds to you, Shaman Sanna. We leave tomorrow."

I was startled at such an easy victory. Since SwiftSure seemed so obliging, I asked her, "May I talk to you about your brother?"

"Ah, and has SeeFar been doing his best to seduce you? Well, it's no bad thing, I'm thinking, and I'll not do or speak a thing to gainsay him. He is that loath to leave Tribe Dauntless, yet it's time and past time he was fathering babes. And you've the fine broad hips for bearing and birthing babies, isn't it so?"

"You don't care if he rapes me?" I asked, aghast.

"Rape?" she said, flaring into outrage, "And who was saying anything about a rape at all? I am knowing my brother's nature, and to be using force against a woman is not in him. Why, aren't all the girls just chasing after him in the summer pastures? Aren't they just tripping him and beating him to the ground to be enjoying his fleshly skills? It is altogether his plan to be teasing you and tempting you, and drawing you to him every day you are with us until it's you that will be creeping into his bed, not the other way round."

"Well!" I snorted. "We'll just see about that, won't we?" And I flounced off.

Chapter 34

The next morning, we rose at dawn and began breaking camp. I looked at the moon and realized that only a fortnight ago I had been in Arrex, preparing to leave for Thon. And then I realized – "Oh," I spoke aloud, "it's my eighteenth birthday."

CureAll turned to me with a broad smile. "Is it that, Shaman Sanna? Great joy to you, and may you rejoice in many another such day." Then she clasped my shoulders and pressed her right cheek to mine.

That seemed to be the salute for the occasion. Everyone in camp managed to come and press cheeks with me in the midst of all their bustle. LoveSinger, RunningFast, WillingStrength, and SeeFar came to help CureAll and me load our tent and rugs onto the pack camel. When I saw SeeFar approaching, I wanted to run and hide, but instead I bent my back to the task. Then they all clasped my shoulders and pressed right cheek to mine, wishing me joy of the day. When SeeFar touched me, a shock seemed to run through me. He felt it too, blinking, then smiling into my eyes. And when he pressed his cheek against mine, he whispered in my ear, "Later, my lissome queen of love." I ignored him as hard as I could, though heat surged through me and my breath went quivery for a moment.

And when the last pack strap had been fastened and the last child secured ---

Everyone was looking at me.

"Now what?" I asked CureAll.

Her smooth young face furrowed with concern. She looked out across the desert, then back at me, and the fetishes dangling from her hair-picks tinkled lightly in the cold still air. She said, "From this oasis to the Place of Meeting, it is only the Shaman who can be finding the way across the Bridges of the Good One, through the Bones, and all the way over the grasslands."

"Me? But I have no idea where we're going!" I squawked. "This is ridiculous!"

I was standing next to my camel, holding his reins. Suddenly thick solitary blackness wrapped me round, and an eerie voice whispered, "But can you find your way in the dark?"

I stood quite still for a moment. Then I spoke.

"SwiftSure, if you needed to muffle my head, couldn't you have found something better than an old camel blanket? It's hairy and it stinks."

SwiftSure snickered and plucked the enveloping drape off me, then spoke. "Camel blanket or silken scarf or only your own white eyelids, something must be covering your eyes for you to be finding your way in the dark. For look you, the Place of Meeting lies beyond trackless wastes of shifting sands and none but a Shaman can find the paths. None but a Shaman will know where the fell taurek lie hidden, and none but a Shaman can trace the maze of the Bones. You are Shaman to Tribe Dauntless, and, do you not lead us, we must stay here and starve."

"Do but be closing your eyes, Shaman Sanna," CureAll suggested. "The way will be coming to you. Mount your camel and be closing your eyes."

What else could I do? I mounted my camel and closed my eyes. All I could see was a red glow where the light shone through my eyelids. My fingers picked fretfully at one another.

"This is useless," I declared, opening my eyes again to see the entire tribe staring anxiously at me.

"Dear, hasty mouseling," said RugMaker. "You are not giving yourself time enough. I have heard it told how, when Auntie HealWell first became Shaman, sometimes she would be sitting, waiting for the leading for as much as an hour. Do you but be sitting quietly and having faith, and most faithfully, the leading will be coming to you."

So I closed my eyes again. Blindly, I tore at a dry cuticle till it stung. My hands demanded to have something to do. I pulled knitting needles and yarn from my belt bag and began a blanket for PeaceBringer. I have done the self-heating stitch for so long that I can do it without watching or even paying attention. My fingers know how it goes. As I picked up the rhythm of the knitting, my frantic thoughts stilled.

And wonderfully, I knew which way to go!

When I stopped knitting to pick up my camel's reins, however, the sureness of direction left me. I tried again. Knitting, I knew where to go. Not knitting, I was lost. Well then, I would walk. Knitting and walking at the same time was as easy to me as talking and eating at the same time. And since I knew where to go, it didn't feel at all as if I were walking blind. Instead, it felt as if a ball of yarn had been unrolled before me, and all I had to do was knit it up as I followed.

I slithered down my camel's shoulder and tied the reins to the back of my belt, then closed my eyes, picked up my knitting, and set out. I heard the sounds behind me as first one, then another of Tribe Dauntless began to follow.

Soon I got the sense that I was walking the top of a high, narrow ridgeline. I opened my eyes, and all around me I saw nothing but great mounds of sand. Tribe Dauntless snaked behind me, single file, following exactly the path I had wandered. When I closed my eyes and knit, I could tell where every one of the thirty nine adults and twelve children of the tribe was, as if their lifelines were also in my hands as I walked. I set out again, but called over my shoulder, "Tell Smith to put that baby into her pommel basket. She's getting too warm clutched to his side like that."

I felt the ripple of surprise and relief that ran behind me. I was doing a Shaman's duty in my own peculiar way, but clearly I was in touch with my tribe and leading them on the proper paths.

Sanna Meets Dauntless Swiftsure

I continued to follow the narrow ridgeline I sensed before me until late in the afternoon when it seemed to spread out into a small plateau.

"There's enough room here to camp," I declared, opening my eyes and turning around.

SwiftSure was on the camel directly behind me. "First you must be marking out the limits of safety for us, for surely, none but you is knowing where the drop begins."

"Very well," I answered her. "And how am I supposed to mark it out?"

"Ahh, well then -- Auntie HealWell was having a spell that stained the sand where safety ended. Have you no such spell in your beautiful bag of trickery?"

No spell in my belt bag, but any number of knitting needles to stake into the sand, and a ball of bright red yarn to string between them. I marked a line around the camp site, and Tribe Dauntless entered in. Animals were corralled in the center of the safe zone, tents were set up near the perimeter, toddlers were leashed to adults by a length of rope. I saw little HappyGirl scamper away from her mother with a laugh of naughty glee. As soon as she stepped over the red line I had marked, it seemed as if her feet slipped out from under her, and she slid down a hidden slope like a careless climber who had come too close to the edge of a drop-off. The sand closed over her like water. Her mother grabbed hold of the rope that leashed the child to her waist and pulled frantically. I leapt forward and joined her, and we dragged HappyGirl back onto our plateau. SwiftSure rushed over to help, and as soon as I had cleared the child's airways, SwiftSure grabbed her, held her out at arm's length and snarled, "Do – not – *ever*

– be going beyond the line set by the Shaman. When you have grown bigger, you may be too heavy to pull back, and we will have to be leaving you for the taureks!"

HappyGirl began to weep loudly. SwiftSure shoved her back into her mother's arms and strode away.

Patting the sobbing child, her mother said, "There, there, my precious bright star. Tonight, RugMaker will be telling the children the tale of this land as she does every year at this time. Do you sit with them and be listening carefully, so that you will learn to be good and not be angering our Headwoman again."

I thought it might be a good idea if I could also learn to be good and not anger the Headwoman. I decided to join the children that night.

Chapter 35

So, as twilight fell, RugMaker stood next to the Headwoman's fire while her shadow danced on the tent behind her. The children and I gathered at her feet, watching the stars begin to pierce the indigo sky and listening to her tale while the grownups made our dinner.

"I'll be telling you how it is then," RugMaker began, her voice like smoke and velvet. "In the long ago times before the Peoples of the Wide Skies were coming to this place, it was a green wilderness of steep canyons and ridges, with the little springs and streams and waterfalls laughing sweet as children. Oh, and the beasts of the forests were flourishing fit, and the pretty birds of the air sang all the bright day long. The Good One was loving this land so well that she brought the first woman and the first man to live here, for she would ever be having all the best for her beloved children. And she told them to be rejoicing in their world and to be kind to one another, and they did so gladly – for a time.

"But the Good One made the first woman and the first man with the power to be choosing, and free they were to be choosing for good or ill. And so the day came when the first woman was wanting to be moving a stone to see what was underneath of it. But don't you know it was too heavy for her. So she was going to the first man where he was lying on the soft green grass in the sweet cool shade and dreaming -- oh, such a lovely dream.

"'Wake up, my dear husband, and do be bringing your wonderful strength to help me with a thing,' she called to him, bending over and patting him on his great broad shoulder.

"But the first man was lying so easy in the grass and dreaming such a lovely dream. He rolled away from her touch and said, 'Do be waiting just a bit, can't you dear wife, till I am finishing this one little thing.' And he closed his eyes intending to be slipping back into sleep.

"The first woman was wild with curiosity to be seeing what it was that lay underneath her great heavy stone, and this was not a time she was choosing to wait.

"'Rouse yourself, good husband,' she said, prodding him in the back with her foot, 'for I am wanting your help this very minute.'

"'Well then,' said the first man, 'today you will be learning what it is to be wanting and not having. Now go away for the while, and be letting me sleep.'

Sanna Meets Dauntless Swiftsure

"The first woman was hurt and angry. 'Shame it is to you, husband. Was not the Good One telling us to be kind to one another?'

"The first man answered her quite crossly, 'And is it kind of you to be stirring me up from my sleep and shredding my dreams like the webs of small spiders? Shame it is to you as well!'

"And so they fell into bickering, forgetting that at any time they might, one, or the other, or both together, choose again to be kind. Then the Good One was coming to them and taking them from the lovely land, and exiling them to harder lives till they, or their children, or the children of their children should again choose to be kind to one another.

"And until that grand day dawns, the Good One was burying her lovely land beneath the fine and slippery sands. Right up to the ridgetops has she buried it, and only the Shamans can be finding the way across, leading their tribes along the hidden bridges of the ridgetops. And look you, the ridges are narrow as a squint, and they wander like a drunken snake, so you must be remembering always to be going only where the Shaman goes, lest you should be stepping off the safety of the ridge and go slipping down under the sand. HappyGirl found out today what a grievous thing that is, and it is only that she is small and light, and her mother is strong and quick, and our wise and gifted Shaman Sanna was right at hand to be saving her that she is sitting with us tonight."

Every eye turned to the toddler, who had been subdued all afternoon. She sucked her thumb and cuddled up against her older sister, who asked, "Why is it that we are coming out here where there is so much danger?"

RugMaker replied, "We must be crossing from our wide grasslands to the cities and trading for their salt and steel and strong straight wood for our lances. For look you, these are things we are needing to live and can be getting no other way. And the Good One has left us these ways to travel because, though we are not often kind to one another, She is always, always kind to us."

We sat silent a few moments, then, when no more questions came, RugMaker shooed us off to our waiting dinners.

Chapter 36

The next morning, we rose when it was just light enough to tell a black hair from a white hair. Again I led, knitting. The sun beat down, and I walked in a sort of trance, following the thread of magic leading me, knitting busily on the nearly finished baby blanket. As we traveled, I began to sense something approaching behind us. I stopped, opened my eyes and looked, but could see nothing. I climbed onto my camel saddle and stood on it, but even with the added height, all I could see was miles and miles of nothing but miles and miles, and all of it bare sand.

SwiftSure called out to me as she lounged on her own camel-saddle,

"And it's a fine brave pose that is, though we are not wanting a statue at this time. What is it you might be doing up there?"

"I feel as if something is following us," I said, "but I can't see anything anywhere."

She sat straight upright. "Do you hurry, Shaman, and find us a spot we can stand together and defend ourselves, for surely nothing moves out here but Tribe Dauntless and taureks. And it is time that the taureks are coming up the slopes for their summer nesting."

I jumped down and stepped out briskly, concentrating on finding a plateau. As I strode along, I began to realize that the thread I was following had various smaller threads branching off from it. Suddenly one flashed a bright green for me. I was so hungry for the color that, without thinking, I turned and followed that offshoot. It grew thicker and brighter as I traced it, and soon I sensed a wider place. Unlike the plateau we had camped on the past night, which had dropped off precipitously in sheer cliffs, this solid land sloped away in front of us like a broad, rounded hilltop. I grabbed the ball of red yarn from my bag and waded forward, marking the increasing depths. When the sand was above my knees, it became too difficult to walk, so I backed up a bit and traced the line knee-deep. We had an area just big enough to bring in all the camels and goats, with perhaps five feet to spare on either side. The animals, sensing danger, huddled tightly together. The warriors dismounted and readied their weapons. The rest of the tribe remained perched out of the way on camelback.

First Forth was standing beside me. "What *are* taureks?" I asked. But before she could answer, the sand in front of us began to churn, and from it rose a great gray dome. As it climbed the slope toward us, the dome rose swiftly higher till suddenly a pair of giant, beetle-like pinchers appeared at the front end. The creature was man-high and coming fast, clacking those horrible jaws.

I snatched out my quarterstaff, screeching, "Where are the soft spots?"

"There are none," FirstForth yelled over her shoulder as she charged with spear raised, "You've got to be shoving something sharp through the shell and be hoping you are hitting a vital organ."

She avoided the taurek's jaws, and managed to pierce the beast's shell, but it pulled away so fast that it jerked the spear out of her hands. It seemed that the beasts could move easily in any direction without turning. I jumped forward, swinging my quarterstaff, and struck the joint of the jaws as hard as I could. There was a crack, and the joint seemed to dislocate. The pinchers no longer closed completely.

The taurek charged me. I jumped back, dropped the end of my staff on the ground in front of it, and raised the other end as high as I could. The creature ran itself halfway up the staff so that its lower parts rose out of the sand. By the Good One it was heavy! FirstForth was there beside me with another spear to jab between the frantically threshing legs three times before the creature tipped itself sideways and slid away. We backed into the comparative safety of ankle-deep sand, as the taurek made little darts and dashes, toward us, then back. There was another one behind it, half as big, but just as ugly. This one made a run at FirstForth, and she played my trick of making her spear-shaft into a ramp for the thing to drive itself up. It was small enough, and the sand was shallow enough for her to flip it over on its back where it stayed, cradled in the sand, and completely unable to right itself. The mandibles clacked desperately, the scores of fin-like legs flailed uselessly at the air.

We had no time to celebrate. Another small one threw itself at us. This one had a spear piercing its shell and waggling with the beast's movements. I swung my staff to hit the end of that spearshaft, driving it like a nail through the body of the beast and pinning it to the solid ground. Bluish ichor began to well up around the spear shaft as the taurek shuddered, then fell still.

To our left, WillingStrength cried out in pain. His right forearm was caught in a taurek's mandibles, and it was dragging him into deeper sand. FirstForth hurled her spear, struck the taurek, but didn't kill it. We struggled through the hampering sand as quickly as we could, trying to reach WillingStrength in time. He was up to his waist when FirstForth threw herself forward and caught hold of her son's outstretched left hand. I grabbed her ankle, the only part of her near enough to reach, and set my feet to try to pull her back.

Then I realized – I'd set my feet on solid earth! I sent my spirit into the ground like a tap into a living tree. Strength and Power flowed into me. I sent it out through FirstForth, on into WillingStrength, and wove us into a chain that would not be sundered. Then, Grounding more deeply into the very bedrock supporting the earth, I found even more power. I took a step backward, pulling our chain of humanity back toward high ground. The taurek would not release WillingStrength, so it was pulled back as well. Another step, and another, I dragged them back through the sand. My ears were ringing. Black spots danced before my eyes. WillingStrength was shrieking with pain. I may have made him part of an unbreakable chain, but his flesh was being crushed and torn. I had to free him from that ghastly grip before blood loss and shock killed him.

I looked around for help. I saw Eldritch Smith caught by the leg and dragged down. His mighty arm raised above the sand one last time as he stabbed his spear again at the creature. Then he was gone. Artful SaddleMaker, Threadbender's husband, was caught by the largest taurek, which clamped his ribs in those grisly pinchers. Blood spurted from the lad's mouth and nose as he struggled in vain to free himself. He was dying as he slid beneath the surface.

The taureks seemed to swim in the sands that supported them as water supports a fish. If we had found a plateau, they could not have climbed up the sheer sides to us, but the sloping sides of our hillock gave them shallows from which to attack. SwiftSure was hurling balls of flame, but the sand shielded the beasts from harm. I had no idea how to fight such creatures, and began to despair. I had led my tribe to certain death.

Then CureAll stood up on her saddle, and threw her hands and voice to the heavens, crying, "I am Dauntless CureAll, daughter of Shaman Dauntless HealWell and Eldritch Sojourner, niece of Headwoman Dauntless FearNaught, cousin to Headwoman Dauntless SwiftSure. By my blood and by the duty I am owing to my tribe, I am calling on the mighty winds to aid us."

A breeze blew, cool on my sweaty face, then it grew, changed direction, chilled and waxed stronger, ever stronger, till at last it was an icy blast coming straight down from the heavens, driving sand like a cutting tool. I clung to my Grounding and stood firm, but how could any others endure such punishment? What sort of help was this, to blow us to our knees and blind us with sand? Then I no longer felt sand scouring me, though the wind continued howling straight down onto us. I bowed my head and opened my eyes a bare slit. The ground at my feet had been blown clean of sand! I raised my head and saw that the sand was blowing away from us, exposing the top of the hill and stranding all the taureks. Smith's head appeared, shaking off sand like an angered bear clawing free from a den.

As the taurek clinging to WillingStrength felt itself being stranded, it released him and attempted to escape. I let go of FirstForth's ankle, and she was after the beast like a terrier after a rat, grabbing the bloody pinchers and jerking the creature uphill. Its flippers scrabbled frantically against the ground, but couldn't shift its weight without the supporting sand.

By then, I had my hands on WillingStrength, sealing off torn arteries and veins, giving him unconsciousness to let him escape the pain. He was a strong and healthy young man, and could be left for a bit while I saw to others who might be nearer death.

Chapter 37

The wind continued to blow, clearing away sand. I shielded my eyes in the crook of my elbow and made my way down to Smith. He was choking and spitting, and clawing at the ground, trying to drag himself (and the taurek still clamped to his leg) up the hill. I touched him and read that his injury was not life threatening. Fury against these creatures that threatened his daughter and stepson was fierce enough to give him extra strength. I jerked his spear free from the shell of the beast that was trying to drag him down, and put it in Smith's hands. Then I swung my staff and again cracked a mandible joint. With his leg freed, Smith did swift butchery, then turned, eyes watering against the wind, limping after other prey.

The wind was abating. I saw that sand had been blown clear of the hill-top to a depth of twenty feet below the surrounding dunes. The taureks were scattered about like so many soap bubbles on the ground. And the warriors of Tribe Dauntless were slaughtering them with joy. I took myself back to WillingStrength and set about re-knitting broken bones, darning crushed muscles, re-embroidering torn blood vessels and nerves. I saved his life. I saved his hand. I considered, then woke him.

"WillingStrength, I can heal you without scars, but I know how men love to show one another the signs of their bravery. Shall I leave a big red scar on your arm to show where the taurek caught you?"

He blinked several times, looked around, looked back at me and asked, "And am I still breathing, then?"

"Yes, son of my heart," said FirstForth who had come to kneel at his side. "Thanks to Shaman Sanna, and Healer CureAll, we are all still breathing. And I am thinking you would be glad of a scar to show off." And she grinned at him, her teeth flashing white in her scarred and blood-smeared face.

CureAll and I went from warrior to warrior, mending what damage we could. Artful SaddleMaker, who had been caught by the ribcage, was beyond our help. SwiftSure took charge of his body and reverently burned it to ash while his wife, ThreadBender, stood by, weeping.

Before I finished my ministrations, the tribe had been organized into work crews. The dead taureks were flipped onto their backs and dragged up the hill. The sand, which had been blown away, had piled up in a great wall encircling us but was sliding slowly back into place as I watched, re-covering the blessedly solid ground. And the taureks were being butchered. Their bluish ichor stained the ground as

Sanna Meets Dauntless Swiftsure

their pinchers were twisted free, their belly plates pried off, their organs scooped out and sorted. Each taurek carried its own sack of water, and these were taken and carefully reserved, as they would stay sweet indefinitely. There were orange lumpy parts and green wobbly parts that were set aside as well. The rest was thrown into piles that SwiftSure burned to ash and stinking smoke. The lining of the shells was a soft, silvery sort of leather. It was peeled out, rubbed with the green wobbly parts, and carefully folded. The less damaged shells were kept, the rest left. When the small one that FirstForth had upended was opened, the lining showed a bright ruby red.

"The male!" she cried. "The male is mine. The Taureks have taken Artful SaddleMaker from us, but we are taking the male for this region! I am having the red hide!" And waving it overhead, she strutted with gratification while a roar of approval rose from the tribe.

CureAll, WillingStrength, and I were resting, watching the babies as the rest of Tribe Dauntless dealt with the bodies of our enemies.

"Why is FirstForth so happy?" I asked.

"Ah, do but look you," said WillingStrength, smiling fondly at his mother. "It is not once in three dozen years that a tribe can be stripping the hide from a male taurek, and the warrior who killed it is most greatly to be honored. We are crushing this nest and killing the male, and there will be no taureks at all to be plaguing this valley of the land for the next dozen years or so. A measure of such safety is always a joyful thing. FirstForth will be making herself a fair skirt from that roundel of hide, and she will be wearing it with pride every time she is donning her finery."

"Oh, and many are the men who will be coming a-wooing her when we reach the grasslands," said CureAll. "And how will you be liking that, WillingStength?"

"Ha! Good luck to them all, say I," WillingStrength replied with a broad smile. "FirstForth has ever been particular about who she might be choosing, and how many warriors will be measuring up to her demands? And for all of that, I might be doing a bit of wooing my own self." He stroked his fingertips across the long red scars marking his right forearm, and smiled rather proudly.

Chapter 38

It was late when the work was finished. The shells of the taureks were filled with their hides and watersacks and tied behind the camels for towing. And, knitting again, I led us back to the main path. We traveled through the late afternoon. We traveled through the golden hour of evening. We traveled through the colored light of a brief and brilliant sunset. And weary to the bone, we traveled under the cold hard stars. I walked and knitted and followed the thread before us till it finally brought me to a wide, secure plateau with a spring spilling water into the barren sand.

I set out the perimeter yarn, chanting the charms of safety and protection, setting the warding and defense spells, protecting my tribe. CureAll worked alongside me, listening as hard as she could to learn my spells from

Thon and Dertzu, though her little face was drawn with fatigue.

We ate cold dinners and put up only a few tents, packing together into them as close as swallows in a nest. And we all slept, even SwiftSure, without stirring all night.

There were groans and moans all over camp the next morning, as stiff muscles were called to respond. A fire was lighted, and hot porridge prepared for all, ordinary waterbags were emptied of their stale sour contents, and refilled with the clean fresh water of the spring. The tents were folded and packed, and as the sun rose, we were ready to begin our march again.

I had finished the blanket for PeaceBringer, so began with some rose-pink silk I had, to knit myself a shawl using the reverse self-heating stitch. It makes a lovely, light and lacey fabric that cools the air around it. I was sweating gallons during the day, and there was little water left in me to flush the poisons from my still-weakened liver.

The stitch was tricky and not all that familiar to me, so I sank deeply into my walking trance. I was startled out of it by a rush of wings. SeeFar had taken off from his camel and was climbing into a sky burned white overhead by the relentless sun. He circled once, then flew perpendicular to our line of march.

SwiftSure rode behind me. I called to her, "Now what?"

"He is but going to inspect a thing he has seen with his fine sharp eagle eyes, sweet Shaman Sanna," she replied. "Do you be walking on, and we shall be following gladly behind."

"And what do we do if he gets himself lost?" I muttered to myself. But I shut my eyes and walked on, knitting and following where I was led. The path bent and twisted and doubled back on itself. We traveled miles. I stopped to take a swig of water and noticed a buzz of excitement behind me. The tribe was looking off to the side, so I turned and looked, too. On the horizon were the silhouettes of hills! So that was where we were headed. But the path led inexorably parallel to the hills. Well, surely this great buried valley would come to an end, and we could get around it. I closed my eyes, took my yarn in hand and set out with more enthusiasm than ever before. I yearned for hills.

But there was yet another obstacle to cross before we reached the hills. I led us onto a slope that rose beneath my feet. I opened my eyes and saw a scene I had dreamed. Ahead of me was a wilderness of broken black boulders. SwiftSure rode past me and Tribe Dauntless followed her into the hard landscape. CureAll came up alongside me at last and said, "And so you are seeing the Bones, Shaman Sanna. And well you have led us to be crossing the sands in only three days and to be coming to the Bones with so much sweet water at hand. I am thinking that SwiftSure will be making camp here and resting sound tonight, so that we may face the barrier of the Bones well rested."

"It looks like a maze to me," I said. "How do you find your way through?"

A smile dimpled her rounded cheek as she said, "Why, merely by following you again till you are leading us to the grasslands. SeeFar has flown on ahead to be telling the other tribes of our coming, and friends will be meeting us at the far side of the Bones. And then Shaman Sanna, there will be joy and celebration and a great, round welcome. But come you now, and let us be setting up our tent."

Chapter 39

In my dream back at the inn, I had seen the Bones as a field of black boulders, but now I saw it was more like an icefield at the edge of a black glacier. Or like a huge black glass platter dropped by some giant, then kicked into a pile. There were no rounded edges. Great shelves and plates of stone were tilted up and toppled together with crevasses between them deep enough to hide a tall man standing on a camel. It was through these crevasses that I led Tribe Dauntless the next morning. Footing was uncertain, and I had to watch every step lest I break an ankle on the sharp stones. But I could see which way to turn only with my eyes closed. So, knitting, I walked along the floor of the cleft, and at every intersection, paused and closed my eyes so I might be led in the right direction.

The sun shone down with furnace-like intensity. The black stone held the heat and radiated it back like a great iron griddle, and not the least whisper of wind blew down in our sunken path to cool us. By mid-afternoon, even the goats looked wilted. I was trailed by the sound of fretful, whiny children, exhausted by the intense heat. I worried about them.

Then came an intersection that gave me a different sort of leading. Our path out led to the left. But to the right led a vivid green ribbon, much like the thread that had led me to the hillock where we defeated the taureks. I paused, then followed the green path to the right.

As we went, the sides of the crevasse began to curve over us at the top, giving blessed shade. And underfoot, the way was smoother, less cluttered with loose stones. A breath of a breeze began to blow into our faces! At last, we came to a place where the trail disappeared into a deep, dark cave that was exhaling cool air. There was room to set up our entire camp in the mouth of this cave.

CureAll called to the rest of the tribe, "And isn't our Shaman Sanna the canniest and best of all the Shamans in all the tribes? For look you, she has led us to be camping tonight in a cave of the Fire Sprites, and with so many hearty bachelors and lovely women in Tribe Dauntless, we shall be dealing and trading all the sweet night long."

Our weary people raised a cheer, and began to set up camp. As CureAll and I worked with our tent, I asked her, "What are Fire Sprites?"

"They are a people like us, yet not so very much like us. They are living in these darksome caves, eating the blind creatures they find therein and mining the beautiful stones. Whenever a tribe of the Peoples of the Wide Skies camps near them, they are coming out to barter with us, and some will be bringing the beautiful gems and wanting to be making babies. Their bachelors are admiring our strong, tall women, and their women are craving the seed of our randy bachelors. I'm too young, but you might be finding suitors with gems aplenty tonight."

"You – you sell yourselves to these – creatures?" I asked, aghast.

"Do not be saying such a scurrilous thing!" CureAll replied, much affronted. "It is in no wise such a tawdry act! But if a handsome Fire Sprite should catch the eye of – of FirstForth, say - and she dallies with him for the night, enjoying the pleasures of their passions, and in the morning he is gifting her with a necklace of gold and gems from off his own shoulders, can you think at all that she has sold herself? Could you ever be thinking such a thing of your friend FirstForth?"

"Well of course not," I said, "but -- "

"And if LoveSinger might be having a length of silk to be bartering, and he and some fair female Fire Sprite do begin negotiating for it, and in the flash and fury of their dealings, a spark strikes between them, would you have them forego their embraces merely because a bit of goods have been exchanged?"

"Well, no, but . . what about babies?" I asked, then remembered, "Oh, wait. Babies are a gift to the tribe. No wonder everyone is so happy to be here!"

We joined RugMaker and SwiftSure to share our dinners. They seemed to be simmering with excitement.

The sun set, the Bones cooled, the air stopped blowing out of the cave and instead seemed to be drawn in by a great, gentle pair of lungs, carrying the smoke of our small fires with it. Stars began to show in the bit of sky visible from the cave mouth. Then I turned and saw stars appearing in the inky depths of the cave itself. Fascinated, I stared as these mysterious lights grew closer, larger.

I took a step forward, but RugMaker stopped me with a hand on my arm saying, "They must be coming to us, Shaman Sanna. If we are going to them in the darkness, they will be carrying us away. Do you be waiting till they can be seen by the light of our fires. I tell the children that it is best to be always keeping a fire between you and the gullet of the cave."

I noticed that toddlers were again leashed to their mothers as they had been out in the mazes of sand and ridges. Three fires created a sort of line across the back of our camp. And I noticed that everyone was standing and watching the lights approach.

Chapter 40

The Fire Sprites set down their mysterious lamps in the farthest flickering of the firelight and approached quickly, almost eagerly, filing between our three fires and spreading out through the camp. They were small, lean, wiry and utterly white-skinned. Not the pale peachy color usually called white, but white as a white horse or a white cat, with traceries of veins showing blue here and there. And their eyes – well, I could see that SwiftSure had a Fire Sprite somewhere in her family background. Every one of them had the same large eyes so dark that they seemed all pupil.

FirstForth, true to her name, stepped out to meet the newcomers. She was wearing a red linen skirt slung low across her hips to show off her taut belly, and a brightly embroidered vest that left her muscular arms bare and showed the top curve of her breasts. Her wrists and ankles rang with gold bangles. I looked around and saw that many of the unmarried men and women were dressed to display their assets. WillingStrength was shirtless and had oiled himself so that every move brought a play of light sliding across his stalwart torso. He had a number of charming children's toys he had carved from the tough, twisted roots of desert trees and was showing one to a pretty lass with a smoldering gaze.

The Fire Sprites were dressed in silvery gray taurek skins, cut to form close-fitting trousers and hooded shirts. The pretty lass pulled back her hood, and long white braids slithered down like albino serpents that had been coiled around her head. Startled, WillingStrength flinched. The lass gave him a look of disdain and walked away. I looked around and saw that all the Fire Sprites had hair as white as their skins. There was an eerie, ghostlike quality to them.

Two women came over to us. The woman in the lead swung a sling off her back and tenderly pulled out a baby. Looking at CureAll in her Shaman's white robes, she said, "This child does not thrive, Healer. Our wise woman can find no flaw in her, but this child was fathered by one of you dark people. Perhaps you can help her?"

CureAll turned to me, but I said, "Inspect the poor waif, CureAll. Tell us what you find."

So CureAll took the child in her arms, and cooing the same inane baby talk that we all use with babies, unwrapped the pale infant, revealing a slight deformity in chest and legs. CureAll turned her face into the gentle wind blowing in from the desert and closed her eyes.

Sanna Meets Dauntless Swiftsure

"Ah, the poor little sweeting," she said. "Her bones are growing wrongly. She is needing something to be strong. Her skin is hungering for something . . . something warm . . . something . . ." She trailed off, then opened her eyes, tears of frustration in them. "Oh, Sanna, it is making no sense to me at all. How could she be needing the bright sunshine to be making her bones strong?"

"Well done, CureAll!" I said. "With all the sun you face daily, I doubt you've ever seen a case of rickets, but in Thon there are parents and children who sleep through the day and work in the darkness, and they suffer just this same weakness of the bones."

Then I turned to the cave-dwelling mother and told her, "Your baby should be naked in the sunshine, morning and evening, every day for a month. No more than five minutes at a time at first, and never in the heat of the day. After a month, ten minutes once a day should be enough, but watch her, and if she grows sad and listless, give her more sunlight."

The small mother looked at me suspiciously. "You are not wearing Shaman's white. I was not speaking to you."

CureAll explained, "Oh, Sanna is a most powerful healer and Shaman. She is not born to the Tribe, so she is not choosing to wear the white, but she is consenting to be our Shaman till I have reached my moon times."

A tiny withered crone standing next to the mother stretched out her hand to me. Smiling, I took it, thinking she might need healing as well. A jolt of power blazed through me like a lightning bolt. Before I could gasp in shock, it withdrew, leaving no trace of its passage.

The mother fitted her baby back into the sling, handed me a packet and strolled off toward the bachelors' tent.

I began to open the packet, but the crone gently stopped me. "This is her gift of gratitude. It is rude to value it while we are with you."

I blushed, quickly fumbling the packet closed again. "I'm sorry. I didn't know. Really, it wasn't necessary . . ."

She patted my hand again, saying, "You are a good child. Now let us sit and talk about healing. There is much I would like to ask you, and I'm sure you will have many questions for me, as well."

In the course of the evening, a handsome Fire Sprite with a silky white mustache and long, long lashes that glinted silver in the firelight came by and began talking to RugMaker about the beautiful rug she sat on. She took him into the tent to show him some of her other work.

SwiftSure strolled out of the cave into the darkness of the open air, then burst into flame and whirled up into the night. Many of the Fire Sprites cheered!

LoveSinger ambled past us, singing, with a woman on either arm, his fine pure baritone voice floating through the air like an elusive fragrance. Young CureAll, the old crone and I all stopped our talk to watch him pass. A delicious shudder rippled through me as his song slipped away into the shadows near the bachelors' tent. CureAll looked dazed. The crone heaved a sigh.

"He's a LongRider, isn't he? We have power in our touch, girls, but LongRiders have the power of truth in their mouths. And when the truth is, 'I admire and desire you,' we all respond to the hearing, even if it's not meant for us. Well, what were we talking about? Ah yes, scorpion stings."

We were late to bed, and when we rose, all but one or two of the Fire Sprites had left. The mother with the sick baby had, much to my surprise and his delight, spent the night with WillingStrength. When an early pool of sunshine poured down into the cave mouth, WillingStrength held the little mite to bathe in it while her mother stood back in the shadows. The baby gurgled and wriggled, and WillngStrength smiled down into her little face, then turned her over to lie along his arm and get sunshine on her back. When she wet on him, he only laughed. After five minutes, he took her back to her mother. As he bent over to hand the baby back, the little mother stood on tiptoe and kissed him on the cheek, then handed him a packet, closed his fingers around it and kissed the back of the fist so made. Then she turned and purposefully carried her baby back between the fires and into the darkness of the cave.

As we retraced our steps along the cleft, I had a sense of benign presences around us, as if the spirits of Fire Sprites followed us. And once, through a deep, deep cleft in the rocks, I saw the glimmer of one of their strange, phosphorescent lamps.

If the day before I had turned left instead of right, Tribe Dauntless would have been free of the Bones just after sunset rather than spending the night with the Fire Sprites. It was just past midday when we finally made our exit. The cleft looked as if another tight turn was ahead, but when I rounded the wall, there was a bay of deep, lush grass. I walked forward, threw myself belly down in it and buried my face in the glorious perfume of greenery and moist soil. Then I rolled onto my back and saw, far, far above me, an eagle. SeeFar had found us. He wheeled and flew away again.

The bay of grass was the entry to an ocean of grass, rolling on straight to the horizon. And the breezes blowing across it were intoxicating! We muzzled the camels to keep them from eating too much green feed at once, as it would make them sick. Then, walking and knitting with my eyes closed, I led Tribe Dauntless into the trackless plains.

Chapter 41

The eagle reappeared, flew over us, then away. SwiftSure squinted up at him. "So the clever SeeFar has found us, has he then? And what is it that he might be wanting, I am wondering. I'll just be taking the little bit of a flight to be seeing what it is of such great interest he would be showing me."

She flew off. Clearly, it didn't take much of an excuse to get her into the air. Flight must have been such a pleasure to her!

I closed my eyes and began walking again. Grass brushed against my shins and knees with every step. It was like wading through a warm, shallow pond. Small birds flew up with twitterings as we approached, and the insects they were feasting on made a steady background hum. The warm, humid air caressed my skin. I had peeled down to a light silk shirt of blue and green plaid, and thin linen trousers. Sweat poured out of me and plastered my clothes to my skin, but the steady breezes kept me cool. Every time I paused to check the tribe, I saw more and more exposed skin. When I saw that FirstForth had peeled down to her singlet and a pair of wide-legged knee-length breeches, I went back and admonished her.

"FirstForth, you are going to get a terrible sunburn. Cover your skin."

"A sunburn?" she asked. "What in all the world might a sunburn be?"

"It's when your skin turns red and sore, maybe even blisters and peels off. It happens if you spend too much time in the full strength of the sun. See?" I said, pressing a finger against the back of my hand, then pulling it away to show how scorched I was becoming.

FirstForth called out to CureAll, "Oh the heedless mothers that we all are! Shaman Sanna is, after all, a baby in our tribe, and she has never been anointed. She is suffering now from the heat of the Good One's sun. Are you having enough ointment to cover her long body?"

CureAll began to dig through the saddlebags on her camel and pulled out a small jar, which she tossed to me. "I am not having enough for the anointing of the great length of you, but enough to cover you from the beltband upward. Do you be doffing your shirt, and FirstForth will be helping you with the awkward bits."

So I stood behind CureAll's camel and pulled off my sweat-soaked shirt and singlet, relishing the feel of the cool breezes playing across my bare skin, and the delicious naughtiness of being half naked in the sunlight. I poured some of the ointment into my hand, and began rubbing it

Sanna Meets Dauntless Swiftsure

onto my face, neck, and breasts. FirstForth, after blinking in startlement at the scar the dragon had left across my torso, took the jar and began working the stuff into my back and shoulders. The ointment tingled and tickled.

"Now don't be forgetting the tips of your ears, oh mighty Shaman Sanna," CureAll teased from her perch on camel-back behind me. I reached up with both hands to rub the unguent into my ears, arched my spine, leaned my head back, and laughed up at her. And over her shoulder, high in the sky, I spotted that damn eagle again!

I clasped my arms over my bare breasts and hunched forward. "Your cousin SeeFar is back, CureAll."

"Oh, and the rude brute that he is, he's spying on you, isn't he? Well, I will be giving him the rough edge of my tongue when next I see him! He should be having better manners than that!"

"Do but pull on your singlet now," suggested FirstForth, "and you may be anointing your arms in all decency. And I too will be speaking to SeeFar, Warleader though he may be! You are no lightsome lass but Shaman of Tribe Dauntless, and he should be courting you with all due ceremony and courtesy."

"I'd rather he just left me alone," I muttered as I pulled my singlet over my head. Then I spoke up, asking, "CureAll, how long is this ointment good for?"

"How long?" CureAll replied, "Why it is good for as long as you are wearing your skin. It is changing your skin so that you will never be burning in the rays of the sun again."

"And our little CureAll is having such a powerful Gift with her potions that she is brewing the best of all ointments to be had," FirstForth remarked. "There are many tribes as will be wanting to trade for her concoctions at the Place of Meeting. Won't she be the busy one then, simmering and stewing all the day long, and her still so young. It's a wise and wonderful Shaman you will be for us, CureAll, my dear."

FirstForth patted CureAll on the leg and strolled back to her own camel. I rubbed the last of the ointment into my wrists and elbows, took up my knitting, and again began following the invisible thread, leading where the tribe should go.

Chapter 42

An hour or so later, FirstForth shouted, "There they are!" and goaded her camel into a gallop. How those ungainly beasts cover ground so fast is a wonder to me. Those knobby legs flail around, the long shaggy neck stretches forward, and the creature just hurtles along!

From camelback, FirstForth could see farther than I could. At her shout, everyone in the tribe had perked up; they were squinting into the distance, shading their eyes, and pointing.

"What?" I demanded of CureAll, who was also peering ahead of us. "Who? Where did she go?"

"We are finding the kindly welcomers who have ridden out to be meeting us," she answered, with excitement in her voice. "And won't we be having the glory when we are showing them our gifts from the Fire Sprites?"

I had forgotten the packet handed me by the little mother. I reached into my belt bag and unwrapped it. It held a pair of earrings dangling clear stones about the size of a peach pit. But somehow, when I turned the stone, there was a glint of golden light in the heart of it.

"Sun stones!" gasped CureAll, "Oh, and aren't all the angels of the Good One smiling down upon you this day? Do you be donning those earrings now, and we will be amazing the welcomers right wonderfully!"

I slid the wires through the holes in my ears and rocked my head a bit to get used to the weight and dangle of the jewels. "How do they look?" I asked.

"They are looking gloriously impressive." CureAll said.

At last I saw these welcomers riding through the tall grass. They had horses! My father was the head trainer for the racehorses owned by the Potentate Ahariza of Dertzu. I had grown up around horses, thoroughbreds as well as workhorses. I knew horses as well as I knew people, and these horses were royalty! They were fine-boned and long-legged, graceful as greyhounds. They carried their small heads high on long, arched necks. They moved so lightly that it looked as if the ground was merely a reference point, not a necessary support. As soon as they spotted us, the riders of these magnificent beasts clapped heels to the horses' silken sides and sped toward us.

As they drew closer, I recognized more than one of the riders. Our headwoman SwiftSure had joined up with this party and was bestriding a roan with a muzzle so small

Sanna Meets Dauntless Swiftsure

it might fit into a teacup. She rode at the right hand of a woman dressed all in white, riding a tall, elegant white mare. Another Shaman. And this Shaman was scowling blackly at me. She looked to be in her middle fifties, with her hair pulled into a gray twist at the back of her head, pinned in place with picks dangling the Shaman's feathers and fetishes. Her white sleeveless vest, short trousers ending above her knee, and neat little white boots left a lot of mature skin exposed. When she reined in her mount about five feet away, I could see her muscles moving like squirrels under a sheet.

"WoundMender!" cried CureAll, throwing herself off her camel and racing up to the intimidating Shaman. The fearsome scowl melted, the mature woman threw a leg over her saddle and was on the ground, hugging the girl. CureAll was crying her heart out, and WoundMender was patting her shoulder and murmuring, "There, there, poor little orphaned mouseling. Oh, the brave, valiant girl that you are. There, there, I am knowing it all."

SwiftSure, meanwhile, turned to SeeFar, who was riding at her left. "Well, you miserable young goat, it's not enough that you should have been spying upon our Shaman, but you must also be bragging about it so that all may be knowing your shamelessness. And now what do you have to be saying to our fine and worthy Shaman?"

SeeFar also dismounted and strode up to me. He was wearing nothing but a loincloth. His skin shone richly tan in the brilliant sun, making his long blonde hair seem even paler, his large dark eyes even deeper and more mysterious. His cocky smile gleamed whitely. He dropped smoothly to one knee in front of me and held up his hands in supplication.

"Oh good Sanna, most powerful of Shamans and fairest of all the lasses I have ever seen, please do be forgiving me for spying on your naked beauty. It was not a thing I could be resisting, nor could any man be resisting it, be he never so old and weary. I have been seeing the outlines of you against your clothing, firm and round as the sweetest of pomegranates. I have been seeing you when the cold has brought the peaks of pleasure upon you, and there was always an answering rising in me. And when I had the chance to be gazing on your twin jewels unveiled, how could I be denying myself? Be giving me what penance you will, and I will be bearing it gladly. It will all be worth it for the one glimpse of your pink and white beauties. And having done my penance, I promise now to begin courting you with all propriety and honor, for I can never be knowing happiness until I have the right to admire your tender glories entirely."

I looked at him, smooth and sleek, lean-legged and long muscled. And I thought of my beloved Jerris as I had first seen him, also naked but for a loincloth, standing on the sales block at the slave markets. Jerris had always treated me with respect and courtesy. He would never have stolen a kiss, an embrace or a naughty peek against my will. (Though the few kisses we had shared had been soul-stirring!) If he had come upon me sleeping and helpless, he would have guarded me, not taken advantage of me. He didn't fill the air with lyric compliments. His eyes and his actions spoke his love. Jerris had been willing to give up his kingdom to marry me, and I had turned him down for the sake of my Magic. Well, perhaps I could have both my Magic *and* the man I loved. As soon as I could, I was going back to Arrex and to Jerris!

I looked into SeeFar's eyes. He grinned, so confident and full of himself that he sparkled. Then I dismounted and walked past him, ignoring him altogether, and went to lay a comforting hand on CureAll's shoulder.

Behind me, FirstForth roared with laughter, and I could hear SeeFar rising to his feet and brushing the dried grass off his knee. He flung himself onto his horse and galloped toward the back of our column, fleeing the scene of his humiliation. SwiftSure and FirstForth followed, and after them, a train of beautiful horses led by strangers.

Chapter 43

WoundMender looked up at me and nodded. We stayed as we were till CureAll had cried herself out. I kept pulling clean handkerchiefs from my belt bag so she could mop her wet face and blow her nose. When she had subsided to little gasps and sniffles, I pulled out a bottle of cold, sweet tea and handed it to her. She drank thirstily. She must have shed a pint of tears.

WoundMender was scowling at me again. "How can you be pulling that long bottle from your little belt bag, bony lass whoever-you-are?"

CureAll spoke up for me, "This is Sanna of Dertzu who was kidnapped by SwiftSure to be our Shaman when Momma was killed. And Momma has been telling her how to be a Shaman. And hasn't Sanna healed herself of Amanita poisoning and worked the Rite of the Passage for FearNaught, and led us safely over the Ridges and through the Bones and even to a cave of Fire Sprites last night? And WoundMender, she'll not be wearing the white because she says that I am to be Shaman and the nuisance of making a white wardrobe is not worth the few years she'll be wearing it. And her belt bag is magic," she finished.

"Aggh, that SwiftSure and her hasty answers!" snarled WoundMender, "And why is it that you are wanting to be Shaman to Tribe Dauntless, long Sanna of Dertzu?"

"I don't," I answered. "I want to go back to Arrex. They'll be worried sick about me by now, and I can't even let them know I'm still alive."

"But you have been acting as Shaman to Tribe Dauntless, leading and healing and naming and all?" WoundMender asked.

"Well, someone had to," I said. "But CureAll will be all the Shaman any tribe could want in a year or so, and then I can get on with my own life."

"I am LongRider WoundMender," she said formally. "Would you be sharing your Spirit with me?" WoundMender held out her hand. Expecting another lighting bolt like the one the Fire Sprite Shaman had sent through me, I hesitantly clasped hands with WoundMender.

This was different. This was warm, strong winds carrying me up like a kite, or like a strong gray goose flying home to the north, with the southerly winds lifting and pushing her along. I understood then why the geese cry out as they fly. I was filled with joyous excitement! I threw my head back and screamed, "Yeeeehah!"

I frightened the horses.

For several days, CureAll, WoundMender and I rode knee to knee through the deep grass, Tribe Dauntless and their friends following contentedly behind. I was delighted to be on horseback again. The pretty bay mare I was riding was as alert and willing as any horse I had ever known. Her slender legs carried me across the miles as easily as if I weighed no more than a feather pillow. In the soft spring nights, I began sleeping outside. And if the air turned chill before dawn, she would lie down with her warm back next to me, and shelter me from the pre-dawn breeze. Her name was several long lines of extremely complicated poetry, which I could never remember correctly. I called her "Red."

We rode for blissful days across the grasslands on our way to the Place of Meeting. It was uncanny to see nothing but rolling hills of grass from one horizon to the other. I felt exposed without some sheltering mountain in sight. But the Peoples of the Open Skies seemed to expand, unfold, blossom out in this space and emptiness. There was much laughter and frolicking.

One evening, when we had made camp, SeeFar and RugMaker were joking, and he teasingly snatched up her waterskin, transformed to eagle, and flew away with the waterskin clasped in his claws. RugMaker grasped the tassels of her aerial rug and gave them a commanding twitch, clearly intending to follow him into the air. She remained earthbound. Frowning mightily, she twitched the tassels again, and again, nothing happened.

"What ever could be wrong?" she cried. "Why am I not flying?"

Sanna Meets Dauntless Swiftsure

The panic in her voice brought me over to her. I dropped down on the rug beside her and patted her hands as they tugged and jerked at the unresponsive tassels. My touch on her skin told me all I needed to know.

"Hush, RugMaker. Hush. Didn't FearNaught lose her ability to fly when she became pregnant? That handsome Fire Sprite left you triplets, dear. Maybe that's why you can't fly. You're a little over two weeks along. Only forty more weeks to go. You're going to be a mommy."

The look she gave me was stricken, appalled. With a wail of grief, she threw herself into my arms. "I didn't think …" and "Not just yet!" were the gist of her mumbled and sobbing complaints. SeeFar circled down and landed beside us, face creased with concern.

"Whatever is wrong with sweet RugMaker?" he demanded.

"Nothing's wrong with her," I snapped. "She evidently didn't expect to get pregnant when she dallied with that mustachioed Fire Sprite. But that's how babies get made. Oh, there, there, RugMaker. You'll be a wonderful mother. There, there."

CureAll and WoundMender had come running at the sound of RugMaker's weeping. She turned to them, crying, "Oh surely I'm not carrying a child. Please be telling me it isn't so."

Puzzled, WoundMender asked, "Well, and what are your symptoms then? Have you missed your moon time? Are you feeling sick in the morning?"

"No. No, there's none of that," RugMaker sniffed.

"There wouldn't be yet," I said. "I told you, you're not that far along."

"You're reading it wrongly. You must be. It isn't so. It isn't sooooo!" RugMaker lamented.

"Well then," I said, "why can't you fly?"

"Ah, so that's the way of it then, is it?" said WoundMender, while CureAll cuddled down beside RugMaker and began crying with her. "The gift of flight is always leaving when the gift of life burdens a woman. SeeFar, my lad, be thanking the lucky stars that brought you to birth as a man. Flight is yours for life."

When word went around that she was carrying not one, not two, but three Fire Sprite babies, RugMaker became the most petted and indulged woman in the tribe. The other mothers almost carried her on their shoulders in pride. RugMaker began wearing the gift her Fire Sprite lover had given her – a silver bracelet set with three smoothed and polished ovals of clear gray volcanic glass. But I noticed she still would give the tassels of her rug an experimental twitch now and then, when she thought no one was looking. And every time the rug failed to fly, she looked sad.

I tried to get CureAll to accept the sun stone earrings given me by the Fire Sprite mother, but CureAll insisted that they had been given to me and I was the one entitled to them. They were heavy earrings, though, and made my lobes sore when I wore them, so I left them in my belt bag.

Chapter 44

I sensed that we would soon be at the end of our journey. Every time I picked up my knitting, I could feel the pulling strengthen, drawing me ever more insistently across the undulating plains. And at last, we crested a rise and saw below us a great camp spreading out along the bank of a river.

"The Place of Meeting," sighed WoundMender, her eyes already searching for familiar forms among the people riding up to greet us. "I am returning to be helping you get settled after you are selecting your campsite." And kicking her horse into a canter, she rode away.

"And now I'm supposed to find that campsite, right?" I asked CureAll. She nodded.

Well, if anyone didn't like the site I selected, we could move. I closed my eyes, picked up my knitting, and nudged my Red mare with my heels. She was so well trained that

I could guide her without reins, just by shifting my weight and nudging with my knees a bit. I rode, obedient to the pull on my yarn, weaving my way among unseen barriers, hearing joyful greetings mixed with murmurs of surprise all around me.

Then we were there. We had arrived at our destination. The leading I followed ended with an almost physical sense of release and satisfaction. I opened my eyes and found myself at the bank of the river in a large cleared space surrounded by established camps. Tribe Dauntless immediately began unloading their tents with the help of dozens of happy friends. Camels bawled, men shouted greetings and slapped one another on the shoulder. Women cried out with joy and embraced their friends and the older sons they had not seen for the better part of a year. Children shrieked with excitement and raced around everywhere, getting underfoot. Red turned her head and looked at me questioningly as if to say, "Well, how long are you going to sit there?"

I threw a leg over her shoulders, slid down to the ground, and took off her riding pad. "This must be the place," I said to her. She responded by lying down and having a luxurious roll.

CureAll was untying the Shaman's white tent from its pack saddle. I pitched in to help, and many other folks joined us. It wasn't until the tent was fully set up, and I turned to grab a bundle of rugs for our floor that I noticed everyone around me was wearing shaman's white. They had been keeping an eye on me, waiting to see when the fact would sink in. Now all the women paused in their work, watching me.

I swallowed. My heart thundered. What was I supposed to do now? "Oh. Ummm. . ." I said, while searching madly through my memories for any training that might help me deal with this. I had seen the Potentate's First Wife welcome dignitaries to court when I was growing up. I had spent many tedious hours in Deportment Class at school in Thon, learning the proper forms of address and behavior when meeting important personages from Borovia, Dianos, Thon, and Arrex. But how was I supposed to greet several dozen critical Shamans? Then I saw WoundMender, her arms full of bedding, and her face grinning broadly. I smiled back tentatively. The stern faces around me softened.

"Thank you so much for helping us," I said. "The tent has never gone up so quickly before. I'm Sanna, a Sorceress apprentice from the Thon Academy of Higher Magic for Young Ladies of Exceptional Talent. And I would be at the Academy now if SwiftSure hadn't kidnapped me to be Shaman when HealWell was killed. I don't know how to behave, so please forgive me if I seem rude. May I offer you something to eat or drink?"

The oldest woman there spoke up, "No, all we Shamans are fasting till after our Joining tonight, and you should be doing so as well. Be sharing your Spirit with me." She held out her leathery, scarred, age-spotted hand. Veins stood up in blue ropes across the back. Bones had been broken and healed lumpily, knuckles were swollen, the skin creased in deep wrinkles. A life's history was written in that hand. I reached out and clasped it gently, fearing to bruise the fragile skin.

The Spirit that was transmitted through that touch left me gasping. Iron will? That woman bent iron wills as easily as I bent an earring wire.

She riffled through my memories without so much as a by-your-leave, inspected my scar from the inside, prodded my liver, healed now from the damage done by the Amanita, tested, weighed and measured me and did not, quite, find me unsatisfactory. What she said out loud was, "For an ignorant young idiot, you are not doing all that badly."

"Now just listen here," I snarled, pulling my hand away. "I didn't ask for this job. I wasn't bred or trained for it, and I'd like to see anyone in the same situation do better. How *dare* you criticize me?"

"Sanna, Sanna, hush you now," WoundMender rushed forward to stand between me and the senior crone and gently gripped my shoulders, sending soothing, calming energies into me. "StrengthWeaver was not criticizing you. By the truth of my right hand, that was the highest praise I have ever heard her to be using."

"That was praise? Then her criticism must leave people in little smoking piles of rubble. I'm not suited for this job, I agree. Anyone who wants it can take it and welcome. Otherwise, it might be more effective to help me do it properly till CureAll is old enough to take over!" I stomped away, leaving our tent unfurnished and all the other Shamans standing around silent in surprise. All except StrengthWeaver, who I could hear cackling with satisfaction.

I wound up sitting next to the river, splashing my bare feet in it and doing my best to get a bridle on my stampeding fury. Before long, I was aware of a presence. I turned to see little HappyGirl sucking her thumb and watching me.

"What is it, sweetheart?" I asked.

"You thad?" she lisped.

"Oh, I've gone all the way through sad and come out into angry," I said. "But I'm never angry at you, you know."

"Yeth." The thumb went back in, then pulled out, leaving a lovely smile behind it. "You good girl."

"Thank you, sweetheart. You're a good girl, too." I smiled back at her.

"Yeth," she agreed complacently, then added, "Thmith wanting you."

"Smith wants me? Will you take me to him?" I asked.

"Yeth," she beamed at me.

So, hand in hand, HappyGirl and I walked through the camp of Tribe Dauntless, and as we responded to the greetings we received, I realized that I loved every one of these brave, honorable people. I didn't know what was coming next, but I knew I could count on them when it came. I might not have the wholehearted approval of the Shamans, but I had the support of my tribe, and that was enough to get me through.

Smith was worried about a touch of rash on PeaceBringer's little behind. I prescribed a daily airing. PeaceBringer soon lolled gleefully naked on a blanket in the shade, while HappyGirl shared incomprehensible baby gossip with her.

A rumble of excitement caught my attention. Someone else was arriving? I stood and looked toward the sound.

A troop of hard young warriors escorted two blindfolded Golmen raiders on their little ponies, leading them to CureAll's tent and all the assembled Shamans. I darted forward to be on the scene when they arrived.

Chapter 45

When I got close enough, I recognized one of the raiders. It was the leader of the band that had saved our little group from the attack of the wild dogs. The fellow I had cured of worms and an infected, ingrown toenail. When his blindfold was removed, he looked exhausted, as if he had been riding hard for days on end. I elbowed my way through the growing crowd so I could see and hear everything.

The one I had healed growled a command, and his companion, a girl, dismounted. Then he said, "Golmen warrior killed Shaman HealWell. This bad, bad thing. Peoples of Open Skies needs Shaman for HealWell's tribe. Golmen give you this Shaman."

The second raider stepped forward. She was small, golden-skinned, and amber-eyed, with long, long black hair caught up in a tail at the top of her head and falling back down almost to her elbows. She was taut and lithe and supremely self-confident. More than anything, she reminded me of some little wild desert cat.

"Look you, I am the daughter of WildFaring JoyMaker," the young woman said. "She was being captured in a raid and taken into the household of Millchao, the chief. He was valuing and protecting her, and when I was born, she was protecting and training me. But the lung fever was taking her this past winter, and without her protections, my gifts are not finding welcome among the Golmen."

"Worthless girl child," declared her companion. "Ride like man. Give orders like man. No one buy her for wife or slave. Good Healer, though."

She nodded toward the man and said, "Uncle Millcairn is thinking you might be taking me to be replacing your missing Shaman. I am knowing the way of the Winds, I am holding the Heart of the Fire, and I am finding my way in the dark. And if you are not accepting me, I'll no doubt be dying within a year. I just can't be keeping my mouth shut when I should."

StrengthWeaver was in the forefront of those gathered by CureAll's tent. She held out her hand and said, "Share your Spirit with me."

The young woman took the proffered hand, and for a moment I felt, in the marrow of my bones, the echoes of the testing of those two minds. Then StrengthWeaver pulled her hand away and declared, "She's WildFaring, sure enough. And a Shaman as well. What name are you having, girl?" she demanded.

"Worthless girl child not have name," her uncle informed us.

"Mother was calling me 'Kitten,'" she told us, "And everyone else was saying to me, 'Shut up.'"

"Well then, WildFaring Kitten, you are welcome home. We will be finding a place for you where your gifts will be valued."

"What you pay for her?" demanded her uncle.

StrengthWeaver twitched her left hand, and like magic, knives and spears appeared in warriors' hands. With a smile that raised the hairs on the back of my neck, she replied, "We are valuing this young woman so very highly that we are paying an extraordinary price. For look you, we are allowing her uncle to be keeping his life. And better even than that, we will be returning him unharmed along with both of his ponies to the edges of the grasslands where our fine strong guardians were finding him."

He looked around at all the wickedly shining edges surrounding him, then nodded. "Good price," he declared.

He and his ponies were taken away to be fed and rested before again being blindfolded and returned to the borders. And StrengthWeaver led Wildfaring Kitten into CureAll's tent.

I had to know what was going on, so I followed, and as I lifted the flap, heard StrengthWeaver say, "And will you be good enough to be showing us your shapeshifting then?"

In answer, the young woman shrank, and transformed to a black and umber spotted cat, with enormous amber eyes. She stretched her front paws forward toward StrengthWeaver, extended long sharp claws, dug them into the carpets, and stretched back luxuriously. Then she settled back onto her haunches, threw one leg into the air, and began washing her nether parts.

I laughed out loud.

Kitten snapped her head around to look at me, the tip of her tongue still protruding, forgotten. Then she transformed back to supple, young woman, lounging on the carpets.

"Is it you I am going to be seconding?" she asked.

"I'm acting as Shaman for Tribe Dauntless," I answered. "At least until CureAll is old enough. But if you can do the job better than I can, then perhaps I'll be allowed to go home and get on with my life. I'm Sanna." And I offered her my hand.

Her hand was rough and callused from hard work. And rather than rummaging through me like the other Shamans had done, her Spirit, like a careful cat, sat back and watched to see what I would do. So I opened my memories of the past year and invited her in. Then I sat back to watch in my turn. She inspected my memories, picking up some of them and turning them from side to side to study like a pretty teapot or a well-made sweater. And when she had finished, she opened her own memories to me.

Life among the Golmen raiders was harsh and violent. The chief was supreme, and dominated his brutal tribesmen by being even more brutal than they. He valued his slave, WildFaring JoyMaker. Any jealous woman who dared raise a hand against her had that hand cut off. So the jealousy simmered and festered, and when JoyMaker died, it burst forth against her daughter. Insults, indignities, injuries became her daily fare. And she could *not* keep her mouth shut. She would tell some warrior that he was a fool without a single thought as to the consequences. She was just as likely to tell the chief's wife that her stew was ill-seasoned. And she was usually answered with blows. If she had not been able to heal herself, she might not have survived at all.

Our exchange took only instants in actual time. But it was time enough to learn how desperate she was to belong somewhere. The tribe that took her in would have her gratitude, her undivided loyalty and the skills of a Healer and gifted shapeshifter. Why shouldn't that lucky tribe be Tribe Dauntless?

Chapter 46

StrengthWeaver snorted at us. "Such courtesy you are showing to one another. When you are as old as I have become, you will not be having the time for courtesies. And there are things now that I should be doing in preparation for the Joining tonight. Eat nothing before bringing your young selves to the meetinghouse at sunset. CureAll is knowing the way."

And with that, the brusque old crone turned and hobbled out of the tent. I smiled at Kitten and suggested, "Since we are so young and courteous, with so much time on our hands, CureAll and I can introduce you to the tribe."

CureAll looked with disgust at the dirty leather trousers and horsehide shirt that Kitten was wearing and said, "You are being so small that you are scarce bigger than I am. Maybe I am having something to fit you."

Sanna Meets Dauntless Swiftsure

She dug through a few baskets and unearthed a loose white muslin robe that flowed and draped gently around Kitten's subtle but oh-so-womanly curves. Its sleeveless cut also showed an ugly burn scar running down the back of her left arm from shoulder to elbow. I thought about suggesting something with sleeves to hide the scar, then I thought again. Kitten looked so young and helpless in that girlish white dress. A bit of sympathy couldn't hurt her case with Tribe Dauntless.

As we were leaving the tent, SeeFar came striding up. He had not spoken to me since I had snubbed his public apology. To CureAll he said, "Here am I, seeing to the feeding and pasturage of all the fine horses and camels and goats of our tribe, as is the duty of any Warleader, and while I am doing my thankless task, I am missing all the excitement. And is it true that the Golmen raiders are bringing a Shaman of their own to replace HealWell? And what would we be wanting with one of those dirty vermin? Tribe Dauntless has Shamans enough and is not needing ---"

Then Kitten stepped out of the tent. SeeFar stood with his mouth hanging open while he took her in, from her tiny bare feet to her shiny black hair. And she looked him over as well, her eyes lingering on his broad smooth shoulders and his long lean legs. Then she dropped her eyes and smiled shyly up at him from under her lashes. The minx! If I ever taught her how to fish, I could skip the lessons on how to set a hook. SeeFar was all but landed already!

I said, "SeeFar, this is WildFaring Kitten, Shaman of the Golmen." I knew she had no need of an introduction.

She had learned all I knew of SeeFar when she had been through my memories.

SeeFar glanced at me as I stood smirking down at him from my several extra inches of height. Then he looked back to dainty, graceful Kitten. I was wearing a pair of wide-legged, knee-length red breeches and a long, wrinkled, marigold-yellow shirt. (Not a good color on me.) All I needed was a pair of oversized shoes, and I could have played the jester in any court in the world. Kitten looked like a pocket-sized golden goddess. SeeFar dropped gracefully to one knee, lifted the hem of her dress to his lips, then raised his head and said, "Here before you is one who would be serving as your devoted servant if you would only be accepting his heartfelt pledge."

Kitten bent, took his hand and raised him to his feet. Then, standing very close to him, she whispered, "Oh, SeeFar, no man has ever been so kind to me."

"The sight of your sweet self is kindness to me," he replied.

I looked at CureAll and saw she was as close to breaking into guffaws as I was. So I said, "SeeFar, why don't you introduce Kitten to the rest of the tribe? CureAll and I have to --- we have to --- do things."

He flashed me a cuttingly brilliant smile. "It would be of all things a pleasure!" he exclaimed. And tucking Kitten's hand into the crook of his arm, he led her away, while meaningless pretty phrases dribbled out of him like water from a leaky bucket.

"She can not really be believing all the things he is saying, can she?" asked CureAll as we stepped back into the tent.

I replied, "*We* know he doesn't really mean those things, and *she* knows he really doesn't mean them, but as long as *he* doesn't know he doesn't mean them, it's entirely likely that he will behave as if he *does*."

CureAll frowned her confusion at me and asked, "If he doesn't know? Oh, I see. As long as SeeFar is thinking that he's the honorable young gallant, he'll be acting like one. Yes, I'm thinking that would be no very bad thing, at that. Do you think she'll be having him?"

"I think, no matter who Kitten chooses, SeeFar will be had," I said with malicious satisfaction.

Chapter 47

The sunset was spectacular, with banks of clouds dark as bruises, showing gold, scarlet, and orange along the edges while rays of light lanced up across the sky. CureAll, Kitten, and I walked toward the bathhouse, all clad in proper Shaman's white. I was still terribly underweight, and missing two meals had been a trial for me. I was glad to have gotten a good breakfast, at least. But the hunger couldn't keep me from wondering what the night's ceremony would bring.

"What can you tell us about the Joining, CureAll?" I asked.

"Every year, the Shamans, and those who will be Shamans, are coming together on the first night of the gathering and joining in Spirit to be sharing all the things that we are learning during the year. And then we are sharing a great, fine meal," she said with a smile as my stomach grumbled loudly. "But here we are, and now you will be seeing for yourself what the Joining is."

The meetinghouse was the first permanent structure I had seen the Peoples of the Wide Skies use. It was set in a grove of birches. Nine of the trees had been planted in a wide circle, and when they had grown tall enough, their tops had been bent inward and bound together. A roof of limbs and branches had been built. The spaces between the trees had been filled with slabs of turf piled like bricks. Grass and wildflowers had taken root in the mud, making the building look like a miniature hill. The door was so small and low that I had to crawl through on hands and knees. Inside, it was dark and crowded already, and more women were coming in behind us. As we shuffled and shifted to find a place, I noticed that there were babes in arm, girls as young as five, teenagers, two pregnant Shamans, women young, middle-aged and old. There were over a hundred females packed into that little building. We stood elbow to elbow and had to brush against one another to move around. But instead of the sense of stifling claustrophobia I would have expected, there was a feeling of cozy warmth. When I was little, Hasmina, the Potentate's First Wife, used to take me on her lap and read to me. This gathering gave me the same sense of cuddlesome intimacy. A gentle humming of subdued conversation filled the air.

"CureAll," I asked, "are all these women Shamans?"

"Yes, and the children will be," she answered. "Know you that we are recognized as Shamans at our naming, and come ever after to the Joinings."

"But there are so *many* Shamans!" I said, amazed. "How many tribes are there?"

"In this encampment we are meeting only Tribes LongRider, Eldritch, Cunning, Artful, and Charming, but among the Peoples of the Wide Skies are hundreds of tribes. Shall I be naming them all for you?"

I shook my head and held up my hands. "No. Please. But I thought each tribe had only one Shaman, like Tribe Dauntless."

"Oh, not at all," replied CureAll. Most tribes are having many and many Shamans. Why, most women of Tribe Eldritch are Shamans. But in Tribe Dauntless, the winds are blowing differently. It has been many a year since Dauntless had more than two Shamans, and for ten years past, there has been only HealWell, my mother. And now you, Sanna. And *now* you, Kitten," she added, turning to the girl with a smile.

"But why didn't Tribe Eldritch loan you a few Shamans just in case a tragedy occurred?" I asked. "Then SwiftSure wouldn't have had to kidnap me."

"You would have a woman be leaving her own tribe?" CureAll asked, aghast.

"Why not?" I responded, reasonably. The women around us turned and looked at me as if I had just sprouted green leaves all over my face.

CureAll sputtered, "But ... but ... but no woman would be willing to be leaving her tribe. How could we bear to be living without our mothers and sisters, cousin and aunts around us? How could a woman be living alone among strangers?"

"I have. Kitten's mother did," I pointed out.

Kitten explained, "Oh. But most women stolen by the Golmen are dying of grief within months. Mother was

Sanna Meets Dauntless Swiftsure

surviving because she was catching the life of me in her womb almost at once, and had to be living for my sake. And you – well – you poor thing - you are not born to the Peoples, and are not knowing how bereft you are."

The women around us murmured sorrowfully. I felt awash in a sea of condescending pity.

"And truly, Sanna," CureAll said, "I am thinking that you are much like a man in a woman's body, going forth as you do without support and love of any of your family. You are not a woman like the women of the Wide Skies."

"I think you are speaking the truth," one of the women standing near said. "SwiftSure was saying - - - "

"SwiftSure would be saying the sky is yellow and the sun is green if she thought it would be getting her what she is wanting," said another eavesdropper, waspishly. "And what she is wanting is to be the glorious, prized Firebird, flying free, petted and pampered and giving never a thought for the wishes of others. She is having pride and fine training enough to be Headwoman for Tribe Dauntless, but I'm thinking she is too selfish to be giving up her powers to be bearing a child. It is assuredly time and past time for her to be having an heir."

Then StrengthWeaver crept painfully through the low entrance, followed by a flash of light as the final rays of the setting sun blazed under the clouds, straight across the river and flat through the door. I had been facing that way, so the last burst of light left me blinded temporarily in the succeeding dimness.

"Are all here?" asked StrengthWeaver, and when a murmur of assent answered her, she declared, "Then we shall begin the Joining. Shamans, be sharing water."

All the fully fledged Shamans produced a waterbag and began trickling it onto the hands of those around them. Kitten, CureAll and I had our hands anointed, and CureAll cautioned us, "Leave your hands wet. Don't dry them off."

Then StrengthWeaver proclaimed, "We are born in water, we are made of water. Every woman's daughter, we are joined by water."

It was the same charm of Joining used during the graduation ceremony at the Thon Academy of Higher Magic, where I had been taking classes. I was stunned and thrilled to realize that women's Magic remained the same all over the world! My sour and prickly feelings faded in joyful anticipation. I held out my wet hands to the women near me, gently, easily clasped theirs, joined Spirits, and became one of the sorority of Shamans of the Peoples of the Wide Skies.

Chapter 48

The next morning, the Headwomen of the other tribes and their senior Shamans were waiting for SwiftSure as she exited her tent. Seeing them, she froze, then half turned as if to duck back into the safety of her shelter. I blocked her way, grinning with malice.

"Ah, do not be so soon leaving us, Dauntless SwiftSure," I purred in imitation of her honeyed brogue. "We are just having the wee bitty of a thing to be saying to you this day."

SwiftSure gaped at me in astonishment.

StrengthWeaver gave me a look that would have soured sugar and spoke to SwiftSure, saying, "Headwoman of Tribe Dauntless, you are standing in need of an heir. You are knowing that any tribe lacking Shaman or Headwoman must be losing identity and joining with another tribe. If you will not be taking a husband this very week, to be getting an heir, then we must be naming the tribe you will be joining with henceforth."

SwiftSure's face darkened in a wicked scowl. I could feel the air heating around her and smell her clothing beginning to singe.

"It won't do you any good to fly away from this, you know," I told her. "Either you decide, or we will."

"How dare you to be telling me what I am to be doing?" she snarled at me.

"I'm your senior Shaman," I snapped back. "And I'm doing my duty by Tribe Dauntless just as you should."

CureAll and Kitten stood at SwiftSure's other side. CureAll touched SwiftSure's arm and said gently, plaintively, "Cousin, no one is telling you to be doing a thing that isn't needful. Would you be letting Tribe Dauntless fade to an end with your final flight? Are you not wanting to care for us and ensure our well-being? What will happen if you are dying gloriously in some conflict?"

"There's not so much of a hurry about it all," SwiftSure grumbled. "I'll not be dying at any time soon."

"So thought my mother, HealWell," said CureAll, "and see now who are your Shamans."

SwiftSure glared at me, glared at Kitten, glared at the assembled Headwomen and Shamans in stubborn defiance. Then I could see a thought had occurred to her. Her gaze fell to the ground for a moment as she considered it. Her ugly scowl softened, to be replaced by a confident smirk. She threw her head up so her white hair floated around her face and looked StrengthWeaver in the eye.

"Since you will be forcing my hand so hastily this day," SwiftSure proclaimed, "then I will be naming as my heir the oldest daughter of my sister, RugMaker."

"This I am endorsing as senior Shaman of Tribe Dauntless!" I called out, loud and joyous. "RugMaker is carrying two Fire Sprite sons and a Firebird chick."

SwiftSure's face was a book. I read anger, jealousy, frustration in quick chapters. Then she burst out with a bittersweet laugh. "And so it is that I may fly as Firebird as long as I shall be living, and RugMaker may have the burdens of training the brat to all the duties of Headwoman. I am finding no flaw in this plan. Will you be having aught else of me, or may I be taking my breakfast?"

"Oh, do you be breaking your fast, you selfish, willful bird," grumbled StrengthWeaver. "The oldest daughter of RugMaker is heir to the Headwoman of Tribe Dauntless. This I am endorsing as senior Shaman of Tribe Eldritch."

The other Shamans and Headwomen also endorsed the decision, then went to find RugMaker and share the good news.

"One more thing, SwiftSure," I said, before she could make her way to her morning meal. "Now that you have Kitten to be your Shaman, you won't be needing me any more. How soon will you take me home?"

"Now how should I be taking you home, willow-lass?" she asked, with an ironical lift of her white eyebrows. "The babe that will be replacing me as Firebird has bereft you of transport. RugMaker's aerial carpet is the only way to get you across the Golmen lands between the desert and the mountains of Arrex, and swollen-bellied RugMaker flies no more." With that, she turned and began walking toward the communal cook-fire.

"Well... well," I sputtered, trotting after her, "Couldn't you give me a camel so I could take myself back? I know I can find the way."

"Oh, of that I've no doubt, Shaman that you are, but I'll not be giving you a camel that will only be slaughtered by the Golmen raiders as you are crossing their lands. And don't be thinking the winds will be keeping you safe, for only by flying, or by running in beast form, has any of the Peoples of the Wide Skies ever crossed to your soft lands," she said.

"Then why shouldn't some other tribe give me a ride on their carpet?" I countered.

"Only in Tribe Dauntless are the Rug Makers so gifted as to be making aerial rugs. And there will be no more aerial rugs unless RugMaker births another of her own skill."

"Then how am I supposed to get home?" I wailed.

SwiftSure stopped so suddenly that I bumped into her. She grabbed my shoulders and dug in her fingers, and snapped into my face, "Whether you are staying with Tribe Dauntless or going with some other tribe or walking away on your own white feet, willow-lass, make up your mind to it, you'll not be seeing your home again in this life."

She shoved me away from her and strode off. I stood, shaking with emotion, my mind as cold and empty as a snowfield. I could hear the bustle of camp, feel the sun and wind on my skin and smell breakfast cooking, but it was as if all meaning had been sucked out of everything. Nothing in the world made sense. If what SwiftSure had said was true, then the last time I had seen my friends in Thon was the last time I would *ever* see them. I would never again see my family, my brother Jonel, my dearest love, Prince Jerris - - -

Red rage flooded into the hollows in my head. It wasn't rational thought, but it was better than the gutted emptiness I had felt.

"NO!" I roared so loudly that I hurt my throat. People turned to stare at me in astonishment. SwiftSure turned as well, and I caught her eye. "I will go home," I whispered, just to her.

She was too far away to hear me, but she may have read my lips. Dark anger flooded her face, and she abruptly turned her back on me in total repudiation.

"I will," I repeated, to myself. "I will go home."

I spent the rest of the day out in the grasslands trying to find some outlet for my raging emotions. Unfair! Unfair!! I ran as far and as fast as I could, then collapsed, weeping, sobbing, screaming with rage and grief. SwiftSure had no reason to lie to me. When I thought about that, sorrow engulfed me, and I covered my head with my arms, tears washing down my face, while I whined and keened incoherently. Then a hot red spike of rage would stab through me, and I would howl my frustrations to the indifferent blue sky, pounding my fists fruitlessly on the soft ground.

Finally exhausted, feeling washed clean inside, I thought calmly and rationally about what I could do. I felt so lost! But then I realized, a Shaman can always find her way. I had become a Shaman, and I could even find my way in the dark. I closed my eyes, and sought for the leading. I stilled my furious heart and opened my mind to all possibilities. I put my need in the center of my awareness and looked at it from all possible angles.

I would have used my Power gem to help me seek out a solution, but I had given it to Jerris. Then I realized I had another Power gem – two in fact. I pulled out the sunstone earrings, held them against my closed eyes, looked at my problem sideways . . . and found my way home! It would take time and work. I would need help and training, but, by Althinia's other elbow, I was going to get myself home!

I walked back to camp in the last of the afternoon. The grass was knee deep and full of life. Brilliant butterflies danced in the slanting sunlight. Other insects hummed, buzzed, clicked. Spiders spun, casting floating silk threads that glimmered in the air. Birds darted about, feasting on the bounty of bugs and filling the soft air with their songs. Rodents scurried, rabbits hopped and wildflowers made the air drowsy with perfume. I was gathering plants and cocoons as I went, and my dirty, tear-streaked face was now relaxed in a smile of satisfaction.

Chapter 49

That night, we held a ceremony of introduction for Kitten and for two young men who were ready to join with Tribe Dauntless for a year and a day. The light had lingered long, and the first star was barely pushing its way through the hazy sky when we began. SwiftSure stood in front of her tent with RugMaker to her right and CureAll and me to her left. Visitors from the other tribes stood companionably around the fringes of our ceremony, watching but not participating.

When the last tardy member of Tribe Dauntless had arrived, SwiftSure spoke. "You are all knowing that returning to the Peoples of the Wide Skies the daughter of WildFaring JoyMaker, gotten on her by some Golmen raider," I saw Kitten stiffen at this. It seemed to me to be a rude way to describe someone's parents "WildFaring Kitten has been acknowledged as rightwise a Shaman by Eldritch StrengthWeaver. As Tribe WildFaring has been lost to us and Tribe Dauntless is needing Shamans, WildFaring Kitten has asked to join with us. Tonight it is time that your new Shaman should be knowing you. Who will first greet her?"

"I will," I said, stepping forward just half a second before SeeFar. I touched my left hand to the notch of my collarbones in the greeting of a woman to a Shaman, and held out my right hand. "Welcome to the tribe, Kitten," I said, grinning broadly. She grinned back and took my hand.

Then, one at a time, each member of the tribe followed suit and shared with Kitten, as they had shared with me so many weeks ago, a bit of themselves, welcoming yet another strange woman into their midst. I felt warmly proud of my gallant and kind adopted tribe.

The next day Kitten took a party of herders and hunters out into the plains for a week. In the featureless, rolling openness, anyone out of sight of the smoke from the camp's fires can get lost. Anyone but a Shaman, that is. And a Shaman never loses track of her people, either. If I stopped to think about it, I knew where each and every person in Tribe Dauntless was. They showed in my mind like little gems on a huge tapestry. Kitten would keep track of her hunters and herders while they were out fattening the stock and filling the larder, and she would bring them all safely back to the tribe.

RugMaker and I watched them go. All the young men and women were whooping with excitement and galloping their mounts like performing riders, each trying to outdo the other with wild and daring tricks. Kitten was in the lead on a rawboned dun stallion, riding like she had grown out of his back. SeeFar was rear guard, as is the duty of a Warleader, and we could see him simmering with frustration. He wanted to be up front with her, with the wind in his hair and bugs in his teeth, flaunting his strength and skill for her to admire. Instead, he was trailing behind in the dust with the responsible adults.

"That bids fair well to be the largest hunting party I'll ever be seeing in all my life," RugMaker remarked.

"Well, every young buck who could has joined up to get closer to our little Kitten," I said, chuckling as the rowdy throng dwindled in the distance. "It's a good thing she's so handy at mending broken bones. There's going to be a lot of showing off on this trip."

"And won't life be ever so much more peaceful here in camp?" she said. "It's glad I am to be seeing the backsides of them."

We were spinning the undercoats of the tribe's goats into yarn. The bitter cold winters caused the goats to grow a thick, downy layer of wool for warmth under a long, coarse outer layer of guard hairs. Rather than shear the goats, leaving them naked to the chilly spring nights, the Peoples of the Wide Skies would wait till the warmer days caused the goats to start shedding that cozy inner layer. Then they would comb out the undercoats using wide-toothed hand rakes. One person would straddle the goat, facing the tail, pin the goat between her knees and take up her combs. Another person would catch the goat's back feet and pull them back and apart so the creature was too off-balance to kick. Then the combing began, pulling out the loose underlayer and leaving the long, coarse guard hairs. Oh the fuss and fury! Oh the screams of goatly outrage! You would have thought we were skinning them alive, though it was no more damaging than a good brushing, and they were more comfortable when we were done. And oh, the glorious piles of soft white fluff we combed out!

I had never seen such long, fine animal fiber and was thoroughly enjoying spinning it up. RugMaker was using her thigh spindle to spin her share. I was in a hurry, though, so I had pulled my double-treadle castle-style wheel out of my belt bag and set it up on a flat place in the sun. As I spun, I kept pausing to pluck hair from my head and carefully feed one hair at a time into the yarn. And I also added a strand of silk from the butterfly cocoons I had gathered. By the end of the day, I had baskets full of yarn, and no more hair than a shaved sheep. I had taken the first step on my journey home.

I quickly wrapped a scarf into a small turban around my tender-skinned skull so no one would know I was bald. Late the next day, ThreadBender came to me and asked me to show her how I arranged my turban. I wrapped her head in the scarf she had brought, and stepping back to view my handiwork, realized that the way it framed her face made her eyes look larger and brighter. And it was a good way to keep long hair off the back of the neck on a hot and sticky afternoon. The bright glass beads decorating the ends of ThreadBender's scarf dangled by her temple, catching the light, and also catching the eye of every passing young man.

In two more days, half the women in camp were wearing small turbans with sparkling beads. Everyone assumed it was a foreign fashion of mine, and no one but RugMaker knew I was bald as a baby.

The next day, CureAll and I began preparing dyes from the plants I had gathered. It took us days to prepare the dyes. Some plants needed to be crushed and soaked in stale urine to obtain the fade-proof color. Others needed to be fermented, boiled down, filtered, chanted over, aged in a rusty iron pot and mixed with secret ingredients. I'm no potions maker. I just did the idiot work and left the finesse to CureAll.

Meanwhile, SwiftSure and the other Headwomen met frequently in conclave to settle matters pertaining to the good of all the tribes. For example, Tribe Charming had only one smith, and he wanted to journey with Tribe Cunning for a year and a day. But a tribe could no more get along without a smith than it could do without a Shaman or a Headwoman. Luckily, Eldritch Smith had been training three likely lads from Tribe Dauntless, and one of them rather fancied a Charming lass. However, she wasn't sure she liked him well enough to marry him. SwiftSure spoke to the lad. She spoke to the girl. She spoke again at the council of Headwomen. Tribe Charming agreed to give the lad an anvil and a set of hammers and the pack camels to carry it all if he would travel with them for two years, whether or not the young lady ever returned his interest. It was a steep price, but SwiftSure wrung it out of them.

SwiftSure was turning out to be a capable, if fierce, Headwoman. She would squeeze blood from stones if it would benefit a member of Tribe Dauntless. She would feed your liver to dragons if she needed to. Dragons never want someone else's liver, though. They'll never be satisfied till you feed them your own.

Chapter 50

Kitten and her hunting party returned with an amazing array of carcasses. They had everything from strings of small birds to several of the wild aurochs – great horned beasts like wild cows. (The meat was tough and strong tasting but worked nicely in stews, and when smoked, it made a jerky that you could chew all day long.) We held a big feast that night to celebrate.

"What are you going to be wearing tonight?" CureAll asked me with some concern as preparations for the party were set in order.

I had my mind on my project, and it took me a minute to figure out what she meant. "Does it matter?" I asked. "Won't this do?" I was wearing the clothes I always wore when dying – close-fitted trousers and a snug shirt with sleeves rolled above the elbows. The trousers had started out a drab brown, the shirt, unbleached linen. Both had been splashed over the years with pigments, mordants and bleaches till "piebald" was the only word you could use to describe them. My hands and forearms were dark crimson from the latest batch of coloring, and my bare feet, between the red dye splashed on them and the mud caked on them, looked like I had been wandering through a butcher's yard.

She looked appalled and said, "No, that will not be doing! The first hunters' feast each year is by way of being a very significant occasion. We are showing off the wealth and glory of the tribe. I am going to be wearing that splendid bleached linen dress with the fair lilies embroidered on the hem and cuffs, and the heavy silken vest with the gold bullion trim and my darling, lovely new sandals and truly every bit of jewelry I own. And you, being the senior Shaman of Tribe Dauntless, you must be shining like the very moon in the heavens! If you are to be coming in your stained clothing, with your hands all bloody red like that, why truly you would be shaming the whole tribe!"

"Oh bother!" I huffed. "I'll have to take the time to clean up, then. I'll see what I can do."

CureAll had a concoction of willow bark that she poured over bandages which she then wrapped around my hands and left on for two hours. I had to sit with my hands still for two wasted hours while my skin bleached. The concoction took off the top layer of skin, so I had to heal myself when the bandages came off. I must say, though, my hands were smooth and white and lovely for the first time that I could remember.

Sanna Meets Dauntless Swiftsure

CureAll and I worked together to dress Kitten. I had a white silk petticoat in my bag, and we found that, cinched up under her armpits, my petticoat made a ground-sweeping, strapless dress for Kitten. Her smooth amber shoulders and elegant neck cried out for adornments. I tried to get her to wear some of my jewelry, but neither she nor CureAll would have it.

"You are senior Shaman. You must be shining like the moon," they declared.

I protested, "But Kitten, I'm only a year older than you. What difference does it make? And who cares how I look?"

"You are the senior, and so you are carrying the honor of the tribe. We all care how you look tonight!" I was told again.

So I went into the tent, pulled on my white wool Shaman's robe, wrapped a white silk scarf around my bald head and arrayed myself in all my jewelry: the Calabrian necklace looking like a chain of gold violets, and the pearl earrings given to me by the Potentate of Dertzu and Hasmina, his First Wife, and the pearl and aquamarine crown given to me by Prince Jerris. And then, there were my sunstone earrings. I had one hole per earlobe and was not about to stab in more just for the evening's festivities. So I threaded white silk cords through the filigreed settings, and tied the earrings against the pulse-points on the wrists of my newly whitened hands.

The feast was quite a show. FirstForth wore her red taurek-skin skirt, and the Warleaders of Tribe Cunning and of Tribe LongRider were waiting on her hand and foot, meanwhile scaring away any other fellow who dared show an interest. Her son, WillingStrength, had on dark brown breeches and a lighter brown shirt with red, green, and yellow embroidery down the front. I had artfully slit the sleeve seams so that his impressive scar from the taurek battle showed every time he moved. Young women were clustered around him all night, listening wide-eyed to his stories and delicately slipping their hands inside his sleeve to run their fingers over the scar. He was blushing and grinning so much he almost forgot to eat.

SwiftSure wore tight gray trousers and a long coat of brocaded gray silk, very closely fitted, with the straight skirt slit up the sides to the waist,. The coat was sleeveless, the better to display her wealth of silver wrist cuffs and armlets set with turquoises and white agates. Multiple silver chains around her neck and waist and even around the ankles of her boots, and a silver and moonstone hair ornament with long white feathers arcing up and over, accessorized her ensemble.

Usually, we just carried a camel saddle over to the fire and perched on it for a seat while we ate and socialized, but with all the other tribes coming to share our feast, there wouldn't have been room. Instead, everyone had brought out all their rugs and cushions and spread them on the ground for seating. It meant shaking out all the dirt and dragging everything back into the tent when it was time to go to bed, but for a feast, it was worth the trouble. So much food was being prepared that precious fuel was spent on *three* cooking fires! All the tribes were gathered, lounging on the rugs, dressed in their finest and gaudiest. And the moon beamed down on us as if She approved.

The three Shamans of Tribe Dauntless came out from our tent to start the feast. A hush followed us. SeeFar, dressed dramatically in black leather, strode up to us, took one look at Kitten's lack of jewelry and, without a word, began loading her up with his own. His heavy golden chain with carved amber plaques went onto her smooth bare shoulders. A lighter gold chain looped three times round her throat and still hung down to her waist. He pulled off his wide gold wrist cuff and slid it over her little hand. She giggled and pushed it up over her elbow and clear up to her biceps where it finally seemed willing to stay. His ruby pinky ring fit on one of her thumbs. He pulled out his blue and green enameled earrings, then realized she had never had occasion to pierce her ears. She put her little hands over his big ones and said, "I must not deprive you of all your adornment, gracious SeeFar. Already you have made to me a princely loan."

"Oh, not a loan, beloved Kitten. All I have is yours, and it gladdens me to bestow it." He very nearly licked her shoes like a puppy eager to please.

Cats like to play with their prey. Kitten, all wide-eyed concern, said, "But kind SeeFar, I cannot, in good conscience, be leaving you bereft. What would you be doing if I should be taking all your goods and possessions?"

"Why, I would be lying at your doorsill and starving for love of you, precious Kitten. And I would be hoping that you might be taking pity on me and agreeing to be taking me as your husband for the year and a day. Won't you just?"

"Not just this night," she replied, twinkling up at him. "For there are many other fine bachelors among the

Peoples of the Wide Skies, and I must be choosing my first mate most carefully. Now, of your great kindness, do not be pressing me further so soon."

His face fell. Then I could see him making up his mind to be the most pleasing bachelor of all time. An amused murmur went up from the surrounding listeners.

"Aren't men wonderful?" I whispered to CureAll. "If you treat them like dirt and never give them what they want, they'll follow you around like dogs."

We promenaded up to the cooking fires and greeted the assembled Headwomen and Senior Shamans. Then, as I had been coached, I declared, "The Good One has blessed us with her bounty. We have food to eat now and food to preserve for the hard winter. Tribe Dauntless welcomes you to share our fortune. As senior Shaman, I pronounce a blessing on this feast!" I was filled with genuine goodwill as I said this and threw my hands wide in a welcoming gesture. The sunstones on my wrists lit up like little lanterns, casting rays of light across the assembled tribes.

I was as amazed as anyone else. Lowering my hands and staring at them, I said, "Well, would you look at that?"

Wizened old StrengthWeaver started laughing, and soon the whole camp was rocking with hilarity. I grinned sheepishly and made encouraging motions to folks to step up and start loading their plates.

Little HappyGirl helped herself to a roasted rib bone almost as long as her arm and walked away from the fire carefully balancing it on her plate alongside one small carrot. "Well, would you be looking at that?" declared her mother, and people laughed.

Four young warriors approached Kitten at the same time, each with a plate-full of delicacies to share with her, and collided with one another in their urgency to be the first to make their presentation. "Well, would you be looking at that?" remarked StrengthWeaver, and chuckles erupted.

All evening long I kept hearing people saying, "Well, would you be looking at that?" and bursting into laughter again. It seemed to be the favorite phrase for the evening.

I turned to RugMaker. "Everyone's laughing at me. Have I shamed the tribe?"

She patted my hand consolingly. "Not a bit of it, surely, for the lighting of a sunstone is a most rare and wonderful skill. We are but sharing in your wonder and delight. And a blessing these little lights are to you, I'm thinking. Isn't it so?"

"Well, a Sorceress can always find a use for some Power gems," I said, and we smiled over our shared secret.

Chapter 51

CureAll was keeping my secret, as well. I needed her help with the dyes for my yarns. And I kept Kitten out of the way by asking her to lead all the hunting parties while I stayed in camp to help RugMaker get her yarns dyed. Kitten jumped at the chance to spend more time out in the grasslands, running wild and free, hunting in her cat-form and being courted and pampered by half the single men in the tribes.

So I had time to study quietly with RugMaker. She had agreed to help me get myself home. She was teaching me how to make an aerial rug!

"A shame it is that you had to be plucking out your hair entirely to be crafting your yarn," she said as we set up rug looms on the shady north side of her tent. "But I was saving the brushings of my hair for years before I began the knotting of my rug. And I'm fretting that you won't be having enough yarn as it is."

"As long as it's big enough to sit on, that's all I need."

"It is needing to be big enough for a full repeat of the pattern," she cautioned me. "And in order to be having the strength to be lifting you, it must be measured by your own body. From your fingertips to your elbow twice over will make the width. And three times over will be making the length. This will be the size of your repeat."

I put my fingertips together and looked back and forth from one elbow to the other. "Well, if I were just weaving the rug flat, I have enough yarn to make four repeats," I estimated.

"The knotting will be using a great deal more yarn than flat weaving," she said. "And it is taking also a great deal more time to be doing the work."

"One repeat will be just fine, then," I said cheerily. "It's not as if I need to carry passengers."

"You might be wanting to be carrying passengers at some time in the future though, kindly Sanna," RugMaker said, quirking one lovely black eyebrow at me. "I am understanding your wanting to be returning to your own home and your own life, but would you not be considering waiting perhaps just the one year and brightening our lives with your company that littlest bit longer? I am loving you like a sister and shall be missing you sorely when you are no longer sharing our tents and meals and bringing health and comfort to all in need."

I sighed, "Oh, RugMaker, I'll miss you too. Everyone in Tribe Dauntless is in my heart - you and CureAll most of all. But I will always be a stranger here. I belong to the tribe, but I'm not *of* the tribe. Do you understand?"

She hugged me. "And wasn't I just saying that I am understanding? But, selfish wight that I am, I would still be knotting a string round your ankle and keeping you like a pet bird to be singing for my pleasure."

I returned her hug and laughed, "Then you obviously have never heard me sing."

One of the fascinating things about the fiber arts is the artistry involved. If the pattern is executed perfectly, but with a poor choice of colors, the finished product will be flawed in some way. I knew a girl who loved pink and orange together. She knitted a pair of mittens in the self-heating stitch using especially jarring shades of pink and orange. The mittens were wonderfully warm, but they made the wearer's hands break out in rashes.

Or if the colors are perfect but the technique is off, the final result will still be less than desired. If I embroider a dress with the invisibility stitch, the wearer can become invisible at will. If my cousin embroiders a dress with the invisibility stitch, portions of the dress randomly become invisible, then go opaque again. (My cousin's husband rather likes the effect.)

My Gift for fibers had led me to choose dark red for my background color, though RugMaker had frowned at me slightly when I did so. The power and energy of the color had felt – right - and I trusted my judgment. Moreover, the casual observer wouldn't realize that I was knotting a flying carpet, since RugMaker's carpet was mostly blue. I didn't want too many people to know what

I planned. In spite of her animosity toward me, I didn't think SwiftSure would want me to leave, and I wanted to avoid the confrontation as long as possible.

Chapter 52

The summer went on. RugMaker grew bigger and bigger in the belly but was never sick or uncomfortable (I saw to that). She was creating rugs to line the pommel baskets for her babies. These rugs were made to wick away moisture from a wet bottom, and neutralize all unpleasant smells. Babies are very good at producing unpleasant smells. I guess everyone is good at something.

We sat on sheepskins as we worked. As our rugs grew in length, we piled up more and ever more skins to keep us at a comfortable height. From the first, I wore the sun stones tied against my wrists, and my fingers learned the tuck and clip of the knotting surprisingly quickly. Soon I could leave the work to my hands and eyes and let my mouth and ears run along by themselves. RugMaker and I talked and laughed, told one another our life stories, shared secrets and jokes, analyzed everyone we knew and figured out how their lives would be ever so much better if only they would behave the way we thought they should.

I ate hugely, and slowly began to get a proper womanly figure again. My hair grew, albeit slowly. And my rug grew with gratifying speed. Summer solstice came and went. If I had been in Thon at the Academy of Higher Magic for Young Ladies of Exceptional Talent, I would have passed into the First Form and been only one year away from my Journeywoman status as a Sorceress. I had no idea how missing the better part of a year would affect my progress. I worried about it. I wondered how Jonel and Cleonie were getting along. Had they been frantic when they realized I had never gotten to Thon? Had they given me up for dead? What had they told Prince Jerris when they realized I had gone missing? Did he grieve? It broke my heart to think of it all. I moped for several days, then decided the best thing to do was get back as soon as possible and set everything right. I gritted my teeth and worked even harder at the rug, often staying at the task long into the fading hours of twilight, my sun stones lighting my way.

Meanwhile, Kitten led SeeFar a pretty dance. He gave her horses and camels and goats and jewelry. Other men did the same. She became a wealthy woman. Giddy with her newfound power and acclaim, she smiled and flirted and played the men like puppets, and they kept coming back for more. SeeFar became so desperate that he even asked *my* advice, seeking me out where I sat working on my carpet.

"You might start courting some of the other girls in camp," I suggested. "Be pleasant to Kitten, but turn your energies elsewhere. She'll be angry at you at first, but it'll make her think."

RugMaker agreed with me, "That's no bad plan, I am thinking. And who should you be courting, then, but our sweet willow-lass, Sanna? For look you, Kitten knows you will not be leaving Tribe Dauntless to seek a bride elsewhere, so any lass you are dallying with here at the meeting place, you will be parting with in the autumn. But Sanna will be giving Kitten the competition for your attentions all the year round. And now that Sanna has filled out so beautifully -- ah, the competition she might be!"

SeeFar looked at me appraisingly. I protested, "Oh, let's not start that again! SeeFar, I swear, if you try to force yourself on me one more time, I'll . . . I'll cut off all your pretty hair!"

He looked chagrined. He honestly looked ashamed of himself! "It's the arrogant, selfish lout I was in my dealings with you, Shaman Sanna," he said. "I did not treat you with one tenth the honor you are deserving, and it's sore contrite that I am. You were helpless among strangers, and I was thinking only of how you could be of use to me. I am knowing now what a scurrilous wretch I was."

I blinked at him in astonishment, then narrowed my eyes in suspicion. RugMaker read my face and patted my hand.

"It's thinking, I am, that my little brother SeeFar is growing up at the very last. Perhaps it's being the one whose feelings are not considered that has made him begin to be considering the feelings of others. Do but be touching his hand, Shaman Sanna. I can be reading his heart in his voice, but you are not knowing him so well as I. Do be touching his hand and reading his Spirit."

I did as she suggested, and saw that she was right. SeeFar was genuinely sorry for the way he had behaved. He was learning his lessons. I wanted to help him.

Then I looked at my rug. Any time I spent in helping SeeFar entice Kitten, was time away from my work. I looked at SeeFar and read the tentative hope in his eyes.

I shook my head. "It might not work, SeeFar. Kitten has had a hard life, and now she's just mad with greed for all the good things coming her way. She might not be ready to settle down at all. You might court me as flagrantly as possible, and she still might not be jealous enough to marry you."

He followed my eyes as I looked back at my rug. He squinted at it. His eyes widened, then he shot a look of inquiry at RugMaker. She raised her eyebrows at him. He looked back at my rug. I could almost read his thoughts. *"It's an aerial rug! And RugMaker is helping. Sanna is going to fly away. And she's my only hope to win Kitten. I could stop her . . . No. I can not make myself happy at the cost of her happiness. She's entitled to have her own life back."*

He gave me a gallant smile. "It's entirely right you are, wise Shaman Sanna. I'll not be troubling you with my foolishnesses any longer." He started to rise to leave.

Nothing like a graceful surrender to win me over completely. I stood with him and said, "Well, let's give it a try. She's taking out another hunting party tomorrow. Let's give her something to think about tonight."

Chapter 53

So we sauntered through camp, arms around one another's waists, laughing and teasing. At dinner, I perched on my camel saddle, and he lounged on the ground at my feet, leaning against my knees. Occasionally I would bend forward to feed him tidbits from my bowl. In return, he would stretch up a smooth, long-muscled arm and hand-feed me some special morsel from his. When I slowly licked the tasty sauce from his fingers, he drew a startled breath and his eyes widened. I looked deeply into his eyes -- and winked. And that's when Kitten sauntered up to us.

"It's the fine friends you two are becoming, I'm thinking," she said.

"Mmmm -- yes, well, you might say I'm finally settling in," I drawled, looking down into SeeFar's upturned, grinning face and languidly running my fingers through his hair. Then I sent my Gift into those flax-pale strands and they began weaving themselves into a braided helmet.

Kitten snorted at me, "Mighty tricksy, that is. Why don't you be plaiting up your own hair and setting another new fashion?"

"Oh, I cut off all my hair to make love snares," I replied, plucking off my headcovering and revealing my frizzy scalp.

Kitten pulled back in astonishment. SeeFar gaped at me a moment, then I saw him putting two and two together. He had been around when RugMaker spun the yarns for her own flying carpet, after all. He grinned and assisted my lie. "Love snares? Ah, so that is the reason for my change in heart. Well, glad I am of it, lovely Sanna, for I have ever found joy in your sweet company." He began walking his fingers slowly, ostentatiously up my shin, his eyes twinkling teasingly as his hand disappeared under my skirt on the way up to my knee.

"Love snares?" barked Kitten. "What manner of foreign trickery is this? And how dare you be using it on my SeeFar?"

I smiled complacently at her. "It's just a simple little charm, Kitten. I can easily teach it to you, though really, you don't need it. You've snared most of the men in camp with your natural gifts. And with so many suitors, surely you can spare one? If I'll be staying with the tribe, I may as well take a husband. And SeeFar pleases me." I caressed the side of his neck and continued, "He's strong and handsome and quite the valiant Warleader. And then there's his ability to transform . . . I think an eagle is the handsomest bird, don't you?"

The outline of SeeFar's hand under my skirt was sliding slowly over the top of my knee and moving higher. Kitten watched it like a cat fascinated by a snake. I gave the wandering hand a playful slap and giggled, "Stop it, you naughty boy. People are watching."

"Humphf!" Kitten snorted. "And are you thinking that is any way for a Shaman to be behaving? Or a Warleader, for that matter? SeeFar, she is making a fool of you!"

"Then it's a happy fool I am," he said, gazing dotingly into my face. Then he glanced up at Kitten and said, "And I'll not be needing you to be telling me how I should be behaving. Nor will I be going hunting with you this next time. LoveSinger has agreed to act in my place."

I sent my Gift into SeeFar's long blond hair again, transforming it into a nest of serpentine locks, rising and swaying threateningly as if ready to strike at Kitten. Then I told her, "Unlike you, I've never been taught how a Shaman behaves, and really, I don't care. I know what I want, and I'm going to have it."

Kitten clenched her fists and stomped away, marching across to a knot of her admirers and beginning to flirt outrageously with them.

I set SeeFar's hair to tickling and caressing his face. He batted my hand away and looked after her with a worried expression. "Do you think she will be casting me off altogether now?"

"I think she'll start casting wiles to get you back. That was well done, SeeFar. There's nothing quite so desirable as the thing someone else values. And remember, kitties don't like to share their toys. Let's go for a walk. If she can't see what we're up to, it will drive her mad with curiosity."

Sanna Meets Dauntless Swiftsure

We stood and I dusted him off, then he hefted my camel saddle for me. I tucked my hand into the crook of his flexed elbow, and we strolled into the darkness. I noticed Kitten watching our every move and scowling.

I stayed up late, making up lost time on my rug. When I came to bed in the tent that CureAll and Kitten and I shared, Kitten rolled over in bed and hissed at me, "I thought you were going to be a friend to me."

"I *am* a friend to you, Kitten. Why would you think otherwise?"

"Aren't you stealing SeeFar from me? Is that the act of a friend?"

I slipped into my bedroll and whispered in the dark, "How can I steal what isn't yours? You haven't taken him for husband. He's free to go with any girl he likes."

"But you are *ensnaring* him! You have stolen him from me by false magic. How could you so betray me when you know how hard life has been for me? And aren't you still loving your Prince Jerris? How can you be dallying with SeeFar when your heart is elsewhere?"

"Some of us are trying to sleep," CureAll grumped. "Fight over him tomorrow."

"It takes two to make a fight, and I'm going to sleep, too," I replied. "Good night, CureAll. Good night, Kitten."

"'Night," CureAll mumbled. Kitten said nothing at all, just flounced her blankets as she rolled over with her back to me. I tucked the blankets under my chin, crossed my hands on my stomach and fell asleep, thinking happily of how I would soon be seeing Jerris again.

Chapter 54

Kitten continued not speaking to me the next day as she loaded her saddlebags and mounted up. I made sure to be standing next to SeeFar with my arm around his narrow waist as we waved to the departing hunters and herders. Kitten rode in sullen solitude, snarling at any of her suitors who dared to disturb her.

I finished my rug while she was gone. I had four hawk feathers that I had magically dyed a year ago, left over from my attempt to make a flying cape. But the spell had been interrupted in the middle, so the feathers constantly changed color, cycling from hawk gray to "floating blue" and back again every few minutes. And the tears I had subsequently shed into the dye vat caused a rainbow iridescence of colors like a starling's wing in strong sunlight. They couldn't actually cause anything to fly, but they could give a little extra lift. And they reminded me of previous successes and of people who believed in me. I worked them into the dangling tassels. And then I was done. I spread my finished work on the ground, and RugMaker and I viewed it.

"Assuredly, it is beautifully done," she said. "The knotting is flawless, and you are working the pattern with perfection. But it's worrying I am over the colors. That dark red is rich and lovely in the eye and carries the ocher, the tan, the black and the blue in good balance, but never have I heard of an aerial rug of such a color. And small it is, as well. Will it be having the strength to be lifting you?"

"There's only one way to find out," I answered, sitting down crosslegged on my precious little mat. "I just twitch the tassels and . . . ?"

" . . . And do be lifting your heart into the air," RugMaker finished for me.

I twitched and lifted. The rug shot up into the air with a jerk, throwing me backward so that I yanked the tassels closer to keep my balance. The front of the carpet lifted higher, faster. I was so far above camp that the people looked no bigger than mice! I kept pulling back on the tassels as I would on a horse's reins. The rug whipped around upside down, then righted itself again in a rapid loop. As I began to climb again, my brain took over control of my hands, and I dropped the tassels to waist level. Suddenly I was racing through the air, high above the camp, afraid to move my hands in the slightest. I took a deep breath, then let it out in a huge sigh. I loosened my white-knuckled grip, and my speed slowed. I opened my hands and let the tassels lie on my palms and gently coasted to a stop. For quite a while I played about, diving, climbing, turning and swooping -- getting the feel of the reins, as it were. *Free!* Oh, at last I was free again! I could just squeeze these tassels and head for home. I was about to do so when I noticed an eagle circling me. SeeFar? I lowered my hands and brought my little rug to a landing. The eagle landed close to me and transformed into SeeFar. He was laughing. "Ah, and haven't you been setting the camp into a tizzy with your sky dancing? A mercy it is that SwiftSure has gone off with the hunters this one time. She would be for burning you out of the sky rather than letting you be going without her leave."

"Did you come to stop me?" I asked.

"No, sweet Sanna. I've only come to be wishing you well. May you be finding a warm strong wind to be blowing you swiftly back to your home and to those you love. And RugMaker and CureAll are wishing you the same in bountiful measure. May your life prosper. May you be finding joy."

Tears stung my eyes. Three minutes ago I couldn't fly away fast enough, and now I was sorry to leave. And come to think of it, I had some unfinished business.

"Maybe I'll wait a few days longer before I go. It wouldn't be polite to leave before saying goodbye. And what sort of a weaver would I be if I didn't tie in my loose ends? I have an idea how we can rush Kitten into marrying you and get SwiftSure to let me go with her blessings."

We flew back into camp side by side at a moderate pace. I landed beside RugMaker, quickly rolled my carpet and tucked it into my belt bag. CureAll and StrengthWeaver were sitting with Rug Maker, who had the red and swollen eyes of someone who has been weeping. StrengthWeaver glared at the people coming to make a fuss about my new rug, and they drew back out of earshot.

"Oh, RugMaker!" I cried, hugging her. "What's wrong? Don't cry!"

"It's the selfish wight that I am," she replied. "Seeing the glorious joy of your flight and remembering that never again will I know that exaltation has brought this storm of tears upon me."

I could sympathize. Having tasted the wild freedom, I understood her sadness at being groundbound for life. I told her, "If it's any consolation, your firstborn son will be a RugMaker, too, and surely he'll be happy to give his mother flights on his carpet. Just be patient. He'll be grown and flying before you know it. Not the same as flying your own carpet, but better than sitting in the mud ever after."

She snuffled, blew her nose and gave me a watery smile. "It's just this being with child that is upsetting my usual cheery nature," she said. "All pregnant women are easy weepers. And the greatest of fools I am to be weeping over that Gift of flight that I have lost, or to be envying you the glories of it that you are now finding. Though my heart was assuredly in my mouth at first to be watching you. I was thinking time and time again that you would be crashing into the earth. And then I was coming to realize that you were but playing, and I was wroth with you for making me fear so. And now I am only glad to be seeing you back, safe and sound again. But Sanna, I was thinking you might not be coming back again to us at all. Why were you not setting out straightway for your home?"

StrengthWeaver squinted at me. "I'm thinking that it is because Sanna is senior Shaman of Tribe Dauntless and has one or two things to be doing here yet."

Chapter 55

Two days later, Kitten and SwiftSure and the party of hunters returned to camp, and when they were within hailing distance, SeeFar and I flew out to greet them. Kitten was leading her heavily-laden horse, flirting with the young men who were always around her like flies around raw meat. (Or perhaps I should say, like bees around a lovely flower.) When she saw me fly in on my carpet and land, and then saw SeeFar land and transform right beside me; when she saw me smile happily at him and kiss him on the mouth, she snarled and transformed into the huntress cat I had seen before. She leapt across the grass like death on four paws and only half changed to human when she faced me. Sharp, curved claws still protruded from blunt, paw-like hands. Slitted golden eyes glared at me from a face of human bones covered with cat fur. And her teeth were long and sharp, distorting her words.

"Mmmine!" she yowled, menacing me with those wicked paws. "He isss mine!"

SeeFar stepped between us and stared her down, scowling fiercely. The bristling fur settled slowly on her neck, then changed into long human hair, falling in a silken black veil almost to her knees. Her face became fully human. Her hands and feet were ordinary human hands and feet again when SwiftSure came galloping up.

"And what am I to be making of all of this, now? Sanna, I see, has become a Rug Maker in her own right, and glad I am to be seeing it, though what good we can be having from such a tiny bit of carpet I am having no idea. But what is it, Kitten, that is putting you into such a fury?"

"She is stealing the handsome SeeFar from me," Kitten shrilled, and her eyes started turning into cat's eyes again. "She has been making love snares with her foreign Magic and is taking his heart away from me. Now she will be flying all over the skies with him and doing who knows what. And it is *me* he is truly loving. He is mine, and she is traitorously stealing him"

StrengthWeaver had reached us from the camp by then. She cackled. "Is it SeeFar you'll be wanting then, WildFaring Kitten, second Shaman of Tribe Dauntless?"

"Yes!" Kitten declared. And grabbing SeeFar's right hand in her own she shouted so loudly that everyone in camp must have heard, "I, WildFaring Kitten, rightwise second Shaman of Tribe Dauntless, am taking Dauntless SeeFar to be my husband for a year and a day."

"What are you saying to that, Dauntless SeeFar?" asked StrengthWeaver.

SeeFar raised Kitten's hand to his lips and gently kissed it. Then he spoke so loudly and clearly that he'd have been heard over the roar of battle, "I, Dauntless SeeFar, am agreeable to being taken as husband by WildFaring Kitten, second Shaman of Tribe Dauntless, for a year and a day."

"Heard and acknowledged," said StrengthWeaver, SwiftSure, and I almost at once. I must have sounded a little too cheery about it. SwiftSure and Kitten gave me sharp looks. Time for my playacting.

I turned my head aside and covered my face with my hands. "Oh, oh the pain of it! The shame of it! Break, my heart! She has taken his love from me without using the least bit of Magic. How can I remain and see their love before me as a constant reminder of my failures? SwiftSure, I can no longer remain with Tribe Dauntless. Surely you won't keep me with you against my will, in constant suffering? You have a better Shaman than I in Kitten. Won't you let me go with your blessings?"

"And what of your word, Shaman Sanna?" she asked me. "Were you not swearing to be staying with us until CureAll entered her moon time? That time has in no wise passed us by."

"Actually," I said, "I swore to stay with you till you had another Shaman to take care of the tribe. You do now."

StrengthWeaver set the tip of her left little finger in the center of SwiftSure's forehead. SwiftSure's eyes lost focus for a moment, then sharpened again. She batted StrengthWeaver's hand away.

"So it's giving me the full remembrance of that word, are you StrengthWeaver? Yes, I am hearkening to it fully. Till a new Shaman could be replacing her was Sanna's sworn word, and that word she has kept full well. You are having the right of it. And the sore thorn in my backside she has indeed been, ever since I did her the honor of taking her as Shaman of Tribe Dauntless. She has served my purpose, and I have no cause nor wish to be holding her further against her will."

Then SwiftSure snarled at me. "It may be as well that you are so soon leaving us, I am thinking, Shaman Sanna, for you and I would be whetting against one another like two knives till one of us is cut into ribbons."

"Thank you, SwiftSure. If I can return for a visit, would I be welcome?"

"Tribe Dauntless is always hospitable," she snapped crossly. "Be coming or be going as you will." And with that, she mounted her horse and rode off into camp.

People were crowding around SeeFar and Kitten, offering congratulations and good wishes. I caught his eye, winked and waved, then sat back down onto my carpet, lifted up and sped off. In the past two days, I had already said goodbye to my friends. I could have gone through a grand parting scene with all the tribes, but I have always found that after you have completed the perfect, wrenching, tearful farewell and walked out the door, you are bound to realize that you left something behind. Then you have to go back, feeling like an utter fool, and either go through the whole scene all over again, or slink away with a flat anti-climax of apologies.

Sanna Meets Dauntless Swiftsure

I sailed through the long warm afternoon and into the evening. Eyes open or eyes closed, the cord tugging at my heart led me straight and fast. I was a Shaman, and I was going where I belonged, back to my studies and back to my love. I flew through the night, my sun stones glowing brightly. My little aerial rug was small, but the power of the dark red color made it fast – so fast. When I peered over the side, I could see the ground race away beneath me. I crossed the Bones before midnight, flashing high above the twisting crevasses that had taken so long to negotiate, turning and turning about through the maze. I hurtled over the sandy wastes, once home to First Man and First Woman, now home to taureks and dust devils. The sky was lightening in the east as I crossed the desert wastes where SweetSavor had died; where the Golmen raiders hunted and pillaged on their way to and from Arrex. And as the sun rose crimson at my back, I began twisting and turning between the high mountain peaks at the border of Arrex.

Within another two hours, I spotted Little Dinwiddy in the distance. I slowed my flight and spiraled in to a landing in the courtyard of The Hen and Chicks.

I stood carefully on wobbly legs and began stretching the kinks out of my hips and back. Suddenly Duggers threw himself through the inn door and slammed to a halt a few feet away from me.

"Sanna? Is that really you?" he hollered. "You *flew*! Can I do it?"

I rolled the rug and stuffed it into my belt bag, then swept the lad into a hug. " Duggers! You've grown!"

He squirmed loose and, almost dancing with excitement, began demanding, "I wanna fly, too. I wanna fly, too. Sanna, please, please, please, let me fly. You're my auntie now. Puleeeeze, let me fly, dear, *dear* Auntie Sanna!"

By then, the rest of the family had poured out of the inn and were all talking at once. Cleonie was hugging me and weeping.

"Sanna, oh Sanna! We didn't know what happened to you. Jonel has just torn himself up over it. You didn't want to go, and he made you, and then the messengers from the court came trying to trace you because the Academy was wondering where you had gone, and he tried to follow your trail but he had waited too long, and he couldn't find any sign of you, and ---"

I interrupted her. "I'm all right, Cleonie. And it wasn't Jonel's fault. Where is he? I'll let him see for himself how well I am."

Her face changed from overjoyed to stricken. "Oh. Oh, Sanna, you were gone for months, and no trace of you could be found, and he had to - well, the Prince – Sanna, Jonel is in charge of the royal escort. Prince Jerris has gone to Boravia to be married!"

"Married?" I squawked. "Where? When? I've got to get there!"

I was dragging the rug out of my belt bag again, but Cleonie grabbed my wrists and held me still.

"They were married in Borovia last week, Sanna. They are well and truly married by now and have been making the great procession through all the towns and villages on the way back to Arrex so that all the people of Arrex may see their new queen. They'll go through another ceremony in Arrex tomorrow, but they are as married as they'll ever be already. Oh, Sanna, Jonel told me all about it – how you and Jerris love one another so dearly but you gave him up for the good of the kingdom. And then you disappeared. What else could he do? He must have a queen and heirs. He's *married* now, to a proper royal princess. Would you change that if you could? Isn't that what you told him to do?"

It was, indeed, what I had told him to do. It was the best for his people. Now that I had some idea of what it cost to lead your people, I knew that he couldn't do anything else. He had his life and his responsibilities to get on with.

And so did I -- useful work as a Sorceress, Shaman and healer. I wasn't the first woman in the world to have her heart broken and it seemed likely that I, like all the others, would survive. I might not want to, but I, too, had responsibilities and a life to get on with. But I had learned, like the firebird, to fly ever in my own ways.

END